CRACH FFINNANT
THE PROPHECY

VOLUME ONE

CRACH FFINNANT
THE PROPHECY

Lazarus Carpenter

Illustrations by Debbie Eve

Words Matter Publishing

P.O. Box 531

Salem, Il 62881

www.wordsmatterpublishing.com

ISBN 13: 978-1-947072-63-3

ISBN 10: 1-947072-63-3

Library of Congress Catalog Card Number: 2018940483

DEDICATION

In memory of Crach Ffinnant

ACKNOWLEDGEMENTS

I first discovered Crach Ffinnant some years ago when scripting a song about Owain Glyndwr for 'The Sleeping Giant Festival.' This festival was dedicated to the life and times of Owain Glyndwr, Prince of Wales and held annually in the Brecon Beacons. The song was well received, resulting in a return visit to the festival the following year. I also had the pleasure of performing it at the Owain Glyndwr Festival, Machynlleth, and the seat of Glyndwr's Parliament in Wales. So grateful thanks to all.

Later I wrote the script and music for a children's play, 'A Fiery Knight's Tale' which is about the rise and fall of Owain Glyndwr. By playing the role of Crach Ffinnant as storyteller in the play, it helped me to further germinate seeds towards this work, 'Crach Ffinnant - The Prophecy.' Grateful thanks to the Gower Heritage Centre for hosting this play.

Special thanks and gratitude to Debbie Eve who created the illustrations for this book, proofread the manuscript and, most of all, for having great patience and determination in managing my madness!

My final thanks to our dogs, Hennie and Noodle, for being there and forgiving me for sometimes being just a little late for their walk.

CHAPTER ONE

For ten years past, I have been an apprentice to Llwyd ap Crachan Llwyd and have learned the ways of prophet and seer. Such a long apprenticeship one may say, as indeed it has been, but all will become clear. Magic and prophecy I am good at, or so the old man told me, and I had excelled, in his opinion, as a healer of sorts. I was a headstrong keen apprentice, streaming question after query, followed by endless thoughts, followed by even more questions. This would drive Llwyd ap Crachan Llwyd to the comfort-induced oblivion of sweet tasting mead, often by the jug-full. It was almost as if the sweetness of heaven's immortal nectar softened life, but the Gods had given him many seasons and with so much time came many stories. I listened and learned a great deal from my Master, I studied and laboured hard. He rewarded me by imparting knowledge and magic that vibrated through our strange world. He told me that we lived in difficult and ever-changing times and that my destiny was to embrace magic, prophecy, and wisdom and to be of service.

Nobody really knew how old he was. Some said over a hundred years, but some would say anything. I would say he has been very, very old for as long as I have known him. Oh, and considerably taller than me. I am a dwarf and have always been so, as it will always be.

My beard is not as long and strong as my Master's but it is growing and magic brings it along. My physical strength, I am proud of and can lift two fully grown men, each on the palms of my strong hands. Mind you, magic helps. I can do many other things. However, these will manifest as my story unfurls. I feel blessed that my legs are strong. Season after season, trudging from one end of Wales to the other, up mountains, down through valleys and back again, and again. It was by my endless shadowing and learning from my Master's wisdom that had prepared me for this moment.

The greatest journey of my life so far was at hand. Venturing far from the familiar terrain of my country into lands unknown to me. Lands and people I had only heard terrible stories about, that of the English.

⸎

My Master, Llwyd ap Crachan Llwyd, had given me the name Crach. Ffinnant is a tiny Hamlet hidden deep in the mountains of Wales and is where I was born. I recall little of my life before becoming an apprentice, but there are remembrances and dreams of past joy and happiness. My parents were of normal stature. Father was a woodcutter by trade. His strength was well known and till this day revered by those who knew him. Mother was quiet, kind and gifted with the sight of prophecy. I dimly recall visitors to our tiny home, seeking counsel and rewarding her service with gifts of chicken, duck, and goose. On reflection, I may have, in some small way, inherited some of my father's strength and my mother's gift of prophecy.

Master had never indicated any of this was true, but why take me as an apprentice unless something hidden deeply within revealed a vision telling of a journey together? He would teach, and I would learn. For ten years, lessons often started early in the morning before the sun rose and continued late on into the darkness. We spent many weeks, sometimes months, away from my Master's small cottage. We walked, trudged, staggered, but never rushed, down the valley and up to mountain top. We often slept in caves, under huge boulders, many times soaked to the skin by lashing rain. Winter was no different from any other season, we just wore more clothes, thus making my little frame heavier. Still, now I was strong and quite fearless for a small fellow, with wisdom and skill growing by the day.

In April of 1375, just as the cock crowed, I plated our food for the first meal of the day as I usually did. I had prepared, served and cleaned up after breakfast, in fact, all meals shared, every day since my first with my Master. I did not know this day would be my last. The mid-morning sun shone brightly through a lush canopy of new leaf, budding above our heads. Shadows danced across the ground as small gusts of wind bristled branches, new and old, above. Cleaning bowls and spoons in the cold waters of the pool formed by a shallow stream, trickling over jagged rocks, I was lost in thought of nothing in particular. I often was!

"Crach!" Llwyd ap Crachan Llwyd stood and beckoned me to join him. "Leave that for now. There is something of great importance that I must tell you. Come here!"

Putting the well-worn wooden bowls to one side, leaving them half- cleaned on the stones by the stream, I rose to my feet. Turning to see my Master, I noticed he looked even older today than was usual. His back seemed more bent and curved, giving him the appearance of a gnarled tree. That aged, craggy, lined face, with prominent, sharp, pointed, angular nose, great straggly beard, and motionless stare, did nothing to alter my image. Only his shining deep-blue eyes disturbed my vision, reminding me of my Master and not that of an old gnarled tree! But I must remember that all he taught me hinged on an ability to conceal oneself in nature. Perhaps this was one of these moments!

"Sit, Crach! Come and sit beside me, there is much to tell!"

Llwyd ap Crachan Llwyd slowly adjusted his ancient posture from one of standing to one of sitting. Not an easy task to accomplish for one of such age and decrepitude but he seemed to effortlessly achieve it nevertheless. I placed another log on the dwindling embers of the morning fire before taking up position as requested by my Master. Sitting down quietly, looking into those entrancing eyes, hypnotic mirrors of this ancient soul, I waited. Many times, when staring into his eyes, I had felt transported to different worlds which unfurled in my mind. But that was not the case this time. His eyes were clear, still looking, staring knowingly and intensely into mine. Putting his aged hand on my shoulder, gently he pulled me a little closer.

"The time has come, Crach!" His long fingers curled around my shoulder, gripping gently. "Your time is now, with many adventures ahead of you. Our time together is at an end."

Llwyd ap Crachan Llwyd gasped at a breath as if searching for more words. Or, I wonder if that was merely my thought due to the fact that he had said so much with so few. Llwyd ap Crachan Llwyd's grip on my back lessened as he began to pat my shoulder in a not so gentle fashion. I wondered what he was saying. I mean, I have always known my apprenticeship would be over some day. But today! Worry was something my Master always insisted is a human frailty to be avoided at all costs. *It stops you breathing in the magic of the moment!'* he would say. Well, this was one moment, and I must say the first for a long time that was clearly and undoubtedly rather filled with worry. What was I going to do? I had never had any plans or adventures not shared with my Master, not ever.

"You have learned much, Crach. There is little I can teach you now that you do not already know. In my long life, you are the fifth and final apprentice and, permit me to say, the only one to have stayed so long and achieved so much. You have become my friend as well as my aide, Crach. How would I have managed to get about so well over the last few years without your help, strength and, more importantly, love?" Gasping, he clutched his chest with one hand and squeezed my shoulder tightly again with the other.

"Are you unwell Master?" I moved closer to him, feeling very concerned.

"No Crach, just old and ready to sleep!" He smiled and squeezed my shoulder again, playfully. "It is time for you to go out into the world, Crach, but there is something of a curious nature that has happened, and I need your help. This is what has brought me to this decision now. Otherwise,

I think, because of our friendship, your apprenticeship may have lasted until I no longer did!" He smiled again.

Of course, I understood very clearly what he was saying. I actually had thought for a number of years that my time with him would be until he was no more. *'But what had happened that he needed my help with? It had to be serious to break this hitherto unspoken pact between us.'* He spoke again, quietly, almost whispering, as if someone or thing lurked in the shadows, eavesdropping his words.

"Great turbulence is facing our country, Crach. Our Princes are long gone by glory of battle or Y Farwdaeth Fawer, the plague."

He was right, the plague had taken one in three of the Welsh as it had in every other country in Europe.

"Our lands and people are long chastised, ridiculed and ruled by the English. Cruel and barbaric earls and barons have enslaved our people for long enough, their hearts are heavy with doom. Clouds of change are looming on the horizon of an uncertain future. A great prince is waiting in the wings, Crach, not yet ready to rule but well placed to do so. He knows not at this time the destiny written for him but will awaken to come forth when the heavens decree, leading our country and down-trodden people to freedom." Llwyd ap Crachan Llwyd raised his eyes. "The skies will reveal all, Crach! Keep your eyes on the heavens and listen as nature will always have the answer! All things are connected at all times, remember, at all times. Justice always prevails. It is the way of all things!"

This was not a new lesson for me but a grand reminder of one he had taught many years ago and reinforced ever since. An ancient law that I had witnessed and one that had proved correct so many times in many manifestations. Yes, a grand reminder! 'But what has this to do with me?' I thought. *All this talk of Princes and great change. What in the name of the moon has any of this to do with me, a dwarf?'*

"You may be thinking, *'What has this to do with you, Crach!'* After all, you are a dwarf, a small man in a much bigger world!" He smiled. At the corners of a wide mouth, the twitching, old, grey beard gyrated an involuntary spasm, conjuring the vision of a horse's tail, swatting away annoying flies. But he was always doing that. I would have a thought, and just seconds later he would give it back to me, accompanied by his beard dancing smiles at my ineptitude. I waited patiently for more.

"Well!" he coughed from deep in his chest and paused. A deep breath gathered his momentum to enable speech. "You are going on a long journey to the Land of the English. Into the very heart of their lives, you will venture." Pausing for more breath to enter his body, Llwyd ap Crachan Llwyd continued. "You will take parchments to my old friend in London, Crach. The writings upon them are in our ancient language, and thus the accursed English will not know the words written thereon. However, Crach, at all times you must remain alert, vigilant, and aware and most of all, awake!" He smiled again, as did I.

We both remembered the times when I had nodded off. There had been so many. But, I mean really, there are only so many hours a dwarf can stay awake. I suddenly stuttered in reply, my anxiety obvious.

"How will I get there? What must I do? I don't know the way? I, I, I!" Now, as panic began to overtake my bewildered thoughts, I paused for breath. Before I had a chance to exhale, he said.

"All is as easy and as simple as night following day." He smiled again, stroking my shoulder. "All is in place for you to start your journey today." His eyes twinkled.

"Today!" I shouted, as sheer panic now thundered from my head to my toes. Now, remember, I am a dwarf. Thus the distance between my head and the ground is much shorter than that of a 'non-dwarf.' I shuddered, every cell of my smallness reminding me they existed.

"Calm yourself, Crach," Master spoke softly. "Do you honestly think I would send you on such a journey without all that you need to do what you must do? And, Crach.... Do it you must!" He smiled again. "You are to meet a shepherd tonight who will take you along the ancient trails through the mountains to Shrewsbury. If you move quickly and sleep little, using the moon at night, you will be there in seven days. And in seven days, you must be there!" He paused to gather breath while I gasped at the mere idea of his suggestions. "You will join a travelling circus in Shrewsbury, staying with them until you reach London."

"A travelling circus!...London!" I cut across his words like a knife through butter.

"Yes, Crach!" He repeated. "A travelling circus and London."

Now I knew my apprenticeship was over and today of all days! But this? Master always taught me to be alert to that which was not expected. Well, I did not expect this and alert now I certainly was.

"Once in London, Crach, you will find my friend's Apothecary and give to him the scrolls. His name is Master Healan, a fellow countryman of ours, a Welshman. This is the name the English know him by, and when you meet him, he will tell you his real name." His look was serious and challenged my stare. "Master Healan will give you shelter and food for a few days so that you may regain your composure after such an arduous journey, travelling and performing."

"Performing?" I stuttered.

"Yes, Crach! Performing." He smiled knowingly. "You do not expect to travel with a circus and do nothing do you? You are a dwarf, my short friend, a dwarf! Dwarves perform in circuses, don't they?"

I did not answer. I simply thought *'Well, this one does not!'*

"Yes, he does!" Master laughed from deep within his belly. Any ears hearing this may have been forgiven for thinking that they heard a stag rutting.

He had done it again! *'Did I open my mouth? I rest my case.'* Ah well, no point in pondering the obvious. Yet here was another issue of survival I recognised instantly, drilled into me by those magical eyes over the last decade.

"Well Crach, telling you 'as it is,' as I have taught you, is the only path in this life. It will be a difficult journey for you, long and adventurous in so many ways. You are the only one I can rely upon to serve this task, and you are ready." He playfully gripped my shoulder, laughing. "When rested after the journey, you must follow your intuition, your destiny in the future will be secured. Not for one moment must you ignore your inner voice."

"Master." I was calmer now. "So you are telling me that in a few hours, I will walk for miles, day and night, over the mountains to Shrewsbury. I only have seven days to get there, and when I do, I will be working in a travelling circus, doing 'the moon knows what'!"

"And don't forget the parchments, Crach! But I must first say more about your need to be free to follow your destiny." He shuffled his body, changing position in an attempt to ease aged muscles. I was now beginning to be even more concerned. It's not bad enough that I go through discomfort and danger, now I have to walk around listening to myself, with no other idea of anything!

"Now all is not to be understood in that way, Crach. "No idea of anything! Ha ha ha!" The belly laugh became silent. Llwyd ap Crachan Llwyd looked stern, eyebrows protruding, stony crag-like cheekbones and nose becoming sharper, vibrating with new found energy. Aged veins along his long scrawny neck pulsed. "What is your destiny Crach?"

Before my addled mind could switch up a notch and words of response could utter forth an answer, he shushed me by a wave of his arm, ending on his lips with a long pointed finger, the fingernail, long, bent and ingrained with the dirt of life.

"Open your ears, my short friend, and remember every word I tell you. Do you understand?" Master's face twitched. Mine did too, a twitch that told him silently that I understood. "You will meet our 'Prince in Waiting', Crach, and you will become his prophet and seer."

"I will what?" I gasped as I stood up in shock and disbelief.

"Sit down, Crach!" He tugged my jerkin firmly, and I fell back to sitting. "Be not afraid of your destiny, because you will be indispensable to our hero on the horizon." He scratched at his chin, thin pointed fingers searching for the irritation on hidden flesh through a matted beard. "Together you will rally our countrymen to the flag, to the 'Great Red Dragon'! Together you will breathe fire and from those embers become free. Then, in turn, you will free our country from the tyranny of the English sword! Together you will scheme and plot to overthrow this evil and exorcise its demise. Together you will see great victory and great defeat, you will feel joy and you will feel pain, but freedom will always be yours!"

Becoming silent, he gasped deeply in an attempt to refill his now exhausted lungs. I sat in silence, trying to take in all my Master had said, and he had said a lot! If all were true, what an adventure this was going to be! It was beyond all dreams ever to invade my sleep, beyond all daydreams when lost in visions. Was this one of those times?...Had I been lost in a daydream and imagined those words?

"Crach!" Llwyd ap Crachan Llwyd stirred again, controlling an obvious excitement and accurately reading my addled mind yet again, he said. "It's all true Crach, all true." He smiled. "There is no more to tell you, dear Crach, and I am sorry if much of the telling may appear harsh. There is a map guiding and informing your true destiny. Remember my words, Crach!" He coughed lightly, producing a rag from his deep pockets, wiping spittle from cracked lips, he continued. "And now you should rest for a few hours. You have not much to pack, and your guide will be arriving as dusk joins us."

He stood, adjusting the worn cloak wrapped around his shoulders, pulling it closely to his bent body, smiled and walked away, stepping across the stream. I sat for a moment, taking in all that he had said and eventually drifted into deep sleep. Visions haunted my dreams until there was only silence and blackness. When my eyes opened, it was late in the day, but dusk was yet to arrive. Master greeted me with a nod and a smile. He seemed very composed, sitting by the fire, a calmness emanating from his being. We ate bread and drank broth in silence—he smiling, me in silent wonderment, shadowed with confusion. My few possessions, Master, had packed in a leather sack which lay in wait for my journey, soon to begin. Dusk was now not far away, and I felt quite tired, not at all prepared for what may lay ahead. My head was swimming in a whirlpool of the unknown.

"Well Crach, there is a little time left before you must leave." Llwyd ap Crachan Llwyd pointed a finger towards a ridge above the treeline. "From that direction, he will come, and soon." He coughed to clear a dusty throat before telling me more about my soon-to-be guide. "Fwynedd is a shepherd and knows our land as well as anybody. He is familiar with all the paths and tracks but, more importantly, holds knowledge of speedy routes unknown to others."

I thought briefly of how pleased I was about that. At least someone would have a badger's nose for where we were going because I certainly did not.

"He is a good man, Crach, but very quiet in manner. Do not take this for unfriendliness. He is a man who, after so many years alone with his flock, finds that little needs to be said, but fervently believes there is always much to be done." Smiling, he bent to poke the logs, stirring smoke to flame. "I have told you all I must, the rest is up to you my small friend. I will miss you, Crach, and it is possible we may never see each other again. Your journey is long and my time on this earth is short. We must share our goodbyes with no regret for all we may now never do, but then were we ever to do anything other than what we do now? Probably not..." His voice drifted into silence.

"This is all rather quick, Master!" I tried to raise a smile, even though a great part of me, deep inside, felt a tearing, ripping sadness. "One day we are here, then gone the next!"

"Such is the way of things" he replied. "Change is ever constant, we can never really know what may happen, can we? Remember our gift of prophecy aids vision to make the right decisions. The outcome of truth is for us to reveal through actions of honest intent."

Sitting down by the fire, he pulled his cloak around a frail, skeletal, aged frame. Cold air drifted along the valley, light was failing and long shadows formed of a day now passed. Dusk had arrived. A fire roared, warming us through to the bone, so welcome as the nights were still cold. I drank more soup and tore pieces of bread, eating most heartily. *'By dragons breathe,'* I thought, *'I have no idea when food may pass my lips again!'* My journey to Shrewsbury sounded as if it would give little time for rest and sleep, perhaps I would eat as I walked, or maybe not! At least I would not be alone, even if much of our journey, by the sound of my guide Fwynedd, would be in silence. I glanced at the treeline above, faintly in the distance, a lonely spectre came into view.

"I think my guide comes!" I pointed to the ridge.

Llwyd ap Crach Llwyd laughed loudly, such guffaw echoing endlessly in a cacophony of chorus along the valley and off into the approaching darkness of night. It ended abruptly in a spasm of coughing, the hilarity of the moment taking his breath. Pausing to gather grace, he took a deep breath, but the smile did not leave his face.

"Have you forgotten that these tired old eyes cannot see that far Crach?" Bursting into laughter once more, he gripped his sides. "Oh Crach, I will miss you!"

"I will miss you, Master! I will miss you." Tears welled in my eyes. "Smoke in your eyes, Crach?" He laughed again, showing a little more restraint, but not much!

The light was dim and night fast approached as the fire roared, casting shadows into the forest beyond. Through a gap in the trees on the far side of the stream, a tall figure of a man appeared, walking purposefully towards us. Upon reaching the stream, just one wide step of such long legs enabled him to stride across with ease. He waved and gesticulated a silent greeting. Fwynedd was strongly built with powerful shoulders, perhaps the size of three of me standing on top of each other. He was a mountain of a man, wearing a beard longer than any I had ever seen. He stood by the fire, towering over me. I stared, taking in his countenance. I had seen many a long beard but never at a length as this one. In my memory, such a beard was sported solely amongst magicians, prophets, and seers. His beard was long and wild, bushy ends sprouted from under a thick leather thong at his waist where the beard lay trapped, held securely in place. Presumably, this stopped it blinding his way when trudging through strong winds. He wore a thick, weather-battered, leather jerkin, tightly wrapped around for warmth. Torn dirty leggings, made from sheepskin, adorned thick muscular legs whilst big worn boots clearly housed large feet. My Master announced.

"So, you are here!"

Staggering to his feet, Master smiled his welcome, putting out a hand to greet my guide. Fwynedd bent down, extending a muscular arm, helping my ancient Master to his tired feet with a firm but gentle pull. They embraced warmly as would be expected of old friends who had not met for quite some time. The embrace lasted for what seemed an eternity to me. Their entwined upper torsos cast strange, eerie, ghostly shadows across the ground, flickering madly in the firelight.

My guide had arrived. It was dark now, shrouding all in night, excepting slivers of light caught from a half moon which, in my presently addled mind, enabled the conjuring of dancing shadows, haunting as far as I could see. Echoes in the distance of creatures who only ventured into the world at night played in my ears. My stomach tumbled, as does a butter churn. My fingers and toes tingled, and my head felt light. I could not understand why I felt so in fear, a feeling most unfamiliar to this dwarf, I can tell you. I felt positively, without argument, upside down.

Llwyd ap Crachan Llwyd, my long-suffering, aged, wise friend, and Master joined with Fwynedd the Shepherd in standing on either side of me, each calmly placing an arm around my shaking shoulders. I began to feel calmer, twitching and tingling started to lessen, my churning gut gurgled but felt less painful. Yes, I was starting to feel more in control, I think? Yes, I was! The top of my head definitely appeared to be feeling somewhat clearer, but still, they held me securely in what seemed like a healing embrace. Time stood still as we three stood, not moving nor speaking, with not so much as a twitch between us. I know not how many moments passed, I only know, as they both gently took their hands from around my shoulders, Crach Ffinnant was feeling grand. All my fears and trepidations of what, at first, felt like the most perilous journey imaginable had melted away and I now truly considered this to be an adventure. '*I, Crach Ffinnant, am ready! This is my time.*' Of course, these were only thoughts in my now less addled mind. Both of my protectors smiled warmly and in unity exclaimed.

"No fear now, Crach! Ready to go?"

Now all three of us laughed heartily until certainly, my

ribs ached. It was time to leave and Llwyd ap Crachan Llwyd, my Master, teacher, and friend for ten years past, took my shoulders in his gnarled hands for the last time.

"Keep the wind at your back, young Crach, and remember all that you must. 'Pererindawd, ffawd ffyddlawn' - a very great pilgrimage." He smiled a smile that would be the last I would see for a long time, if ever again. "I will always be with you, Crach, and when not in this life, as the universe one day will decree, I will walk beside you in spirit from the 'other world.'"

Smiling warmly, he pulled me closer and my final moments in his care and tutorship were over. I could not speak, as no words could I find to say goodbye to him. It was almost as though his final words had spoken so much that none were needed. I would never forget those words, and he did keep to them, as all will see. Fwynedd the Shepherd, my guide and protector for the next seven days and nights, embraced my Master and nodded silently in my direction as he strode with purpose into the darkness. Crossing the stream, I stopped and turned for a brief moment to wave a final farewell to my Master, but he was gone.

CHAPTER TWO

How a man can walk so quickly and sure-footedly over rock, bog, stone, through gorse and forest, blindly in such darkness is, I can tell you, is beyond me. My short legs, as strong may they be, had to move very swiftly to keep up with Fwynedd the Shepherd who was my guide across mountains, over the Marches to Shrewsbury. He did move quickly and with great accuracy of step. I had achieved a good rhythm in pace, even though my stride was less than half of his. After a little while, keeping up with him became easier. I was beginning to enjoy the energy I felt coursing through my small body and to my surprise, even the silence. Fwynedd had not uttered a word, with the exception of an occasional grunt or a tug at my sleeve, since leaving my Master by the fire.

I noticed he never looked down to where his feet should land, nor indeed did he seem in the slightest concerned as to what lay beneath these seemingly blind strides through the darkness of night. I had no idea as to how long we had walked, nor the distance, but given I had no clue, to begin with as to my path to Shrewsbury, it mattered not. Fwynedd suddenly stopped mid-stride, dropping to his haunches. I nearly fell flat on my face as my body crashed into him, thumping to a halt. He stared into my eyes and given he was on his haunches, stood at the same height as me. Well almost!

"By d-dragon's breath!" I stuttered in shock.

Fwynedd gently placed a large muscular hand on my shoulder, squeezing it firmly with a holding grip. Glancing at his eyes shining in the half light, angular nose and sharp features shadowed a broad smile, informing me of a need for silence. Quietly moving from haunches to sitting, his hand disappeared into the unknown depths of an old leather bag which was strung from his shoulder. Swiftly, like a wizard producing a rabbit, a chunk of stale bread appeared in his hand. Smiling, Fwynedd tore our repast roughly in half, passing over my portion with one hand whilst stuffing the remainder into his own mouth, and still not a word. A blanket of darkness cloaked all I may have seen, so I saw nothing, except for fleeting shadows out of the corner of my eyes, dancing in and out of sight. Stale bread, crusty and hard, even to my strong teeth, proved difficult. Pleased that my stomach had been filled to overflow by the final meal with Llwyd ap Crachan Llwyd, I chewed and churned the bread around my mouth as slowly the staleness softened. May I say at this point, my jaw ached from such chomping on bread not at all palatable, even to the roughest of tongues?

My guide, Fwynedd the Shepherd, chewing the last of his repast, again dug deeply into the depths of the leather bag. Silently he handed more stale bread in my direction.

Swallowing hard, his Adam's apple moved rhythmically up and down his thick neck as chewed food worked its way to the stomach. Belching loudly, he smiled and gasped more air before releasing yet another resounding burp. Echoes of escaping wind, a thunderous cacophony of sound so scary and difficult to describe, disappeared into oblivion but not before bouncing around in my ears through the darkness and silence of night. Ensuing laughter burst forth loudly from both of us, adding more echoes through the darkness. Somehow, unconsciously, yet in a state of silent knowing, we recognised the need for quietness, our guffaw quickly and effortlessly hushed into knowing smiles. We ate in silence with the sounds of the night returning to awaken alertness.

How far had we travelled? I had no idea. As to how far we had yet to go, I had no clue. Perhaps such ignorance on my part served to protect me from worry. I do and have always had, this tendency to worry, often needlessly. Surprises always have had such an unsettling effect upon my person. For the first few years whilst in the care and tutorship of my Master, Llwyd ap Crachan Llwyd, mostly all was sedated, quiet and filled with very hard work. As I said before, rising before dawn and working until late in the darkness, was my life. One of the ways he taught me was to surprise me. He taught by surprise, believing, as have I now for the last ten years, it is the only way we shock ourselves back into reality, given much time is spent in daydreaming and the like. Of course, I have spent a long time lost in my dreams that haunt the daylight. Did my Master not remind me to 'stay awake'? Worry often sent my mind whirling off into daydreams, spontaneous thoughts, creating pictures and voices, filling my head. Master was right, I do daydream too much. It took me a long time to understand, but even though I did, worry would sometimes invade every cell of my small body, quaking from deep within the boots I stood. So much did I know and so much I could do now so well, as learnt from my Master's ceaseless lessons, but I could still not stop myself worrying. Until, of course, a point was sufficiently revealed of whatever surprise it was because I could then see there was no need of worry. Why? Because I understood and thus worry dissipated as knowing took its place. Well, this journey, newly begun, did so with worry. My concerns that had been subdued and sedated by Llwyd ap Crachan Llwyd and Fwynedd as we had stood by the fire were now returning with a vengeance.

A question in this dwarf's head now is simple, a twofold quandary. *'Does my stomach tumble like a butter churn again because of 'worry' or have my innards taken affront by the invasion of stale bread?'* In the darkness, I see not what is being eaten but only taste hardness, flavourless, dryness. Perhaps green mould of the type I had been taught by my Master to use on wounds and infections of the skin now swam in my gut. Shuddering at such possibilities resulted in yet another fit of worry. A light tap on my shoulder, another, then in quick succession, becoming more and more akin to silent drumming. Daydreaming shattered back into the now, I opened my eyes at the precise moment I realised I had not known they were closed. Fwynedd, still squatting, stared meaningfully into my deepest being. He had so many qualities that were similar to my Master, especially in the way he invoked a calmness around him and an ability to seem as if he was looking into the depths of that at which he stared. This dwarf knew of such things.

Fwynedd quietly rose to his feet, towering above me.

Looking up at him brought a sharp crick to the back of my neck. *'Goodness he was so tall!'* The air was colder on my face and hands, whilst my breath created wispy serpents as warm air left my body. I saw his head was now covered with a dirty, stained, thick sheepskin hat which protected him from the cold and I looked at his sharp features, silhouetted against the first light of the morning sky. Fwynedd slowly strode off up the mountain. 'Time to go!' I thought, whilst gathering my only possessions without effort. I mean to say, I only had my small bag. The contents unknown to me as my Master had packed all whilst I had slept. My short legs spun into action, rapidly gaining pace but unable to match his stride as I took my place in the shadow of Fwynedd the Shepherd. My eyes sparkled as the new dawn on the horizon created shadowy spectres, dancing under trees and over rocky precipices, glistening atop streams—the new day bringing light into the darkness of night. 'How much further to Shrewsbury?' I wondered. 'Winds away.' I answered quietly in my head. 'Six more days and nights.' I breathed deeply, cold air awakening my lungs again. 'Winds away!'

Driving rain, incessant rain, stinging my face and more, soaking through my cloak and jerkin to the cold skin beneath. Just as the dawn arrived with its golden glow, shining through great fluffy clouds, the sky above my small dwarf-like head became dark and overcast. Fierce winds drove away the bright dawning of this new day, revealing dark clouds speeding across the sky. I am very used to getting wet through and, if I am honest, I mind not the rain but 'by dragon's breath' when it lashes in such a way, becoming a weapon of nature, I would rather be in the shelter of a warm, dry cave. Slipping and sliding over damp and sodden paths, gorse branches pricking my legs and hands, not to mention walking at a pace an observer may be forgiven for thinking was an accident waiting to happen, is not really my idea of fun. Perhaps I should say, '*I was this accident*,' given that Fwynedd moved like a deer, swiftly and sure of foot. With his cloak pulled tightly to his ears and only a sharp nose and piercing eyes to be seen, head and shoulders bent into the wind, my guide strode ever onward, as I struggled on in his shadow. My boots were sodden now as I squelched with every step.

Through the falling rain, Fwynedd silently waved a long arm over his head, egging an increase in pace. I complied, but two steps later tripped on a boulder, falling face-first with the hard ground harshly greeting my chin. '*Now that hurt*,' I thought, as I slowly climbed back to my feet. Fwynedd was at my side in a stride and by a breath held my shuddering shoulders as I staggered to stay upright.

He bent towards me and for the first time since our meeting, Fwynedd the Shepherd, ever silent, did speak. I say speak, more of an inaudible whisper really.

"Are you well, Crach?" Holding me firmly upright whilst looking deeply into my eyes, he whispered again. "Are you well, Crach?"

Silently I nodded with a forced smile invading my face, which was now in grave discomfort, aching and stinging. My chin, fortunately, padded by my beard, took the brunt of the fall but it was not much of a cushion. If it was at all possible to see through this hair on my chin, I am sure there would be a bruise the size of a horseshoe. Fwynedd held my shoulder in his strong hand, and we slowly began to trudge onwards. I rubbed my aching chin, blinking in the rain, welcome of his support. I still felt a little giddy, although no real harm had been done, but falling unexpectedly flat on one's face would make a horse giddy, so why not me? A voice, hidden in a thought, flew by my mind *'Say I, Llwyd ap Crachan Llwyd!'*

As we reached the ridge, Fwynedd pointed silently into the distance at a dark shadow on the rock. 'Could this be what I think it is?' My chin tingled under a sodden beard when a sudden twinge of pain reminded me of life. 'To feel joy is life, to feel pain is life. *Without knowing both, life is not lived!'* My Master's words, deeply etched in this dwarf's soul, echoing lessons of old in my mind.

'Yes!' silently recognising the shadow, it was as I suspected. *'A cave!'* I smiled a welcome to the warmth and security now waiting in front of me.

Fwynedd strode over the threshold into the cavern, and I thought *'from storm to warm,'* smiling to myself inwardly at such poetic humour. Even the idea of this cave raised my spirit. Once inside nature's shelter with the rain behind me, calmness entered my every pore. Turning around, scanning the cave floor for wood to burn, I saw that Fwynedd had already gathered a bundle of twigs and branches in his strong arms. I watched, and within the time it took me to consider where we may be, Fwynedd had piled twigs, then betwixt flint and blade drawn from the leather pouch hanging at his belt, sparked and blew a flame. A small flicker of orange danced as he gently blew and the fire caught. Twigs, dry from the shelter of the cave, lit with ease as Fwynedd snapped branches into smaller chunks, placing one or two on the fire. A warm yellow glow reflected across the cave walls, giving light to our sanctuary. I took the wet cloak from my shoulders and undid the thongs that held my jerkin together. I hung the sodden cloak from a branch extending from a gnarled old tree stump that had somehow ended up here in this cave. Perhaps the old stories were true about lost trees seeking refuge in caves when death approached. True or not, it was proving very useful. Taking off my wet jerkin, I felt a pang of relief, it must be either I have grown, or it has shrunk! I laid it next to the fire and sat down. I could not help but almost stick my feet into the burning logs, I was so desirous of warmth. Casting temptation of pain to the back of my mind, I satisfied myself with a quiet smouldering, wet feet steaming whilst flickering shadows danced across the cave walls.

Quietly and with industry, Fwynedd was boiling water in a small pot, adding chopped herbs and roots, stirring all slowly with a knife blade. He looked up at me smiling. Now that I was considerably drier, warmer and brighter, I also smiled. Fwynedd the Shepherd spoke again.

"We will drink and rest!" his words still a whisper, gravelly and hoarse.

He certainly was, as my Master had said, '*a man of few words.*' He continued to stir the pot, now bubbling furiously. Ushering steam wound its way aimlessly to the cave roof, sucked into oblivion, becoming invisible. A pleasant aroma filled the cave as unseen wisps of our earth's grace filled my nose. Fwynedd covered his hand with a blanket to protect vulnerable skin, as skilfully he removed a steaming pot from the fire, placing it gently on the ground. He then took the blanket from around his hand and sprawled it across the cave floor. Sitting cross-legged atop the blanket, a long, strong arm reached for the hat on his head. As Fwynedd became hatless, thick dark hair, almost as long as his beard which was still tucked in by the belt, cascaded over broad shoulders and down his back. He moved his hair from craggy worn features, securing its wildness behind his ears. Smiling, he said,

"It is dry in this cave, and we have made good time and pace, Crach." His croaky voice, rasping silent whispers, continued. "You do not realise how long we have walked for, do you?" He smiled again.

I thought to myself before answering him. *'A day at most.'* Confidently, I replied to this simple question from my guide.

"A whole day's marching, I would say!"

Upon hearing my answer, Fwynedd the Shepherd, my guide and my Master's old friend, exploded into laughter, almost seeming to burst. His eyes bulged, expelling tears which dripped down his weather-battered cheeks, now rosy from the heat of the fire. In my embarrassment at his reaction and not wishing to seem like a fool, I casually placed some wood on the fire. I looked up at him, still taller than me sitting down, and said.

"Surely it has only been one day!"

He laughed again, only this time a little less raucously and with slightly more control. *'What had I said that is so funny?'* I wondered. Gathering his wits, Fwynedd spoke quietly.

"So, your Master did not teach you how nature will warp our time, change our space, to arrive before we realise we have left?"

"Of course!" I replied defensively. Llwyd ap Crachan Llwyd had taught me everything he knew, and I knew all about 'warping ways.' I gasped a sigh of surprise.

"You mean we have been walking for longer than one day?"

Before he even began to answer, I remembered that the whole essence of 'warping ways' related to not knowing a 'warp' had occurred until it had. *'Like time stands still!'* I thought.

"Exactly, like time standing still. Exactly!" Fwynedd smiled as he repeated my thoughts, whispering in that gravelly voice again. So he too could read my thoughts, just like my Master! My thoughts are not my own!

Fwynedd began to snigger again, lips and forehead twitching, before bursting into laughter. This time I joined him, it was funny, and the joke was on me.

"So how far have we come, Fwynedd?"

I had a feeling I knew, of course, but confirmation was something I now needed. Perhaps this journey was going to be easier than my fears and jittery self-foretold.

"Six days and nights, Crach. Six days and nights!" Fwynedd smiled knowingly. "When all is meant to be, we know all is in harmony. Nature is the only truth in all things."

I knew this and now realised that indeed a 'warp-way' had opened in the universe. This truly was as Llwyd ap Crachan Llwyd, my Master had said. *A very great pilgrimage!*

"We have journeyed far and yet no distance at all in the scheme of things." Fwynedd scratched his forehead. "From the mountains of Gwynedd, across ridges and along valleys, day and night, our pace sure. Through mists, from dawn to dusk, into Powys and over the mountains to the Welsh Marches, Crach. Over this ridge, my little dwarf friend, lays Shrewsbury, your destination, and our parting!" He smiled.

Yes,' I thought, *'warp-way indeed!'* I turned to look towards Fwynedd who was now relaxing against the cave wall, his long legs stretched out in front of the fire, twiddling his beard betwixt intertwining fingers, he was smiling quietly. Such a journey in real time would take seven days. Through the 'warp-way,' we had done it in less than two. Magic in the universe was at hand and true destiny at my feet. Fwynedd, eyes closed, drifted sleepily within the warmth and shelter of our refuge. My eyes, now heavy and tired, lost focus in the firelight as I fell into caverns of sleep. Tomorrow, I would be saying farewell to Fwynedd and be arriving in Shrewsbury with the next part of my adventure in readiness to unfurl before me.

Crach Ffinnant

CHAPTER THREE

Dawn was breaking as half-light danced at the edges of my eyelids, sleep now behind me on this new day. For a fleeting moment, I thought I had dreamt about the 'warp-way.' After all, it is not only rare and most magical but also a sign that the universe shared our journey by opening up a vision, thus achieving ultimate destiny for the 'seeker.' *'Always expect the unexpected,'* my Master's voice echoed deep in the thoughts flowing through my mind. Well, it was certainly unexpected. Perhaps I should have expected it! Now I was getting myself in a muddle. Trying to analyse my Master's teachings often gave me a headache. I was getting one now, across my temples. I'd better think of something else. I didn't have long to wait.

"Crach." A whispering kindly growl echoed in the cave as Fwynedd brought me down to earth, my attention now his. "Drink this," he told me, passing me the pot swimming with herbs, now cold from last night's fire. He then gestured I drink it all down quickly. I did as he bade but not without getting a mouthful of soggy herbs stuck in my teeth, balling on my tongue and making me gag. "Eat the roots, Dwarf! They will give you strength." I did as he said and it tasted not too bad, I suppose, if not a little bitter. I recognised wormwood and sage, their flavours well known to me. Concoctions my Master, Llwyd ap Crachan Llwyd, had forced me to drink over the years were full of sacred herbs and roots, and he had taught me their uses in healing and magic. I knew them well, but the one I remembered distinctly was wormwood which helped to suspend time. It was all becoming very clear to me now. Nearly a week past, I had sat by the fire drinking broth made by my Master. Our journey seemed hard at first. Inclemency in the weather had made travelling very uncomfortable and trying to keep up with Fwynedd the Shepherd was arduous, to say the least, but these days past melted as if into two moons at the most. Wormwood, the secret ingredient!

I had slept and awoken in many caves during the past ten years. My Master knew where they all were. I knew too, but I had never left Wales before, and here I was waking up in a strange cave, buried in the high hills of the Welsh Marches. Shrewsbury was now almost in sight, the first part of my long journey nearly complete. England and the English lay in wait. I swallowed the last piece of root, having chewed it to a pulp, but it still took a few hard gulps before finally, it dropped from my gullet, bouncing painfully into my stomach. *'By all that is pain, which took some swallowing!'* Early morning sun casts light through the cave entrance, catching my eyes and invoking temporary blindness in its wake. Blinking several times, my vision cleared.

Fwynedd quietly began to pack and rolled up a sheepskin blanket. Securing the roll with a long hide thong, strong weather-beaten fingers held two ends of the leather dexterously whilst making a knot. Pulling at the thong to check for tautness and satisfied that all was well with his wares, now secure inside the large leather bag, he slung it over his shoulder. He was ready to move on. Taking his silent prompt, I began to pack my few belongings and was relieved to find my jerkin, cloak, and boots now dry. Fwynedd took a stride towards me, gently kneeling so I could see into his eyes without cricking my neck. A consideration for which I was most grateful. Placing a hand on my shoulder, he and I quietly stood looking out of the cave onto the rolling moorland below, now glistening in the morning sun. In the valley beyond, thick forest cloaked the hillside and a small swift-moving river wound like a snake along the valley contours. Lush new growth of spring sprouted from the ground, bushes, trees, and branches, for as far as the eye could see. Bright green, budding shoots, everywhere. The heavy rain ceased during the night, leaving droplets dangling from branches. Foliage shone as dampness began to dry out. Small clouds of steam rose like mist as all was warmed by the early morning sun. Fwynedd the Shepherd kneeled by my side and pointed a long finger towards the valley below.

"Walk to the river, Crach, and cross at a place shallow enough for you to ford. Worry not, as the river is swift in part but shallow, although you may get your feet wet again!" He laughed quietly, catching my eye, winking as he grinned. "Do you see where the river forks, Crach?"

With my eyes following the line of the valley, I easily saw the river as it divided into two channels. One flowed close to the forest, whilst the other continued down the valley.

"I see the fork, Fwynedd," I said.

He smiled, again pointing to beyond the fork in the river.

"If you walk for five hundred paces and keep to the edge of the forest, you will see a drovers' path. Follow the path uphill through the forest until you reach the top of the ridge." Dropping his hand, he continued. "Upon reaching the ridge, you will notice that the trees begin to thin out. Walk right to the edge of the forest." Raising his arm again, he pointed to the treeline on the ridge. "From there you will see Shrewsbury at the bottom of the next valley. It could not be easier, Crach, could it?"

I smiled and thoughtfully replied.

"Considering how far we have come, Fwynedd, it is no distance at all."

Scratching a bronzed cheek, he smiled again.

"You will be there before dusk, Crach. Remember to search for the travelling circus, it should not be too difficult to find."

'Performing dwarf!' I remembered my Master's words. How all this was to occur evaded me at the moment. After all, this was all part of my destiny, whatever that was to be! I laughed quietly to myself.

"It is time for our 'farewells,' Dwarf Crach." He looked at me seriously for a moment, eyes piercing and bright, staring directly into mine. "You have many miles to travel, your pilgrimage continues. I too have much to do, my friend, and also have many miles to travel as well as a flock to gather in." He bent down and picked his hat up from the floor, shaking it vigorously against his side before placing it on a dishevelled shaggy head. Fwynedd pushed his hair behind large ears and standing up, looked down at me. He took my shoulders firmly in his hands. "No words now my fine dwarf, none are needed."

I felt quite alone, and he had not yet left.

"Thank you, Fwynedd." I placed my hand on his and repeated. "Thank you."

He smiled. "We will see each other again, Crach, but it will be some years hence. I hope you will remember me when we do."

"I will always remember you, Fwynedd the Shepherd, always." He squeezed my hand one last time and stepped out of the cave.

"Farewell Fwynedd!" I called, as large strides took him quickly away down the hillside. I watched as he bobbed and weaved over rock and around bush until my trusty guide could be seen no more.

Picking up my leather bag from the floor and throwing it over my shoulder, I said my goodbyes to the cave, grateful for the shelter and warmth we had shared. Taking a deep breath, filling my chest and awakening my feet by twiddling my toes inside my now very dry boots, I stepped outside and made my way down the hillside towards the river. The ground was still sodden in parts from previous days of torrential rain, at times making my walking difficult, often slipping and sliding on my bottom. For some reason, gorse did not seem to like me and pierced my flesh whenever the opportunity arose. I must be grateful for the mercy of nature, at least it was not raining today. I trudged on. I reached the river quite quickly and followed its banks as Fwynedd had instructed. Her waters were high and swift as the recent falling rains had swelled the flow. Rushing water, taking on the form of white horses, cascaded over rocks, twisting and turning by an unseen current, flowing ever onward. It did not look to me as if anywhere was safe to cross, the waters seemed furious! The side of the riverbank was very up and down, as was I! One minute I was scrambling up a bank, the next sliding down. I nearly slipped into the river a few times, unable to cease my trip from becoming a tumble, my footing uneasy and most treacherous in the mud. Turning a bend, I could see in the distance the fork of the river, narrowing before it became twins flowing in different directions.

Stumbling ever onwards with some trepidation, I saw large stepping stones across the river, barely visible in the flow. Getting closer all the time, my sight of the stones changed from one of doubt that I would not get across to the other side, to one of certainty that I would. The nearer I got, the more I realised the river was lower here, and I could see that crossing by leaping over the stones was indeed possible. I might not even get my feet wet! I felt a sense of relief as I stood on the bank, looking at the first stepping stone which was well within reach, even for my short stride. Six large boulders had been in this place since time began, providing a bridge to enable travellers to get from one side to the other. I suppose it was forever like this, nature always providing a way.

I stepped confidently onto the first boulder. Although it was slippery beneath my feet, I managed to maintain good balance, enabling me to leap swiftly to the next. I landed with ease but was expectant of losing my footing. Luckily my boots gripped on to the rock long enough for me to be able to leap and land, stone by stone, again, again and again, landing on the opposite bank without difficulty. Turning back to look at my path over the river, I noticed Fwynedd had been right, it would be easy, and it was. I did not get my feet wet! He was wrong about that! Walking on, slipping and sliding, as I followed the bends of the river, its twin left us behind, making a way elsewhere to a destination unknown to me. I wonder if the river knew.

It was so much warmer now, so I removed the cloak from my shoulders, slinging it through the strap on my bag. Thick forest skirted the banks of the river, and as Fwynedd guided, I searched for the drovers' trail. Deciding to take a little break, as indeed I felt this was richly deserved after making such good time, I sat by the river feeling the spring sun warming my face. Closing my eyes for a moment, an orange glow appeared under my lids, reflections of the sun reminding me of her power and the grace of light. With my eyes closed, I attracted thoughts and visions of the things daydreams are made of.

I was a small boy and, as I am a dwarf, a very small boy! My dreams first began when I was about seven years old back in my parents' cottage in the Hamlet of Ffinnant. My father used to say, 'The boy is dreaming again!' Mother would defend my daydreaming, telling him I was learning to see! Perhaps Father thought having one 'seer' in the family was enough. Mother was often busy helping others at a time when food should have been on the table, much to Father's frustration. Father was a muscular, strong, quiet man who was well used to nature in his trade as a woodsman and he loved my mother very much indeed. He was always patient and kind, and even though some of his words may at times have seemed harsh, they were always given for the right reasons.

Sitting at our evening meal one night, Mother announced that I would need a teacher in the future to help me go beyond where she was able to take me. Father looked at me, saying it was nature's way of choosing my destiny by making me a dwarf and thus a seer and prophet. He dreamed of me becoming a woodsman like him, but my size made that quite impossible. Mother had said that I would not be able to start an apprenticeship until I reached my seventh year and she was insistent to Father that any future teacher must be of the best lineage. Father patted my head, telling me 'all in a day's work, my boy, all in a day's work.'

My daydream ended with a start. As I opened my eyes, splashing, streaming, gurgling sounds from the river brought me back into the now. Oh, the now! *'Goodness me, how many paces did Fwynedd say it was from the fork in the river to the drovers' path?'* I had a feeling that I was making myself confused and furthermore, getting lost. No, I could not be lost as I had not passed the trail. I remembered Fwynedd had said the trail was five hundred paces from the fork in the river. *'How many had I come already?'* I wondered. The answer was, I simply had no idea at all. I, Crach Ffinnant, had not been paying attention, being too busy scrambling up and down riverbanks. Suddenly a thought occurred to me. *'Was this five hundred paces of his stride or of mine?'* Given I stride three paces to his one and I knew this to be so as 'by dragon's breath,' I had been in his shadow for days. Even though the 'warp-way' had shortened our journey, it had not shortened his stride or lengthened mine. So, in dwarf terms, his five hundred paces become fifteen hundred paces for me. I still did not know how far I had come to be here, where I am now. *'A solution exists for every problem, Crach, and it is always a simple one!'* Llwyd ap Crachan Llwyd's words rang through my mind. Pondering on such wise words, as my Master's always proved to be, I considered that firstly, I had drifted off into a daydream, something I had been warned against, and secondly, I had been told to remain alert at all times, but I had not!

So that is the reason for my problem in not knowing either how far I had come or indeed how far I had yet to go. *'Now what is to be the solution?'* I wondered. I smiled to myself at my own stupidity. I had not passed the drovers' path yet, of that I was certain. So, however distant, it would not exceed fifteen hundred paces. I just did not know how far I had come and asked myself *'did it matter?'* The answer was simple, and again I smiled at my ineptitude. It did not matter, I had not passed it, and therefore, it was not far. *'Why worry, Crach?'* I asked myself, *'silly little dwarf!'* Gathering my wits, I stood up, slung the bag over my shoulder and started walking again, following the contours of the riverbank.

Again, steep banks challenged my fortitude as I slid down muddy ones, losing my balance. Often I encountered the edge of the forest meeting the riverbank and whilst roots and branches proffered a rail for support, gorse attacked my person with spines as sharp as razors, pointed like spears. A rogue branch hooked onto the strap supporting my bag, pulled me right off my feet but provided me with an anchor, preventing my slide into the river. *'Small mercies!'* I thought.

Levelling out, the bank provided sure footing, and I was able to stop feeling so up and down. With dense forest to my left and the river to my right, I walked on. I noticed the treeline becoming sparse, thinning out and further on, maybe at a distance of twenty paces, I spotted a path into the forest - the drovers' path. This trail, trodden by shepherds for centuries, would guide my feet through the forest to the ridge where Fwynedd said I would see Shrewsbury in the valley below. Confidently, I turned left, away from the river, stepping on into the dark, thick forest. The drovers' trail, my pathway towards destiny.

Branches hung over the path, reminding me of a wooden cave. Sunlight danced through the treetops to the glade below. This was an ancient route, and I could feel the spirits of those who had walked before me. It was a magical place with moss covering the forest floor, carpeting rocks, stones and tree roots. Lush shades of green provided me with a vision of beautiful tapestries I had seen in some of the big houses visited with my Master. The path became steeper and pools formed around tree roots where rain gathered, muddy in places, causing me to step from stone to rock jutting up from the path. This way I did not get wet feet. As you have probably gathered by now, I hate wet feet! Although it was steeper and sloppier underfoot, the forest was becoming thinner with the light from the sun brightening the shade. I had reached the ridge, just as Fwynedd said I would. With the forest behind me, I was blinded momentarily by the glare of the sun. I stood at the edge, feeling the warmth from the sun's rays across my face and shoulders. With blindness gone, I stared into the valley below. In the distance, I could see the silhouette of a town. Shrewsbury! I had arrived.

CHAPTER FOUR

Stepping down the hillside towards Shrewsbury, my spirits rose considerably. I always felt better when I could see where I was going. A strange feeling came across me as I walked towards the town, then I recalled my Master's words, *'the accursed English.'* There would be a lot of English in Shrewsbury, and suddenly I thought of something really quite important within the scheme of things, I had never seen an Englishman. I knew some of their language because Llwyd ap Crachan Llwyd had taught me several words and phrases. I had also heard it spoken by some. I must be careful not to give myself away. It was important to blend in, and that is hard enough as it is, as I am a dwarf. But how would I accomplish blending in unseen with little of their language on my tongue? I know! I would pretend to be dumb!

Thinking about it, life could possibly be easier as a dumb

dwarf, even if clearly fraught with all sorts of frustrations. There would be ridicule too. Considering my options, on the one hand, people laughed and joked about us dwarves at the best of times and on the other, were afraid of the supernatural powers we are said to have. So, a dumb dwarf with great physical strength, which I am proud to say I have, might just make folk think twice. In any case, it would mean that my being unable to speak their language could go undetected, part of my disguise, per chance. It should be fairly easy to act like this in a travelling circus, but I must find the circus first.

The sun, risen to its highest point in the sky at this time on a spring day, brightly lit and warmed my path as I walked along the track towards Shrewsbury. Recent heavy rains had left their toll here too. Great indented furrows ran along the track, reminders of heavy wagons rolling into the town, no doubt bringing wares to the market. Hoof prints sunk deeply in between the furrows, revealing ghostly imprints where rain formed pools. I stepped over furrow and furrow, springing to the edge of the track and back again to try and lessen my contact with the mud. Wagons must have passed this way earlier today, judging by such slop.

Upon approaching a bend, I saw a horse-drawn wagon slowly coming my way, heading out of town. A large Welsh Cob, with a proud chest thrust out, was breathing strenuously. Its thick bushy tail swished from side to side as he struggled through the mud. Strong legs, muscles stretched, veins prominent with blood pulsing to every sinew as it pulled the heavy cart laden with huge wooden barrels. There looked to be far too much weight on the wagon, some of the barrels barely hung on and were only loosely bound by thick ropes. A very overweight man clung to leather reins, huge hands at the end of thick set wrists rested precariously on fat knees. A droopy, broad-brimmed, battered, old hat perched loosely on top of a very fat face. Getting closer, it was clear to this dwarf that the driver was rather worse for the quaffing of ale. Judging by his size and the state of him, he must have drained a barrel on his own. I laughed quietly under my beard. As the wagon drew closer, the cob snorted and whinnied under strain from its heavy load. It tripped on a furrow which made this fine stallion stop dead in its tracks. Thus the wagon jolted to an abrupt halt. Instantly, two of the loosely bound barrels fell to the ground with an enormous crash. One burst into pieces, strips of wood splintering as the contents exploded, allowing gallons of ale to form pools amongst the furrows before sinking into the mud. The other rolled, undamaged, into a hedge.

"Dam and blast!"

The fat man came back to reality as he blasphemed. He was unable to stay seated as the wagon jolted and, like the barrels, was sent flying to the ground. He landed in a heap, face first, into the mud. His cursing became almost lost as he bubbled incoherently. His hat had been flung off into a puddle as he fell and I witnessed the fattest, baldest head that I had ever seen. He was the colour of beetroot, with a great jowl hanging loosely over his collar, spittle drooling from a tight little mouth that was almost unseen, hidden by limp flesh. The horse again whinnied and carried on undisturbed as the wagon wheels turned, sinking into the mud, squelching and splattering, drenching this heap of a fallen body upon the ground which now moved slowly, like a great boar rising from a deep slumber. He continued to curse as he rubbed mud from small piggy eyes with great fat fingers. He was clearly having great difficulty in his attempt to raise his bulk from

41

the mire.

I stepped to the side of the great horse and reaching up, grabbed at the loose reins, pulling them taut, the bit jolting in its soft mouth. Quietly the cob stopped and stood perfectly still, tail happily swishing, rest-time assured. Behind us came sounds of grumbling and groaning, accompanied by cursing as the heap scrambled in the mud. I turned around to see the huge man struggling to his feet, picking his battered hat from the sludge. Looking first at me with a glancing look of surprise, he then turned quickly, surveying the shattered barrel before noticing the other stuck in the hedge. He turned back towards me and shouted in English with a slurred voice, spittle dripping from the side of his small tight mouth.

"You, Dwarf... You frightened my horse, you, you!" He coughed and spluttered. "Look at this damage! Who will pay for this? You? I think not!" Putting the dirty, battered hat back on his fat head and turning toward the shattered barrel, he screamed. "Look at this, just look at it!"

I looked at the fractured barrel, smashed to smithereens, scattered here and there across the sodden track. I knew some of his words, not all, but enough, I can tell you, to realise this fat heap of a drunkard was blaming me for the mishap. A mishap that would not have happened at all had he been of sober mind. Drunkenness did very strange things to folk, the most noticeable, of course, being an inability to speak coherently, whether or not the language could be understood. The signs are the same in every language. In every language, quaffing ale in great quantities ends up with nobody able to understand what is being said by the drunkard, often leading to great confusion and violence. But what I did understand, all too well, is that he was blaming me. His fat finger pointing menacingly at me did the trick.

I managed not to speak, although I nearly did. Remembering my vow of silence and feigning dumbness, I gesticulated innocence and bowed graciously, removing my hat. He shouted some obscenity that I did not understand, whilst continuing with a wagging finger proffered in my direction. Again, I mimed my innocence, acting out the accident in front of my accuser. I suppose I must have looked amusing, to say the least. Pretending to be the horse, I mimed hauling the cart and tripping in the furrow. In mime, I quickly changed from horse to cart, thence to pointing at the barrels. The fat man laughed hysterically, holding his sides and dribbling, his chubby face looking fit to explode. I ceased my antics and stared at him. Another interesting observation about those who quaff gallons of ale is their ability to instantly change from anger to humour and back again. I sincerely prayed he would not return to anger and in order to perpetuate my safety, I mimed 'me leaping out to stop the horse,' then 'me as the horse stopping in my tracks.' Throughout my antics the stallion stood motionless, tail still swishing. He turned his shaking head and whinnied, stamping a hoof into the furrow, he whinnied again. *'Was he laughing too?'* The fat man laughed loudly once more, slapping his sides.

Thinking on my feet is what my Master, Llwyd ap Crachan Llwyd, had taught me and I was doing just that right now. I hopped, skipped and jumped towards the hedge. The fat man belly laughed again. Playing the 'fool' or 'strongman,' or 'both'? He was about to make his own mind up about me. Wrapping my arms around the barrel, taking its weight into my belly, I lifted it with ease. The muscles in my legs tightened as I slowly placed the barrel back onto the wagon.

I could see out of the corner of my eye that the fat man was impressed by my strength. Moving swiftly, I wound the rope around the remaining barrels to secure the load. *'They will not fall of now!'* I thought, finishing off the final knot with a twist. The fat man hobbled and staggered in my direction, still laughing.

"How, you are strong Dwarf!" He coughed and then smiled a knowing grin. "I could use someone like you!"

He chuckled heartily whilst patting me on the back. Worse the wear for ale he may have been, but he still had a powerful hand! My back will probably be sporting four fingers and a thumb mark, giving evidence to his playful assault upon me, for days to come.

"Well done Dwarf...Well done!" Coughing, he continued. "My name is Carter and carting is my trade."

His speech, less slurred now, made me think sobering up was in his runes. Hardly surprising after he had fallen headfirst into the mud, a sobering experience for anyone, man or dwarf! Smiling again and steadying his huge frame against the wagon, he said.

"I am sorry I blamed you, Dwarf. I must have fallen asleep at the reins. Too much ale!"

He spat into the slurry, shouting again. Why is it that when people know you are dumb, they assume deafness and shout accordingly? I gesticulated I was not deaf, and he laughed loudly.

"Do you need work, Dwarf?"

Straightening himself against the wagon for support, he continued more coherently and less loudly.

"You saved my bacon. I am sorry I shouted at you." Sweeping his hat from the fat head, he bowed in my direction.

"Thank ye Dwarf, thank ye." he bowed again before replacing his hat, the brim flopping over his face.

I mimed my decline of his offer of work and silently pointed toward Shrewsbury.

"We travel in different directions, Dwarf!"

Shouting once more and slapping my shoulder, he started to clamber back on top of the wagon. I put my hands under his haunches, and by giving a little shove upwards, precariously balancing on the barrel, he gathered his competence.

"Here Dwarf!" He flipped a coin in my direction which I deftly caught in my right hand. "For your trouble!"

Slipping the coin in my bag, I watched as he raised the reins. With a quick lash, cracking on the stallion's flanks, accompanied by him shouting "Get on!" he nodded farewell with a smile on his big round face. The stallion strained in its harness, chest heaving, strong legs digging into sodden earth, it moved off, dragging the heavy cart behind with Carter perched on top, cracking the reins again. I watched them disappear into the distance as I sat down for a while to gather my senses. '*Well that went quite well,*' I thought....Being dumb had worked, and not one awkward question had been asked, although I cannot pretend not to have been worried when he shouted at me. I had not found too much difficulty in understanding his words either. Now, that pleased me. So my qualms, though not without foundation, were groundless. Playing the 'fool,' whilst demonstrating my strength, had matched well. So, my disguise was set.

Spring sunshine cast long shadows, a sign of time passing through this day. Rising to my feet whilst slinging my bag over my shoulder, I faced Shrewsbury and headed off towards my future. Not far now! In front of me, a bridge signposted entry to the town. Its wooden structure hung over rocks in the river, securing a boundary to the town's limits. Upon crossing the bridge, a wider than normal track became the main street. On both sides stood small buildings of wood and clay with thatched roofs. A few people wandered in and out of doorways, going about their daily business. I was startled momentarily as a large dog appeared from nowhere who started to bark and growl at me. Snarling and drooling, it dropped to its haunches as if to attack. Sensing the danger, I stopped in my tracks, stepping backwards, I stared the dog firmly in the eyes. The snarling eased, and the slobbering stopped as it rose from its attack position and sunk into submission, wagging its tail. Breathing a sigh of relief, I stroked the dog as it licked the back of my hand.

The barking had caused alarm, and a window shutter was flung open, crashing into the wall.

"What's up Scrap?"

A middle-aged woman's head appeared at the window. Her face was grubby and dirty, scraggly hair poked from beneath a scarf covering her head. A knitted shawl hung loosely over big shoulders, ample bosom heaving against the sill. Seeing me stroking her guardian, she shouted.

"Who are you?...A dwarf, a dwarf!" She became even more agitated.

"Get away Dwarf, don't bring your bad luck around here, and get away!" Then slammed the shutters with an almighty crash.

CHAPTER FIVE

The further I walked down the street, the more folk started to appear from here and there – from doorways, spaces between hovels, from behind wagons. Most of them gave me a wary glance and a wide berth. I simply looked away as it was probably better for me not to engage with their eyes as abuse may follow. I thought it wise to maintain a low profile- in more ways than one! A golden sun was starting to set, casting long shadows across the street. As I continued along my way, I passed under a window, it flew open, and a voice from above shouted

"Below!"

A bucket of slops missed me by a hair's breadth, splashing onto the ground in front of me. I leapt back in shock and instantly looked up to where the offending offal and human waste had sprung. The voice saw me and disappeared as quickly behind slammed closed shutters as it had appeared. Echoes of 'Dwarf!' screamed from above, then silence. *'That was close!'* I thought.

The gutter was awash with garbage and waste. The stench was so overwhelmingly evil that I was forced to cover my nose and mouth. With my collar pulled up closely around my face, only my eyes peeped over the sheepskin hood pulled tight over my head. I walked on. Fires burning in the hearths of hovels and houses cast smoke into the air. The wholesome smell of wood-smoke did something to mask the evil aromas from the gutter, but not much! Music in the distance caught my ears, with sounds of the beating of drums and the blowing of whistles. Perhaps the travelling circus was around the next bend?

This was going to be very interesting. So far I had been shunned, insulted by association of being a dwarf and laughed at for my antics in mime but I had also been admired for my strength and good humour, and I had been offered a job. I had been in England for less than two hours and seen more people than in the last two years. I had certainly experienced ridicule as I never had before. When in the company of my Master, Llwyd ap Crachan Llwyd, he would never allow such things. He always told folk who made strange observations to be very careful. *'Dwarf magic is very strong!'* he would say. This always seemed to do the trick but now I was alone, without his protection and, of course, I had decided to be 'dumb.' So far this tactic had proved worthy.

Rounding the corner, I found a large group of folk gathered around a fire-eater. He was juggling fiery brands, five flying flames in all. This must be the travelling circus as predicted by my Master, I was sure of it. A canopy strung on ropes between two large wagons gave the performers some shelter and provided a stage for the audience to watch in amazement at what would unfurl for their entertainment. The fire-eater somersaulted in the air as all the flying flaming brands shot upwards and as he landed firmly on the ground, each one was caught with such accuracy before the juggling began again.

I struggled, dodged and weaved my way at waist level to the front of the crowd, passing fat women and drunken men. Aromas of unwashed bodies and dirty clothes assaulted my senses as I pushed through the crowd. Finally, I stood in the front row with a clear view of everything. Suddenly, a very small man, red faced and wrinkled, standing to one side of me, spied me standing next to him.

"Dwarf!" he exclaimed, stepping backwards. The woman at my other side looked down and screamed.

"Ugh, a dwarf!" She also stepped back a few feet.

From being crushed by others' thighs and legs, space rapidly appeared around me as more people moved away. I thought to myself, *'Surely I'm not that frightening, am I?'*

Final flames cast out from the fire-eater's hands as his show reached a crescendo with more somersaults, the brands shooting higher and faster. Night had arrived, and the flying brands gave light, casting fleeting illumination across the circus. The folk around me kept their distance, even though they were hypnotised by the fire-eater.

All this chit chat about us dwarves being bad luck is nothing more than 'chit chat' and has little foundation in reality. Admittedly, we are gifted with such things as great strength, the power of magic, prophecy, healing and even comedy. But 'evil' and 'bad luck'? I should say not. *'Good and bad exists in all people, and it is their choice to be one or the other,*' so says Llwyd ap Crachan Llwyd. It seems to me that folk chop and change their minds to suit circumstances, just as 'Carter the carter' did when one minute he thought I was responsible for his mishaps and the next, a 'saviour,' providing solutions and humour. Yes, folk chopped and changed their minds and manipulated circumstances to get what they wanted. Often with little consideration and, mark my words, especially where dwarves are concerned.

As the fire-eater took his bows, a delighted audience applauded and cheered. Wonder of wonders! A dwarf stepped to one side of the makeshift stage, beating a drum almost twice his size. Another appeared opposite, playing a long flute. Music, unheard before by me, rang through the night. As an increasingly fast jig began to play, some of the audience began to dance, taking on the appearance of manic puppets, jumping and kicking heels, waving frantic arms in all directions. The dwarves played on and on as more and more of the crowd became tickled into dance. Dust flew in clouds, feet stamping and heels flicking, ale slopped and rained from jugs held by drunken hands. Fortunately, I was not battered, kicked or cajoled during this flippant mayhem, which I would have suffered had I been of normal stature. Not that, in my opinion, there is anything abnormal about the stature of dwarves. All is in the eye of the beholder. As I said, there are also advantages to being a dwarf. Glancing at the short musicians, I noticed how the dwarves smiled at each other as deft fingers danced up and down a flute and small, strong hands beat a hypnotic rhythm on the drum. Still, they played faster and like puppeteers, manipulated and controlled their increasingly intoxicated, out of control puppets—the crowd!

I must say, it was a joy to watch. I found it all too much to bear and exploded into laughter which quickly developed into a side-splitting guffaw. My feet were tapping in time to the music. I laughed again, and I am sure that all could see my amusement if they chose to look my way. With this fleeting thought, I calmed and controlled myself in an attempt to smother my hilarity. I did not want to draw too much attention to myself and a belly laughing, hysterical dwarf, standing alone amidst this prancing crowd would accomplish that in no uncertain terms. I breathed deeply, perhaps too much so as I was reminded instantly of so many unwashed puppets and overflowing drains, mingled with wood-smoke. What an unholy pong!

Suddenly more jugglers appeared in the centre of the stage—a trio of dwarves. So, with five dwarves in front of me, as you can imagine, I no longer felt alone nor indeed a spectacle attracting unwanted interest. This was perhaps going to be easier than I had first considered. I wondered if my Master had known this. He probably did as he seemed to know everything, both seen and unseen. The fire-eater reappeared, plunging blazing brands down his throat, flames extinguished, seemingly swallowed. Drum and flute played on as a huge monster of a man took centre stage, hauling an enormous iron-balled chain in one hand, with a most beautiful maiden perched upon his shoulder. She was a mermaid with long blonde hair reaching a slender waist, concealing a slight frame. Her skin colour was like alabaster. Her oval, shiny face had the brightest of green eyes, piercing, and all seeing. Her lower body was that of a fish with golden scales encasing a slender form, glistening blindingly in the light of the firebrands. A most glorious split tail fin dangled at the strong-man's waist.

The giant's black, matted, thick hair, streaked with grey, covered an enormous head, whilst a bushy, wiry beard hid a huge square chin. His craggy chiselled face, sharp nose and prominent, large, black eyes sat beneath grey bushy eyebrows. Heavily weathered and tanned, his muscular body, dressed only in a leather vest, stood like a mountain, still and monstrous. With legs like tree trunks, firmly planted, he swung the iron ball and chain from side to side as if it were a huge pendulum, whilst raising the beautiful mermaid up and lowering her down again with ease in his other hand.

The whole stage danced, shimmering with energy, performers embracing their grand finale. A dark-skinned woman drifted into centre stage as smoke from firebrands sent wispy clouds, fogging the performers, giving a ghostly ambience to all seen. She wore a long purple cloak with the hood hanging loosely over her silver hair, stray strands blowing in the light breeze which was beginning to chill the air. At each side of her stood a wolf. One jet black, one as white as a full moon. Strong muscular creatures, majestic yet fierce in their natural beauty. Amber eyes shone, staring intently at the now crazed audience, cavorting in a mayhem of dance. The crescendo was reaching a spectacular peak, 'Dwarf the Drummer' beat three loud bangs and every performer suddenly stilled, like statues. Three more beats followed from 'Dwarf the Drummer,' performers bowed deeply, the audience applauded, clapping and screaming in appreciation.

"We will be here in Shrewsbury, your wonderful town, for one more day my friends. Just one more day!"

A booming voice echoed through the night, emanating from a big-bodied man, seemingly fat, a bulbous, purple nose, a drooping moustache, dressed in the finery of half armour and doublet. I thought to myself, he must be the Circus Master as such dress I had only seen on Knights and Earls.

"Tomorrow night, my friends, is our last show for your delectation.

We bid you a good night!"

Dwarf, the Drummer, gave three sharp taps, performers bent low once more, and applause came fast and furious. The crowd, happy, drunk and jovial, staggered, dispersing in all directions, chatting and laughing on their merry way home to warmth and sleep. The spring night air had taken on a sudden chill, and I pulled my hood and muffler taut, shielding from the cold. All the performers began busying themselves, cleaning up, stacking boxes and reeling in ropes. Alone now, with the audience gone, I stood watching them, lost in my imagination of what I may do within this travelling circus, if indeed this was the one. My Master had said I would be a *performing dwarf.* 'Performing what?' I pondered.

Dwarf the Flute was busy putting out the firebrands which had earlier illuminated the stage. Wolf-Woman fed her charges by a wagon, their heads buried in large wooden bowls. Strong-Man, with Mermaid still on his shoulder, climbed into another wagon.

"Hey, Dwarf!"

I turned around quickly, startled by the familiar booming voice speaking loudly again.

"Yes, you!"

Standing a few strides away with huge, muscular legs stretched widely apart, adorned in all his finery, Circus Master smiled.

"Looking for work, are you? What can you do?"

Chapter Six

'The skies will reveal all, Crach! Keep your eyes on the heavens and listen as nature will always have the answer. All things are connected at all times, remember, at all times! Justice always prevails. It is the way of all things!'

Llwyd ap Crachan Llwyd's voice echoed in my head. The Circus Master adjusted his doublet sleeve.

"Well?" he said.

I nodded, remembering I am supposed to be dumb. No reason had popped into my mind to alter this chosen disguise. I nodded again. He warmly smiled down at me, twisting his drooping moustache around a chubby leather-gloved finger. A large golden ring adorning the index finger shone. Quizzically, his eyes, bright and silent, assumed questioning again. Wiping his mouth with his gloved hand, he boomed.

"Dumb be you, Dwarf?"

I nodded again, leaving him in no doubt I am indeed dumb. "So what can you do, my little friend?"

Wiping his damp mouth again, Circus Master kneeled down in front of me, our eyes meeting at the same level. *'Here was a man used to conversing with dwarves,'* I thought. Remembering my runes, I fumbled blindly in the bag hanging from my shoulder. Showing them to him, he smiled and laughed loudly.

"How can a dumb dwarf explain meanings when he can't speak?"

He had a point I had not considered. I gesticulated that I could mime meanings, he laughed again.

"You will be there all day." He said, "Folk will not be able to understand, even though you will raise a titter, no doubt!" Staring intently, he asked, "Is there anything else you can do?"

Jumping to my feet, miming my strength, I moved to the edge of the stage and picked up a large barrel with ease. He laughed again.

"Now that is much better!" Circus Master scratched his chin. "We could create a new act with our strong-man and see if you could do other things to help out." He ceased scratching. "How does that sound?"

I nodded in agreement, smiling. Raising his great bulk from bended knees, he continued.

"You will get food, shelter and a share of the coins we are given."

I nodded and raised my thumb to illustrate contractual understanding.

"Well Dwarf, we have an agreement. What are you called?"

I pointed to a crack running in the ground and then

towards myself. "Crack!" He said smiling.

I nodded my pleasure and relief at firstly, his speedy recognition and secondly, I did not have to think of any other mimes. I was tired now, and sleep was not far away.

"Strange name, is it not?" He scratched his chin again. "We can use it. It is unusual, but nevertheless, it would work. Yes, I like it. Crach it is!"

He turned around and bellowed towards one of the wagons. "Wasp!"

Dwarf, the Drummer, leapt from the wagon. So his name was Wasp, and Circus Master thought Crach to be a strange name! I smiled inwardly. Wasp scuttled across the grass, almost slipping and sliding to a stop in front of the Master. He graciously bowed.

"Master." His voice, quite squeaky as a mouse, was most quiet but respectful.

"This is Crach. He is joining us. Look after him Wasp. Something to eat and a bed I would suggest!" He slapped me on the back. "See you all in the morning!"

Circus Master walked off, humming to himself. I had a new friend, a fellow dwarf! Wasp motioned me to follow him as he skipped back towards the wagon from whence he had sprung. I entered the wagon, assisted by a 'pull-up' from Wasp. Inside was warm and cosy with sheepskins covering the wooden floor. Two of the other dwarves slept soundly. One of them, I thought, was Dwarf the Flute, whose snore mimicked the instrument he played when awake. Snores rose and fell, whistling in amusing tones. Wasp kicked him softly on the back, whispering.

"Quiet Crow!"

I had difficulty in hearing Wasp, and I was awake. Now

if Crow was sleeping, surely he would not have heard Wasp complaining and the kick, well he need not have bothered as Crow snored on. Wasp invited me to sit next to him on sheepskins on the floor. Reaching deep into a cupboard, built into the wagon's wooden side wall, he produced some bread and cheese which he laid on a wooden platter in front of me. Passing me a knife, Wasp gestured silently for me to eat while at the same time helping himself to a large piece of bread and a chunk of cheese. I ate heartily as I was feeling very hungry, not having eaten anything since early that morning. It seemed so long since food had passed my lips. Fresh bread and cheese, without mold, was a most tasty repast indeed to be shared between dwarves. We ate and ate in silence until all was gone, then washed it down with a jug of small ale which Wasp poured from a flagon perched on top of the cupboard.

Wasp clambered to his feet and disappeared into the back of the wagon, emerging moments later holding a large sheepskin. He passed it to me, pointing to a space on the wagon floor where I was to sleep.

"Sleep Crach," Wasp whispered. "Sleep."

Laying my bag down to use as a pillow, I snuggled under the fleece. Moments later, I leapt out from beneath the cover and stripped off my clothes, it was far too hot. *'By dragon's breath,'* it was hot. Returning to the warmth under the sheepskin, curling up into a ball, I drifted towards sleep while considering that, all in all, this had been a successful day. All was unfurling just as Llwyd ap Crachan Llwyd had predicted.

My dreams took me back to the safety of Wales and the security of my Master. Rolling mountains and valleys flashed as visions deeply emblazoned my mind. Clouds sped across a blue, blue sky. Bala Lake stretched in front of me, and smoke on the horizon drew me towards a mist. As the mist cleared, I found myself sitting alongside Llwyd ap Crachan Llwyd. A fire was roaring amidst large stones laid in a circle. Smoke was drifting, curling upwards and creating mystical shapes that, once formed, were quick to vanish within the ether of all that is. Master turned to me, tossing his head and fingering the long beard before, in that all too familiar croaky ancient voice, he spoke.

"All unfurls Crach, just as it should."

Twisting his thick grey beard between gnarled aged fingers, coughing quietly, he continued.

"Your journey has gone well, and you have done much better than you may think. I told you it would take no time at all and here we are! You are wise to be dumb for your adventure. Remember to be so until reaching London, but there you will need your voice. Enjoy performing, Crach!"

"Wake up Crach!" Circus Master's voice boomed in my ear. My shoulder was being shaken vigorously, and I sat up with a start. Rubbing sleep from my eyes, I awakened to the sight of Circus Master. Gone was the finery of last evening, replaced by a brightly coloured shirt, hanging loosely over breeches of leather covering huge legs. He was smiling with a broad grin.

"Eat dwarf!" he laughed out loud. "After food, let's get you to work. We have a show tonight!" He turned on his heels whilst booming instructions. "Crow, Wasp, everybody - come on! Let your light enter this day!" I watched as his back disappeared behind another wagon.

Five dwarves sat eating breakfast. Wasp, of course, I knew, and Crow I now recognised from last night but the others I was yet to meet. Strong-Man and Fire-Eater sat cross-legged on skins adorning the ground. Sheepskins lay scattered all around an enormous black steaming cauldron, suspended over a blazing fire. Mermaid was nowhere to be seen, but others sat eating while chatting amongst themselves. A very tall thin man, with not a hair on his body to be seen, leaned over the hot cauldron, spooning thick porridge into a wooden bowl. Sitting quietly was a lady sporting a beard, not unlike mine. She ate daintily, licking porridge from a wooden spoon. I had never seen a woman with a beard before, although I had heard of such things. Trying not to stare, I averted my gaze and then saw the strangest person a waking dream may ever have offered to an imagination. Skin as white as white, more so than Mermaids. Bright pink eyes pierced all they captured. Long white hair reached beyond a slender waist. A face, beautiful and handsome, yet somehow sad, ate heartily. A man wearing a bearskin around him, muscles bulging from heavy shoulders, sat astride a stool. Enormous hands wrapped around a wooden bowl, tilted towards his mouth, draining every last drop of porridge.

"Over here, Dwarf!" Strong-Man shouted. "Come, eat. Blaze pass me a spoon and bowl."

Pale-Man rushed into action, beating Blaze to the bowls, picked up a clean one along with a spoon and held them on high, confirming my invitation to breakfast. Taking the bowl while nodding my thanks, I spooned porridge from the cauldron, filling my bowl to the brim.

"Here Dwarf, sit here next to me!" Fire-Eater waved to a space betwixt he and Strong-Man. "Welcome to our band of troubadours!"

I sat between these two giants as if shadowed by mountains, feeling like a tiny valley dwarfed by creation. Porridge, hot, thick and creamy filled an emptiness deep inside me, bread and cheese from my nocturnal repast, long digested. My new companions muttered with smiles, nods, and winks, welcoming my appetite as I heartily and quickly drained my bowl. Strong-Man, upon seeing my empty bowl, slapped my back.

"More Dwarf, have more!" He pointed towards the cauldron, still suspended and steaming over the fire.

"His name is Crach!" Wasp introduced me as loudly as his whispering voice allowed.

All nodded acknowledgement of my name, banging spoons against bowls, accompanied by a chorus of 'Welcome!' I smiled at all present, nodding and gesticulating joy to be in their company. Filling my bowl for the second time, I settled down to finish breakfast.

CHAPTER SEVEN

"Time for work!" Circus Master's voice boomed, although he was nowhere to be seen. "Work!"

Strong-Man and Fire-Eater jumped up immediately upon hearing the second command to 'work,' almost squashing me momentarily as I was unnoticed by either of them.

"Sorry Crach!" Strong-Man reached down, gripping my collar with a huge hand and hauled me upwards before plonking me down on my now trembling feet. "All well now, Dwarf!"

Laughing loudly and nudging Fire-Eater into hysterics, his large hands dusted me down from head to toe. Fire-Eater jovially slapped my back as they ambled off in the direction of the 'voice.' Pale-Man gathered up the empty breakfast bowls that lay scattered on the floor around the fire, discarded by my new companions. Wasp picked up spoons as everyone else traipsed nonchalantly after Fire-Eater and Strong-Man.

Still trembling slightly from my recent 'crushing encounter,' I wondered whether I should follow the others when my thoughts were interrupted by a flying wooden spoon, ricocheting off my elbow. Turning quickly, rubbing my sore bone, Wasp greeted me with a grin, clearly finding his 'hurling missile attempt' of getting my attention somewhat amusing. Waving his arms, gesticulating I should follow him, provided a solution to my 'direction quandary'. Following Wasp as instructed, we joined Pale- Man who was busy scrubbing the remnants of breakfast porridge from dirty bowls in a small wooden tub. Laying alongside another wagon was White-Wolf with his head buried in the remains of a deer carcase, quite oblivious to all around. He wagged his bushy tail in contentment and was not tethered which filled me with a little anxiety, and I found myself staring.

"White-Wolf is not a problem, Crach!" Pale-Man exclaimed, looking up from pot washing. "Knows us!" he added.

I thought to myself, it might know you, but it does not know me. It is bigger than me too, a fact that was true for all of us dwarves. A small snack we would provide for it and nothing more. Wasp added reassurance, ceased from stacking clean bowls and turned to face me.

"Wolf is safe with us, he won't eat you!"

He laughed loudly, miming and reinforcing his answer by gnashing teeth together, grimacing and shaking his head. Pale-Man joined in the joke. They both began to laugh again as the wolf lifted its head and glanced with huge eyes directly at me! Shaking a huge head, long pink tongue lolling over very sharp white teeth, it took a last glance at me before burying its muzzle again. Gasping relief for a moment, I shocked myself back into a panic. Black-Wolf sauntered from the far side of the wagon, licking its lips, blood-stained jowl quivering. Wasp and Pale-Man sniggered under their breath at the sight of my tensing muscles, freezing my stance.

Black-Wolf's aimless saunter stopped, he halted in his tracks, sat down on muscular haunches and looked intently into my eyes, or so I thought. His coat, thick and long, as black as night, gave the appearance of a 'wizard wolf.' Suddenly, jumping up and turning, he quickly disappeared behind the wagon again, his tail waving a goodbye. *'By dragons breathe,'* I thought, *'that is one enormous wolf.'* I sighed in relief for its lack of interest in me and laughter filled the air again. After we had cleaned away all the bowls and spoons, stacking them in the wagon (well, I say we, I actually just stood and watched as Wasp and Pale-Man completed the task while still laughing at my fear). The three of us then joined the others.

Circus Master leaned against a barrel, twiddling his large perfectly trimmed moustache, standing with huge thick legs crossed. A bulk of a man who commanded respect by his demeanour alone. All stood quietly, listening to every word as instructions for the day were delivered in a matter of fact, no-nonsense fashion, in that now all too familiar booming voice of his. So far I had not heard him speak quietly at all, he shouted everything in a voice that was the loudest ever heard by this dwarf.

He gave orders to Strong-Man, instructing my inclusion in his part of the show and telling all that another dwarf in the troupe heralded more good fortune for the circus. Such joy filled my heart as here was a man who deemed dwarves to be 'good luck' and not 'evil' as most considered. It seemed to me that my time performing in this travelling circus may certainly be less fraught than the fears that had haunted my soul since the moment that Llwyd ap Crach Llwyd sat in the light of day, telling of a destiny to be fulfilled, mine! It was just three days ago that I had joined the circus. How time flies by when magic emanates all around, hours into minutes, days into hours. Now I am 'Crach Strong-Man the Dwarf'.

Strong-Man and I spent all morning preparing and rehearsing for the evening's show. I am able to lift very heavy loads, it is one of the gifts from my father, the woodsman. My physical strength has never been doubted. Strong-Man was no exception, marvelling as I tilted a wagon effortlessly with one hand, while Crow balanced precariously on the other. Mermaid, perched on a barrel, graced our rehearsals with her beauty, laughing gently as we did something amusing and applauding our mutual feats of great strength. We attempted various stunts successfully, achieving all without effort, all as part of the magic unfurling. My first show this night, rehearsal completed, a little time to relax along with my new companions. All is well, just as my Master predicted.

Dusk approached. Wasp lit firebrands, sticking them upright in the ground surrounding the performing area thus providing light for all to see the show. Pale-Man, Crow, Blaze, and Strong-Man suspended the canopy betwixt two wagons, giving shelter for the performance should the weather become inclement. Looking up into a clear spring sky, I knew it would remain dry with no rain tonight. Fire-Eater kneeled by his wagon, seemingly in deep thought, eyes closed, not one muscle twitching in his face nor indeed on his taut torso which was covered only by a strip of leather from shoulder to waist.

"He does that every day before performing!" I looked

around and was surprised to see Circus Master, his voice now quiet and not booming. "It is some kind of trance, maybe magic. I don't know."

He continued quietly, explaining that nobody knew very much about Fire-Eater. Where he came from, what he had done in the past, nobody knew because he never told stories like the others. But one thing he was certain of was that Fire-Eater could create and manipulate fire in ways never seen before as achieved by a man.

"It is as if he is blessed with the 'dragon's breath'!" Circus Master whispered.

I knew all about 'dragons breathe,' Llwyd ap Crachan Llwyd had taught me well. I had also met two of the remaining dragons that lay deep in the mountain caves of Gwynedd. They were majestic and magical, perhaps the last of their kind, although stories told suggested otherwise. My Master had taught me their magic and how to communicate in their ancient language. If Fire-Eater had been blessed by 'dragon's breath' then he could conjure flame from nowhere that is magic. Suddenly, Circus Master became his usual self and boomed across at Strong-Man who was busy securing the canopy with thick rope.

"Tighter, if you please! Tighter!"

His voice echoed through the dusk while the moon rose high in the night sky above us. Tonight, we would see by the light of a full moon.

Chapter Eight

Fiery brands, flaming brightly in the moonlight, cast
shadows, dancing here and there, flickering, appearing
and disappearing, images of spectres fluttering around the
performance area and covered wagons. We were all prepared
and ready for the show, waiting unseen behind the wagons
by an audience yet to arrive. I sat on a sheepskin, perched
on a wagon, sipping water from a wooden bowl. Circus
Master, adorned in finery once more, stood proud, drooping
moustache groomed, boots polished, clad in the half armour
and doublet of a gentleman. A wine-red cloak, as dark as the
blood of man, hung loosely from one shoulder, pinned by
a broach of gold, drooped across his broad back, trailing on
the ground. He stroked his hair, twisting it around gloved
fingers. I noticed that the broach matched the large gold ring

on his glove, the same one he wore last night. He looked very dignified, almost regal, as a knight before a joust.

Fire-Eater sat in silence, seemingly not with us at all. Off on one of his dreams probably. Now that is, of course, something that I can relate to, given that I love to daydream too. But he was not daydreaming, he was going through exercises he used to prepare his mind and body for action. Wasp, Crow and the other dwarves sat cross-legged in the wagon, playing a game with small stones. All were dressed according to their roles. Two dwarves wore carved masks of wood, one of an angel, the other of a devil, their beards hid from sight. Blaze was wearing a fiery cloak across his shoulders. Fumbling with a rosary between his fingers, he leaned casually against a barrel, chatting quietly to Pale-Man. Wolf-Woman stood gazing at the horizon, lost in thought. Two wolves, black and white, sat calmly by her side.

Strong-Man dozed, laying prostrate across sheepskins on the wagon floor, oblivious to game-playing dwarves, a slight snore giving away his escape into fleeting dreams. A rope fence, strung over barrels, surrounded the circus. The audience would enter through a gap in the fence where Mermaid sat awaiting their arrival to relieve them of the entrance fee. Resplendent in a golden cloak, hair cascading to the floor, she waited patiently.

A large man, with an equally large wife, giggled and chuntered, digging deeply in pockets for a coin before passing it to Mermaid who smiled. The radiance of Mermaid's smile captivated the large man, but not for long. His wife dragged him roughly away by his chubby arm, held tightly in her equally chubby hand, cuffing his ear and muttering some obscenity about his parentage. The first of this evening's audience had arrived. In no time at all, a stream of folk passed coins to Mermaid as they walked into the circus to find a piece of ground to call their own. In all shapes and sizes, they came, some dressed in finest attire, some in rags, the audience gathered in wait. Some carried children on shoulders, others held small hands of offspring, laughing and excited at the prospect of the show about to start. Sounds of nattering and giggling amongst the crowd echoed through darkness now descended, a full moon providing light so that all may see. Circus Master whispered to us.

"To work, my fine friends. Our show begins."

He stepped from behind the wagon, boldly taking centre stage. Wasp and Crow stood offside, and each began to play flute and drum. Wasp beat his drum loudly, three times, and the music stopped abruptly. Circus Master raised his arms in the air, bellowing loudly, announcing the evening's welcome to the throng that surrounded him on three sides.

"I bid you welcome, my fine friends!" Wasp beat his drum again, three sharp bangs. The audience, silent now, watched on as Circus Master continued. "Tonight is our last night in your fine town of Shrewsbury. This night, under the light of a full moon!" He pointed skyward. "You will witness a spectacle that you will remember for all time!"

The crowd cheered. Wasp beat his drum, and the crowd became expectantly silent, shuffling with excitement, children on shoulders, fidgeting, little faces shining in the moonlight. Circus Master announced proudly,

"Ladies, Gentleman, Children! Please bid welcome to Fire-Eater."

The crowd roared enthusiastically, clapping hands and cheering wildly. Circus Master stepped quickly to one side. Wasp started to beat the drum, Crow tootled on the fife, Fire-

Eater took centre stage, bowing lowly. The audience cheered again. Fire-Eater raised his hands in the air, lifted first one leg and then the other, stamping each firmly down, planting bare feet on the ground. Uttering a silent incantation with eyes tightly closed, arms outstretched, palms uppermost, white smoke began to appear from his hands, circling upwards in the moonlight. The crowd stepped back in awe. A voice shouted, "WIZARD!"

As the audience applauded, the white smoke changed to grey and then back again. A red flicker shone on the palm of each of Fire-Eater's hands. Suddenly, flicker turned to flame, appearing firstly akin to a candle before bursting, blinding, orange shafts shot into the air. Cheering and clapping, the audience screamed in delight, some cringing, fear of unknown powers filling their minds. Fire-Eater was indeed awesome to see and was now throwing his hands in the air, flames from each creating rings of fire that danced above his head. Wasp and Crow played on, stamping their feet and taking up song. Rings of orange, white and crimson flame danced around Fire-Eater as they sang.

'Flaming fire, burning free
Creating light for you and me
Dancing flames, burning bright
Turning, spinning, into the night.'

The gathered throng hummed along with Wasp and Crow's song and in no time at all, as Fire-Eater spun never-ending rings of fire, they began to sing. Over and over, repeating chorus after chorus, the audience sang on and on.

'Flaming fire, burning free
Creating light for you and me
Dancing flames, burning bright
Turning, spinning, into the night.'

Wasp banged his drum three times and out went the flames in a puff of smoke, as the once blazing rings instantly disappeared. Fire-Eater bent low in appreciation of the applause filling his ears and echoing into the night. Children screamed with delight, clapping fiercely. Parents and others stamped their feet, hailing affirmations of joy. Fire-Eater swiftly slid away to the left of the crowd as Circus Master, as if by magic, appeared in the centre of the stage. Wasp beat his drum again three times. Circus Master bowed, and the audience cheered.

"My friends!" His voice boomed, and the audience stilled. "From flames of light to arrows of truth!" Raising his arms in the air as high as such a portly frame could manage, he continued, exciting frenzy in all who heard. "Now please welcome the man who alone shoots arrows as fast as ten archers." The audience cheered. "An archer with eyes as a hawk!" Circus Master bowed to the audience, stood erect and raised his arms again. "Welcome Blaze!" Circus Master left the stage, bowing to the audience as he went, extending his arms in welcome to the next performer.

Wasp and Crow struck up a tune. Blaze now stood centre stage, holding a longbow which was as tall as a man. Silver hair cascaded over his bronzed shoulders, strong muscular arms held a bow in one hand and a fistful of arrows in the other. He wore an archer's leather jerkin, emblazoned with flashes of red and golden arrows, embroidered back and front. He stood motionless on long legs, full boots reaching muscled thighs. Blaze bowed to the audience. They cheered! Wasp beat the drum. Lifting the bow, placing a projectile carefully to string, Blaze aimed upwards, drew back the arrow and 'snap,' the arrow disappeared skywards. Watching intently in silence, the crowd with necks tilted backwards, stared in wonderment at essentially nothing! There was, after all, nothing to see as the arrow had flown high up into the heavens. Crow and Wasp began to play a haunting melody as Blaze produced an apple from his pocket and held it between long fingers with an outstretched arm. The audience watched as suddenly the arrow, the arrow he had fired into space, came down and pierced the apple between Blaze's waiting fingers. Holding up the apple, the arrow was to be seen as having cleanly pierced through the centre of the core. The audience seemed stunned into surprise and disbelief before exploding into rapturous applause. Blaze strung another arrow, drew back the bow and fired again high into the night sky. Down it came, another apple bearing evidence of magical marksmanship by Blaze. The audience erupted into more applause whilst Wasp, and Crow both danced as they continued to play.

Pale-Man and Strong-Man, carrying a large straw target between them, stepped boldly onto the stage, setting it down on a wooden stand in front of the audience. Blaze aimed his bow over their heads, with arrow charged, bowstring fully drawn. Many in the audience ducked, thinking Blaze was aiming at them. Wasp beat the drum and 'snap,' the arrow was gone. As quickly as the arrow had disappeared, it returned, 'thwack,' smacking into the centre of the bull's-eye. Again the night was filled with applause, echoing out into the ether and the music continued. Several times, from different angles, Blaze repeated feats of marksmanship, stunning the onlookers into a trance-like state of amazement, their eyes bulging, fixed, not a blink between them. The drum beat crashed and echoed and with a low stiff bow in thanks to the audience, Blaze was gone, concealed in a puff of smoke. Circus Master spun onto the stage, clapping his hands and smiling at the audience, knowing success was already painted on the faces of the throng. Slowly but surely, as was always his way, winding the audience towards frenzy, he addressed all.

"You have seen the 'magic of flame,' you have seen the 'arrows of truth' and now...." He paused momentarily to wipe his sweaty forehead on the back of his gloved hand, "and now, the 'mystery of the wolf,' fierce and feared by all." Wasp beat the drum three times. "People of Shrewsbury, welcome into your hearts, Wolf-Woman! Circus Master slid quietly from the stage.

Applause came rapidly and enthusiastically, the crowd now almost in a frenzy of expectation after that already witnessed. A new tune emanated from the dancing dwarves, swooning left and right to haunting tones. Smoke drifted across the stage then, like fog floating down a valley, parted.

Wolf-Woman stood motionless, cloaked in purple from head to foot. A wolf sat at each side, one as black as night, the other as white as driven snow. Majestic, fearsome and huge, standing, staring. A loud gasp came as the audience demonstrated their fear and respect, taking a pace backwards. Wolf-Woman lifted her arms, cloak slipping across her shoulders, reflections of light from the firebrands illuminating her long golden dress, she tilted her head backwards and howled. The music ceased, and silence drifted throughout the night all but for her howl, long, haunting and born deep from within her soul. Black-Wolf sauntered slowly to her extreme left, White-Wolf to her right. They turned simultaneously and sitting on broad haunches, lifted their huge heads towards the moon, emitting a deep-throated howl which filled the night sky, echoing in every person's ears, near and far.

Smoke drifted in clouds across the stage as Wolf-Woman continued to demonstrate her relationship with wolves. Not a word did she utter throughout the performance, she simply howled, grunted, barked and snarled commands to which both wolves responded without hesitation or question. They leapt in the air, attacking an invisible foe, they rolled on the ground with Wolf-Woman, as does a wolf pack at play, and they ran amongst the audience, wagging tails and barking with delight as folk tried to avoid them. Howls, barks, and growls were the only sounds. Wolf- Woman barked, and both wolves returned to her side and sat staring, huge golden and black eyes looking out into the audience. Wolf-Woman, together with both wolves, lifted their heads to the sky and howled again. Thick smoke enveloped them as Wasp beat his drum three times. Circus Master stepped through the smoke, clapping huge, fat, gloved hands. The audience cheered, and children screamed with delight as he raised his arms to muster silence. The crowd complied.

"Strength, my friends, comes in all shapes and sizes." He waved a gloved hand in submission and awe at the audience. "Please consider, if you will if what you are about to see is not the greatest feat of strength ever seen by man!" The audience applauded.

Well, now it was my turn! We had rehearsed hard and long, and I felt confident for my part, but this was the real thing. I quaked slightly in my small boots. I was hidden behind the wagon, dressed in a leather jerkin, my hair held back and secured by a thong tied in a bow, waiting for the cue which would launch my career as a performer, just as Llwyd ap Crach Llwyd had said. I, of course, as you know, had grave doubts about much of what he had said before the start of my journey. However, those hearing my story in the telling will also know much has happened to persuade me otherwise. I stand confirmed in the belief of my Master's prophecy. Strong-Man stood towering at my side in a full leather suit, taut over enormous bulging muscles. Circus Master continued.

"Please welcome to your town the tallest man and the shortest man, the strongest men ever to grace your company!" He applauded as Wasp beat the drum and the audience clapped.

Our cue to the stage rang through the beat of Wasp's drum and with utmost surprise, my legs ceased to quake, and as if no thought was required, I stepped in front of the crowd. For the first time in my life I was a performer and here, now, under a full moon, my strength would be proven to all who could see. Crow played a jolly jig, accompanied by Wasp beating loudly, drumming rhythmically, as Strong-Man and I lifted a wagon high in the air. I lifted a large wooden wheel with one hand above my head whilst Strong-Man swung an enormous iron ball at the end of a short chain, round and around his head. I was really starting to enjoy myself, in fact, it is true to say that I had not had as much fun in years and the applause seemed to make it even better.

Energy coursed as a fast flowing river through every cell of my small body. This small body, in such a state of concentration, and yet not, showed strength equivalent to that of three full-sized men. Our combined strength, phenomenal as it must have been to watch, seemed easy to us and required little real effort, simply concentration with ease. Our finale of strength was near. Wasp crashed the drum as smoke washed across the stage. Strong-Man stepped into the centre and bellowed at the audience, requesting six volunteers to step forward. Well, between them there was every shape and size imaginable standing with us on the stage. All six of them waited, fidgeting and twitching, perhaps wondering what sort of experience to be remembered for many years to come was about to take place.

Strong-Man took hold of two of the men by the scruff of their necks in his left hand. One was as round as a barrel, the other well-built and muscular. In his right hand, he held two very plump men, bloated by ale and pie, faces flushed purple. I knelt with arms outstretched, laying my palms uppermost on the ground, beckoning the remaining men. Each stepped onto my hands, and I felt their weight, heavy at first, as indeed they were. In my mind, I could see feathers floating, and I began to feel their lightness. Wasp and Crow began a merry tune and together Strong- Man and I lifted our charges. He lifted his, their feet dangled helplessly. One man lifting four! I took a breath and raised my arms with a man precariously balanced on each hand. Straightening my back and legs while standing up, I took them higher. The audience was wild with excitement, and the drum beat resounded in our ears.

Our finale over, we stepped back into the smoke, leaving the volunteers, now with feet back on the ground, seemingly lost and forlorn. Pale-Man quickly helped the shaking men off the stage, urging them away into a waiting crowd of back-slapping friends and family.

Circus Master stepped forward. The applauding audience

clapped louder, almost frantically, encouraging more of the same. Raising his arms, gesticulating a need for quiet, slowly the audience responded and became calmer, settling in for the main finale about to unfurl. He raised his arms as high as it was possible, waving at the audience, golden ring on gloved hand glistening in the moonlight.

"Friends, parents, children, people of Shrewsbury. We, the 'Magic Travelling Circus,' invite you all to join in song and dance!" The audience cheered and screamed for more. "Dwarves, strike up the music!"

He waved towards Crow who, beating his drum three times in succession, began to dance as Wasp tootled his flute. Music filled the air, and the audience began to sway from side to side in time with the melody. The performers sang from behind the stage as the music became louder and louder.

'All of us here in dark of night
Have seen magic dancing in light
Mystery of fire, truth of arrow, standing tall
Wonder of Wolves, strongmen big and small
We wish you well in all you do
In grace we bid farewell to you.'

Sounds of joy filled the night as, one by one, performers stepped onto the stage. Fire-Eater, spinning rings of fire around his head, bowed as he stepped forward. Clapping and screaming, the audience thanked him for his part in the spectacular. Before the applause could subside, Blaze leapt onto the stage, spinning his long bow, somersaulting and landing on his feet to stand erect next to Fire-Eater. Hands clapped, feet stamped, and the audience danced on.

Smoke fluttered across the stage, fogging all, as Wasp and Crow played on. Wolf-Woman, with Black-Wolf and White-Wolf at her side, stepped daintily to centre stage and curtsied. The wolves raised their huge heads to the moon and howled loudly, deeply filling the night with their haunting voices. Frantic dancing sent clouds of dust into the air, ale swilling from jugs splashed on unsuspecting neighbours lost in their own dreams, children laughed, screamed, folk wanted more. Crow and Wasp played on as we, the cast, sang.

Now it was my turn. Strong-Man lifted me up onto his broad, muscular shoulders. We stepped out proudly in front of all gathered and both bowed, me being very careful not to tumble off! I laughed loudly at my near fall and Strong-Man, feeling my anxiety, straightened to balance himself, and me too! Circus Master raised his arms, and the music and singing ceased abruptly. He addressed the audience, thanking all for coming, expressing gratitude, bowing low. The audience cheered for one last time as we all bowed and left the stage.

Folk and their children wandered away, some noisily, others quietly, with their minds full of what had just been seen. Children tugged at sleeves, questioning in disbelief, demanding an explanation. Parents frustratingly dragged overtired and excited children in an attempt to ignore questions they could never answer in a 'month of holy days.' The show was done. I, Crach Ffinnant, truly am a circus performer! My first show behind me and destiny unfurling. I was starving!

CHAPTER NINE

The next morning as the cock crowed, up came the sun. A good fine day was promised to us by the heavens. We had all been up since well before dawn, packing away canvas, barrels, and ropes. All circus equipment was now stowed onto the wagons and tied down securely in readiness for our journey from Shrewsbury. Strong-Man and Blaze harnessed two powerful horses to each wagon whilst Pale-Man gave them all a full nosebag of corn. They were well nourished this breakfast. Our troupe was almost ready to leave, but first, we too must eat. It had fallen on Wasp to prepare our porridge this morning, the gruel was cold and ready-served in bowls, waiting for collection by each of us. Sitting in a large circle upon the ground, the bowls emptied rapidly to the sound of scraping spoons as our gathering breakfasted. I ate heartily, needing all my strength for the day ahead, lumps of cold porridge sliding easily down my throat.

Crow rushed around us, gathering up the now empty bowls, piling them up for cleaning, balancing each precariously one on top of the other. He staggered from foot to foot, hidden from view behind so many stacked bowls which rocked from side to side, but with a stumble and a trip, they all crashed to the ground. Our hail of laughter sent him into a frenzy, stamping his small feet in frustration. I helped him to gather up the bowls which had scattered hither and thither, laughing quietly to myself but unable to say a word, of course, because I was supposed to be dumb, a disguise which presented some difficulty at times! Choking on my unspoken words, I passed the bowls to Wasp who was hurriedly scrubbing them clean. Crow put his pile next to mine, laughing now, as we all had, at his own clumsiness.

It would soon be time to leave this place of Shrewsbury as the last bits and pieces were being placed in each wagon. Four huge, lumbering, wooden wagons in all. Eight horses, harnessed and tethered, waited patiently whilst finishing their breakfasts, soft muzzles foraging deeply for any remaining corn lurking in the corners of their nosebag. One, a beautiful black and white mare, stamped her hoof, sending small stones flying in all directions, frustrated that her breakfast was exhausted. Another horse, the largest of them all, shook its huge head from side to side, now wishing the empty nosebag gone. Pale-Man moved swiftly on long straggly legs, striding from horse to horse, removing nosebags from the waiting charges.

"Time to mount up, my fine friends!" Circus Master's voice boomed. Strong-Man mounted the first wagon, taking the reins in huge hands. Circus Master sat mounted upon a pure white stallion, watching carefully as all moved into action at the sound of his voice. His finery from the previous evening gone, he wore a large black hat, sporting a peacock's feather, a black cloak hung loosely, concealing all but breeches and thigh- high black leather boots. Standing erect in the stirrups, glancing across at one of the wagons, he urged Crow and Wasp to move a little faster.

"Get a move on dwarves, it will be dark before we get going. Hurry!" Circus Master cracked his riding whip in the air.

Wasp and Crow jumped up onto a wagon, helping each other to climb aboard.

"Crach!" Wasp shouted at me. "You ride with us!"

I scrambled up to join them, assisted by Crow's extended hand. Pale-Man, with reins already in hand, sat on another wagon, Strongman aboard the third, with Blaze driving the last. When we had all mounted and were prepared to move, Circus Master bellowed.

"Let's go!"

His white charger reared high, and upon landing, dust powdered the air as the magnificent stallion broke into a trot, flared nostrils snorting, tail swishing from side to side. One after the other, whips cracked, reins lashed across haunches and the wagons rolled, following clouds of dust left in Circus Master's wake.

It was a bumpy ride. The wagon jolted as it rolled out of one rut into another but at least the sun shone, and it was much warmer today. Fluffy white clouds drifted casually across a blue sky, little wind blew, and the heat from the still rising sun felt pleasant on my skin. Crow snapped loose reins and whistled quietly to himself. Wasp dozed in the back of the wagon, small snores issuing forth, buzzing like a tired bee. I sat next to Crow and stared at the lush greenery of England. It was not what I had been led to expect by my Master, Llwyd ap Crachan Llwyd. I suppose it was because we thought the English were so evil and dark that their country would be also. But this was a beautiful place to behold indeed. Rolling hills and lush forests reminded me of Wales, and for a moment I found my mind drifting back to my homeland.

"A good day to journey, Crach?"

Crow stopped whistling, smiling at me as he continued. "We will camp for two nights before our next show."

"Where are we going?" I mimed, scratching my chin while pointing into the distance and trying to look quizzical.

"Worcester!" He answered, cracking the reins again.

I had never heard of this place. Mind you, I had never heard of Shrewsbury either until my Master sent me on this journey.

"Is it a big place?" I gesticulated, spreading my arms and again appearing quizzical by raising first one eyebrow and then the other, hoping this would aid my 'dumb' question to be understood. Crow seemed to understand my every expression. Oh, what joy I now felt! I was getting so used to pretending speechlessness that it felt quite natural and my friends appeared to have no difficulty in grasping meanings encapsulated by my actions.

"Bigger than Shrewsbury, more people too, thus probably a much bigger audience than last night. We always earn more there, but it can be a bit dangerous at times." Crow replied.

His words rang in my ears. Well one word to be precise, the word 'dangerous.' I did not like the sound of that. I did not like it at all.

'Dangerous in what way?' I wondered. Crow must have seen fear on my face as he continued.

"Don't worry, Crach, Master always protects us. As there

are a lot more people in Worcester than in Shrewsbury, it means more opportunity for us to encounter folk that may not be too nice, especially to dwarves!" I remembered how I had been shunned and verbally attacked when entering Shrewsbury, not to forget my close encounters with buckets of slops hewn from windows, accompanied by abuse, before shutters were instantly slammed shut by an unknown assailant. I knew we were either revered for our magical abilities or hated due to tales of curses becoming true when issued by dwarves. Well, there is always some truth associated with rumour, but man could often demonstrate more evil intent than any dwarf was born to even consider. Men were vicious, unkind and many times acted without thought. Dwarves never acted without thinking first. It's in our blood to be naturally cautious. Quick to thought and slow to act gives us time to consider a correct response. We do not like violence, and that has nothing to do with our size. I had always thought of brutality as being needless and futile. Although I was yet to learn that in some situations there may be no other choice. Crow started to whistle again, Wasp snored in the wagon, whilst I leant back against a sack and began to daydream with the warmth from the sun aiding my drifting mind.

Rolling mist filled my dreams, mountain tops towered high and deep valleys so very far below. Suddenly, I found myself sitting in a cave, warming my feet in front of a brightly burning fire, giving light to all within. Rain pattered on the wet ground outside. I knew this place, it was familiar, and I had been here before.

"Of course you have been here before, Crach!" Said Llwyd ap Crachan Llwyd. My Master's voice echoed around the cave. "Daydreaming again, Crach, my fine dwarf? And it has brought you to me!"

I turned and saw a spectre above me beginning to materialise from the ether. As it cleared, a shape formed and there stood Llwyd ap Crachan Llwyd, smiling.

"Hello, Crach." My Master kneeled down, slapping me playfully on the shoulder as he had done so many times before. "I told you we would meet again, and this is the second time we have done so in your dreams. It will not be the last!" Smiling again, he warmed his hands over the flames. "Warmer in England I will wager!" He laughed loudly.

"Sometimes difficult to remember you are dumb, is it Crach?"

He gripped my shoulder playfully and laughed. I looked up at Llwyd ap Crachan Llwyd who was beside himself with abject glee - at my expense, no doubt! Giggling from ear to ear, he suddenly looked considerably younger than in my last dream into which he had leapt uninvited. But that was his way. My Master is as good as his word, he truly is watching over the progress of my destiny.

"So Crach, you are to go to Worcester next. Mark my words carefully now, Crach!" His smile disappeared, and he was an old man again, frowning, his bushy eyebrows like two furry caterpillars meeting each other in the centre of a wrinkled forehead. "Thus far, the trials and tribulations experienced by you have been, in essence, in preparation for your future steps."

He kneeled down beside me and gripped my shoulder in a very fatherly way. I noticed a glow deep in his eyes, now sunken with age. He smiled.

"Crach, watch out for an English Knight wearing a blue plume in a silver helmet. One who rides a horse as black as the night sky? Whatever may happen will challenge your patience as it has never been thus before. You must, at all costs, stay dumb. Remember, Crach, speak not a word, no matter what may happen."

Suddenly he was gone, and I was alone in the cave, staring at the place where my Master had been only a moment before.

A great tiredness filled every pore of my body when I felt a jolt so fierce that every one of my bones shook and upon opening my bleary eyes, it was Wasp's snores that filled my ears.

"Dammed horse!" Crow cursed. The horse righted itself from a stumble in the ruts set deeply in the track beneath its hooves. "Come on! Get up there!"

Crow slapped the reins loosely across the horse's flanks. It pulled hard against the harness, and the heavy wagon jolted once more into motion.

"A good sleep, Crach?" Crow enquired.

I nodded agreement and sat up from the sack, shaking my still sleepy body back into some semblance of awareness to current reality. But the voice of Llwyd ap Crachan Llwyd still echoed deep inside my mind. *'An English Knight wearing a blue plume in a silver helmet, atop a horse as black as the night.'*

CHAPTER TEN

For two days we travelled the road to Worcester, camping last night by a fast flowing river. Now, late in the evening, staring ahead, I could see on the horizon silhouettes of buildings, distant chimneys with smoke rising skywards. I pointed at the horizon, grunting my silent question towards Crow.

"That is Worcester, Crach." Laughing loudly, he stood up in the wagon, holding the reins on high. "I was born there, Crach!"

He was very excited, hopping from one foot to the other as he tried to steer the horses. It's a good job that those horses were so used to their tasks, as the two beauties that pulled our wagon completely ignored Crow's frenzied misguidance. He jumped up and down, and I did consider that he may leap off the wagon in error, so I held out a hand to steady him. Crow playfully slapped my hand away, lost his balance completely and fell head-first off the wagon, landing in a less than graceful heap on the ground below. Had Crow not been a dwarf, of course, he would not have had so far to fall. As it was, he fell twice as far as would a man of normal stature.

A cloud of dust appeared as Circus Master reined back his white stallion, coming to a stop next to the heap on the ground that was Crow. He dismounted quickly and rushed to him. Bending over, Circus Master gathered the crumpled Crow into his arms, cradling him back to his shaking feet. Crow was stunned by the fall and not a smile could be seen now as he rubbed a lump on his head that was growing by the second. Circus Master dusted Crow down with large gloved hands, as would a father picking up a wayward child after a tumble.

"What happened here, Crow? You fool of a dwarf! If you had fallen under the wheels of this wagon, it would have been death!"

Despite our Master's protestations, he was not angry with Crow. He really was concerned for his safety and well-being. Circus Master fussed over him, checking for broken bones while rolling up sleeves and trouser legs, rubbing his small limbs in order to recirculate the blood stopped in its flow by the shock of such a fall.

"Looks as if all is well Crow, apart from this lump on your stupid head." He lightly tapped Crow's forehead with a chubby gloved finger. "No real harm done, I wager!" He lifted Crow back up to the wagon, dusting him down one last time.

As Circus Master returned Crow to his seat, he looked me straight in the eyes and whispered. "Take the reins Crach, whilst this fool rests from his fall." He turned again to Crow.

"Well, what happened Crow?"

Crow looked sheepish and tried to avoid Master's eyes,

staring at the ground.

"Well?" Master questioned again.

"I'm home again Master. I'm home!" Master smiled at Crow's answer.

"So you got a bit too excited again, did you?" Master laughed loudly. "You will never learn, will you? Every time we come to Worcester, you fall off the wagon in blind joy. It would be something I could understand if you had family who still lived Crow, but you do not." Circus Master smiled and patted Crow on the back. "You are a silly dwarf, but I don't know what I would do without you, without any of you for that matter."

He turned and taking mount of the stallion, sat erect in the saddle. Holding the reins in my hands, I was ready for my first attempt to drive a wagon. In his haste to ensure Crow's safety, Circus Master had forgotten to ask me if I knew how. Still, a dumb dwarf must have a go at these things. It's probably easier than trying to mime which I had never done before either. *Do you have any idea how huge this wagon and its two horses are to a dwarf? Well, if you have never looked through the eyes of a dwarf, then you wouldn't, would you?'*

Circus Master turned the stallion on its hooves, dug in his spurs and trotted to the front of the wagons. I cracked the reins and, to my astonishment and delight, my new charges walked on, followed by the wagon jolting forward with a lurch. Crow sat next to me, nursing his swollen head, looking just a little dishevelled following his recent encounter with the ground.

We rode on for another hour under the last rays of the sun before entering the stone-walled town of Worcester. It was the time of the annual fair, and the road was busy with traders and farmers, wagons, sheep and cattle, all making their way into the town. The circus joined the convoy as clouds of dust rose from the road, making Crow and I cough. Wasp finally awoke from his slumbers. Here was a dwarf that could sleep through storms and the earth shaking. I had never known the like.

Even though the light from the sun was now gone, we were afforded some illumination from the lamps that shone from many of the windows of the wooden thatched houses and cottages. Ramshackle shelters stood between larger dwellings. Craftsman worked in open-fronted shops, beating leather, smashing anvils, orange and white sparks disappearing into the night. Burly men manhandled huge wooden casks of wine onto waiting wagons. The biggest building I had ever seen stood in front of us. It was so tall, seemingly reaching up towards the heavens.

"It is the Cathedral, Crach!" Crow raised his head and smiled. "The monks there gave me sanctuary and helped me when my parents died. It was them who got me this job with my Master. That was ten years ago, Crach. Ten long years!"

Glancing at Crow's eyes, I could see some sadness as he spoke of his parents, now long gone in the mists of time to the 'other-world,' but not in the mind of Crow, the Dwarf. I squeezed his arm gently while miming my compassion for his loss. Yet he was so ecstatic when we were approaching Worcester? I was mildly perplexed at his mixed emotions but, no doubt, Crow would tell me all in the fullness of time. He smiled as I squeezed his chubby arm and said.

"So many happy memories you know, Crach, so many."

I pulled in the reins, and the horses came to a stop behind Strong- Man's wagon. The four wagons, together with eight tired horses, stood in line, waiting for Circus Master's instructions. The high sides of the Cathedral towered above us, casting a huge shadow over the light that shone from so many windows.

"This is our usual spot, Crach." Crow pointed towards a large space next to a high stone wall adjoining the Cathedral. "Same place every year." He continued. "Time to get unpacked and set up the circus for our show tomorrow!"

He jumped down, seemingly forgetting his recently bruised head following his fall from the wagon. He waved his arm, commanding me to follow. Gently I lowered my small self to the ground, feeling very sore from so many hours riding the rickety rut-filled road from Shrewsbury to Worcester.

Pale-Man was busy digging deeply into a large sack of oats, filling the horse's nosebags. Strong-Man, Blaze, and Wasp unloaded the big sail canvas in readiness for erection between the wagons to provide a canopy which would shelter us in our performances later tomorrow. Crow and I released our horses from their harnesses and tied them to the rope strung between two poles. Circus Master's white stallion already had his muzzle deep in a nosebag, foraging for every grain, swishing a bushy white tail in contentment. Pale-Man, having hung a nosebag on each horse, now busied himself with folding and stacking harnesses into the wagon which previously held the heavy canopy.

"Let's get some food ready for us, Crach."

Crow jabbed playfully in my ribs as I followed him to the rear of one of the wagons. Crow climbed up and started to pass cooking wares down to me. Firstly, there was the big cauldron that would hold our porridge. Secondly, a huge wooden ladle and finally, a stack of bowls, together with wooden spoons. Placing them on the ground carefully, I stood up only to hear

Crow shout.

"Catch!"

I turned quickly just in time to see a sack of oats flying through the air towards me at speed. I held my arms out, stretched every muscle that my height allowed and caught the heavy sack, its weight sending me crashing to the ground. Crow burst into hysterical laughter, holding his sides and jumping up and down. He then slipped on the wagon, sending him sprawling to the floor, landing next to me in a heap. Now it was my turn to laugh! We were both laying prostrate on the ground, giggling, when a shadow of a huge man cast itself on the ground across us. When I looked up, there stood Circus Master staring down with a stern expression on his plump face.

"Mucking about again, dwarves?" He stood with his arms outstretched. "Get up and get on with your work. There is much to be done, and we have no time for children's games. Now get up!"

I staggered to my knees and gesticulated an apology towards him. He smiled at me and then turned towards Crow, bellowing a question loudly.

"Dwarf! Are you a musician or a jester?"

Suddenly, Circus Master burst into laughter, while at the same time attempting to be serious, but it was impossible, he could not stop now. The three of us laughed and giggled until Circus Master, in the midst of frivolity, shouted,

"Enough!" Trying to keep his face straight and posturing seriousness, he barked "Back to work!" as he strode away, laughing and scratching his head.

After the meal, cooked and served by Crow and assisted by me, we washed the bowls and scrubbed the cauldron clean. Crow disappeared in order to practice his music with Wasp whilst I went off in search of Strong-Man to see what tasks still awaited in preparation for the forthcoming show tomorrow.

It had been a long day and night and was now well into a new day, but finally, all was prepared, and we had but a few hours left before the evening's performance was to begin. Pale-Man and Blaze, accompanied by Crow and his drum, had disappeared into town in order to promote the show. I was quite tired so took the opportunity of sleep for a little while, finding solitude between two sacks on a comfortable sheepskin at the back of one of the wagons. Such warmth and comfort led me quickly to sleep.

I was awoken a little while later by Wasp shaking my shoulder and whispering.

"Wake up, Crach. It is time."

I smiled and nodded my gratitude for his waking me while urgently scrambling off the sacks and sheepskins. Climbing down from the wagon, I took the huge ladle hanging on the water barrel and scooped cool fresh water, drinking furiously to quench my thirst. What I did not drink, I splashed over my head. Now that woke me up properly! I shook my head and rubbed my face back into life.

Well, this evening's show was in front of us now, and with this thought, I shivered with quiet excitement. It was now time to find Strong-Man. We had both practised well during the day, and he was pleased with my efforts. Circus Master watched all rehearse and made comments here and there, always supportive and encouraging us to become better and better at what we did. Mind you, it was in his and all of our best interests to perform well so that the audience enjoyed the show and thus rewarded us accordingly. Blaze lit the firebrands around the performing area whilst the rest of us donned our outfits. It would soon be time for the show to begin!

Chapter Eleven

I had never in all my life thus far seen so many people gathered together in one place as I saw in front of me this evening. Maybe three hundred, with more standing around muttering and laughing, but unlike the audience in Shrewsbury, many here were dressed in the finery of their wealth. A group of young men, attired in clothes befitting gentlemen, stood at the front swigging wine from flagons balanced in the crook of their arms, teetering on thirsty lips. They appeared to be quite drunk already, speaking to each other in voices so loud that all standing near could hear their words. Raucous, belittling slurs spun from their mouths, chastising a poor ragged man standing close to them.

"Stand aside, churl!"

One of the group, a tall young man, dressed in a fancy crimson-coloured tunic with blonde hair hanging untidily across his shoulders, shouted as he pushed the man to the ground.

"You stink! Have you ever washed?"

He kicked out at the ragged man but missed and in his intoxicated state, slipped and fell flat on his back. This brought a cheer of both condemnation and justice from those standing near who were witnessing the unpleasantness. His comrades howled with laughter, pointing at him, as the blonde aggressor struggled to his feet and dusted down fine clothes, now stained with thick grime. The blonde man was furious on hearing the gibes from his friends. Waving his hands in rejection of their jeers, he grabbed at the ragged man, lifting him by the scruff of the neck from the ground so that the poor man's feet dangled in fresh air as he struggled against the strong grip of the younger man.

"Let him alone!"

One of his friends, who was of the same height as the bully and of similar attire to that of the wealthy, cried out in defence of the ragged man as he stepped forward, taking the blonde man firmly by the arm. The 'defender's features were sharp and handsome, with high cheekbones and young beard growth on his chin.

"Cease this bullying, Edmund! For pity's sake, the man is smaller and weaker than you, and this is unjust!"

He pulled Edmund away and pushed him in the opposite direction, resulting in a further fall to the ground, much to the appreciation of the onlookers who screamed in laughter once again.

Circus Master appeared, seemingly from nowhere, and cracked his whip high in the air over the head of Edmund, the blonde bully.

"Stop this!"

He shouted loudly, with a firm expression etched across his

face. Strong-Man stepped to one side of Circus Master, Blaze to the other, brandishing a stave made of oak which stood taller than himself. On seeing the strength and force now challenging him, Edmund scowled and muttered under his breath before re-joining his friends. Circus Master addressed the audience in his loudest voice.

"The show will start soon, my friends. It will be of spectacular amazement, with feats of strength and wonderment of magic. But for now, be patient, dear folk of Worcester!"

The audience cheered as Circus Master, Strong-Man and Blaze bowed and disappeared behind a wagon. The show went well, and we all performed to the best of our ability, bringing nothing but credit to our Master. Rapturous applause was received from the enthused audience. The group of young men had, for the most part, behaved themselves during our acts. That is all, but for Edmund, who had continued to heckle onlookers and performers alike. He just did not seem to be able to keep his mouth closed or keep to his own counsel, choosing every opportunity he could to belittle any other. He was the worst sort of bully I had ever come across and was made extremely unpredictable by the quantities of wine he had consumed, some of which having missed his ever-open mouth, now adding to the stains on his tunic.

As the finale of our show came to a close to more rapturous applause, we all took it in turn to bow, much to the appreciation of the audience who slowly began to return to their homes in the darkness of night, chattering and laughing as they went. A few stragglers remained, amongst whom were the young gentlemen, including Edmund. They stood huddled closely together, talking to each other now much more quietly than before. The young gentleman who had defended the ragged man must have been in disagreement with the rest of them as he pulled himself away from the group, remarking loudly so all could hear.

"I will have no part of this! Gentlemen do not behave in this way!" He stood to face them all and again asserted himself. "You are wrong by your intended actions and bring disgrace upon your houses and families."

He stepped further back as Edmund stepped forward.

"Have a care, Glyndwr, or I will stick you like a rabbit!" Edmund threatened, shaking a finger into the 'defender's' face, challenging for authority. In a flash, Glyndwr moved like lightening, grabbing at Edmund's wagging finger and twisting it, bringing Edmund to his knees, wincing with pain.

"You have a care, Edmund, and never address me in that way again!"

Speedily and almost unseen, his hand that had gripped the once wagging finger of Edmund, slid into a hard slap across his cheek that all heard. Edmund stepped back as his hand shot towards the dagger hanging from the leather belt at his middle. Glyndwr, as swift as an arrow, stepped into the full body of the blonde bully and pushed him hard, grabbing the dagger by the hilt before Edmund was able to reach it. He brought his left fist up and struck Edmund hard in the face, drawing blood from a now shattered nose. Edmund fell to the ground with one hand holding his face, blood dripping through his fingers. Glyndwr stepped back and stood tall against the bully.

"Let this be the end of this stupidity. The end!"

Glyndwr addressed Edmund firmly, and all could see that the fight if that is what it was, was now at an end. Edmund was helped to his feet by another of their group. Holding his bleeding face, which was now becoming swollen from the strength of Glyndwr's blow, Edmund stared firmly into Glyndwr's eyes with a fixed gaze.

"I won't forget that, you Welsh churl!"

Edmund yelled, before walking away a short distance where he stopped and sank to his knees, wincing with more pain. Edmund was now left alone on the ground with his discomfort. Glyndwr also stood alone, strong, tall and fearless. I thought *'Here is a man who fights injustice. A brave man who is Welsh, a fellow countryman.'* I looked at him with great interest while also deep inside my mind was a strange feeling of knowing. Circus Master appeared at the precise moment Glyndwr dispatched Edmund to the ground. He stood quietly taking in the scene. Several of the dishevelled young gentlemen, still muttering, stood milling around.

Glyndwr stood alone.

"Come now gentlemen, it is time for you to go and be about your business. The show is over!" Circus Master said firmly as he walked towards them.

Edmund responded.

"Mind your own business, riff raff, or I will cut off your ears!" Blood still dripped from his broken nose. He started to walk towards

Circus Master menacingly, his hand again hanging over the dagger which was back in his belt. Circus Master stepped forward with his hand firmly gripping the hilt of his sword sitting in its scabbard. In his intoxication, Edmund had not seen the sword, but as his eyes cleared, he stopped dead in his tracks, now realising the difference in the length between the blades of his dagger to that of Circus Master's sword. A wise decision. Glyndwr stepped between them and held up his arms.

"Gentlemen!" He said. "It is late and far too much wine has been drunk. Words have been spoken that, in sobriety, may not have been said."

Circus Master's hand still hovered at the hilt of his sword. He stood still, firmly holding his ground whilst staring intently at Edmund. Strong- Man, Blaze, Pale-Man, in fact, the entire company, including myself, Crow, Wasp and the other dwarves, appeared and stood behind Circus Master. Edmund screamed his insults at all of us.

"So churl, you have an army?"

Then Edmund burst into laughter at the sight of us dwarves.

"An army of half-men! Ha! Do you think this will frighten me?" He laughed raucously again.

His comrades stepped away and stood by Glyndwr, who was looking on at the scene with some amusement, perhaps aware that Edmund was about to reap what he had sown by hurling such insults.

Strong-Man stepped in front of Edmund and lifted him fully from the ground with one powerful hand around his throat. Edmund's feet dangled, almost lifelessly, as he clawed the air for breath, unable to shake off Strong-Man's grip.

"Let him go!"

Circus Master ordered, and instantly Strong-Man released his grip on Edmund's throat, letting him fall breathlessly to the ground. Glyndwr left the group of friends and walked slowly over to where Edmund lay gasping for breath. Slowly he helped a half-choked, rather greyish looking Edmund to his feet.

"Come now Edmund, enough is enough!"

He held him by the shoulders, staring into his eyes, which

were now swollen, and pleaded for peace this night. I stepped forward, without any thought for my own safety, and stood at Glyndwr's side. Digging into my pocket, I produced a rag which I silently offered to Edmund so that he may wipe the blood from his face.

"Thank you, Dwarf!" said Glyndwr as he took the rag, smiling down at me, before passing it to Edmund.

We all looked on as Edmund wiped his bloodied face with his swollen eyes full of contempt. The group dispersed, leaving Edmund and Glyndwr alone with our company. Whilst Glyndwr did not seem to mind, Edmund called after them to wait, but his request fell upon deaf ears as they continued to walk away, muttering amongst themselves.

Circus Master instructed us to return to our work as the conflict had now passed. As I turned to walk away, Glyndwr held on to my shoulder. I turned to look up at his great height, and he smiled down at me, his hold changing to a gentle pat.

"Thank you, little friend. I am sorry for Edmund's brash and loutish behaviour."

Edmund was about to protest at the comments but found his mouth firmly closed, shielded by the hand of Glyndwr he was unable to say a word. Glyndwr continued.

"That was a fine show!"

Upon hearing the gratitude expressed, Circus Master stepped towards us and thanked Glyndwr with a bow.

"Thank you, kind sir!" He bowed again. "You are a Welshman, Sir?" Glyndwr nodded agreement and turning to me he said.

"Tell me, where are you from?"

I was just about to mime an answer when Circus Master interjected. "He is dumb and unable to give an answer in speech, he can, however, act his words." Smiling with affection, he said. "Is that right, young Crach?"

I nodded my agreement, smirking. Glyndwr continued.

"My fine dwarf, Crach is a good name, a name to be proud of I'll be bound! Is it not a Welsh name?"

I nodded my head and smiled up at him, acknowledging in quiet agreement, then turned quickly to see if Circus Master had heard the question and noted my response. An instant feeling of panic filled me that this simple error may have destroyed my disguise, but he had not heard, of that I was sure.

Glyndwr was tall and very handsome. He had fine sharp features with an almost regal appeal radiating quiet authority, certainly filling me with a feeling of inexplicable deep security. The only other man in whose presence I had ever felt such awe and security was my Master's, Llwyd ap Crachan Llwyd. Circus Master bade us a 'goodnight' and reminded me not to be long as there was much work to do before the circus could get back on the road again. He strode purposefully back to the wagons where the entire company busied themselves with packing for the journey.

Glyndwr kneeled down and looked into my eyes, his strong hand slight on my shoulder. Smiling, he said.

"You know, I have dreams of a dwarf!"

My eyes nearly burst forth out of my head, bulging like a frog in springtime. *'Could this be the man alluded to by Llwyd ap Crachan Llwyd in his prophecy?'* He continued with raised eyebrows.

"But the dwarf in my dreams could speak, Crach, and you are dumb. He looks like you and is as strong as you are. He is also a healer and a prophet."

I was choking inside upon hearing these words describing

me but my disguise blinded the truth. I looked away from him, casting my eyes towards the heavens and whispered as the wind.

"I can speak....I can."

Glyndwr took my bearded chin in his hand and gently turned my head to face him. He whispered in return, acknowledging the need for secrecy, yet not knowing why.

"So you are he!"

I nodded in agreement. Smiling, I whispered. "I think I may be, my Lord."

He smiled and continuing to whisper closely in my ear, he said, "Something tells me, my new friend, that we will meet again but time is not at hand as we stand now. I must away to London to continue my studies at Lincoln's Inn. What of you, Crach?"

"Eventually, London," I whispered.

CHAPTER TWELVE

The Circus travelled the road to London, stopping to perform in towns and villages along the way. Our biggest shows were in Gloucester, Oxford, Buckingham, and Windsor, and winter was now not far away. For nearly three quarters of a year, I had performed and lived as a dumb dwarf in this travelling circus. It had become my home and the performers, including Wasp, Crow, Blaze, Strong-Man, Pale-Man, Mermaid and Circus Master, my family. Crow was right, Circus Master looked after everybody, never turning a blind eye to any of us, and always there when we needed him. In return, we all performed well at every show. It would soon be Christmas, and the weather was harsh, bitter and wet as our caravan of troubadours entered the gates of my final destination in the first chapter of my destiny as predicted by Llwyd ap Crachan Llwyd—London!

The gates of the city were guarded by the King's soldiers who carefully checked all the contents of our wagons closely before allowing the circus caravan to enter. We slowly trudged wearily through the gates which were surrounded on all sides by wooden ramshackle houses with smoke billowing through holes and makeshift chimneys upon thatched roofs. It was filthy and muddy. Flowing uneasily were pools of excrement which filled the gutters, blocked in places by all forms of cast-off rubbish. The smell that invaded my nostrils reminded me of my first moments in Shrewsbury, only worse.

Rolling slowly through the mud, our caravan passed through streets that were hustling and bustling with folk busy about their daily tasks. Groups of armed soldiers marched here and there, seemingly keeping a close eye on everything to maintain order. I saw a big burly soldier bearing the King's insignia on his tunic, stretched across a broad chest, kick out savagely at an old man who was begging at the side of the road. In my homeland of Wales, we would never treat a person in such an uncaring way. Never had I heard of such cruelty and certainly had never witnessed it as I was doing now. The old man rolled into the gutter, grasping his middle where the soldier's boot had struck him unnecessarily and mercilessly. The soldier kicked him again in the small of his aged back, making the old man curl up like a baby, groaning in the gutter, tears of pain, resentment, and fear streaming from his tired eyes. The King's soldier then stepped over the old man and turning on his heel he drew phlegm from deep down in his big chest and spat. The spittle landed in the middle of the old man's face, spraying onto his cheeks. He strode off, leaving his victim prostrate with ne'er a backward glance.

The streets were full of beggars and raggedly dressed

people, many with no shoes, shuffling around in the cold, looking lost, hungry and frightened. Two riders in half armour rode around a corner in front of us on proud, spirited black horses. They trotted towards us, mud and stones flying from heavy hooves which struck the earth forcibly and with purpose. A few paces behind, riding a black charger, sat a young knight with a silver helmet adorned with a blue plume, wafting in the wind as he rode. As they came closer, I thought I recognised the harsh bitter features of the face under the helmet. I was as sure as 'day follows night' that it was the man Glyndwr had saved them from—Edmund, the bully from Worcester. He wore the helmet and plume, and he was riding a stallion, just as predicted by Llwyd ap Crachan Llwyd in his prophecy.

The three horsemen were almost upon us. As they were in haste, perhaps they might ride by—perhaps not! Two of them trotted past, focussing on whatever their mission may have been without so much as glance at us. It was definitely Edmund under the helmet with the blue plume, following behind the other riders. Our eyes met as he glanced over and I saw clearly his misshapen nose, the scars from his tumble with Glyndwr back in Worcester some months ago. Edmund pulled hard on the reins, the bit chaffing in his stallion's mouth as it reared to a halt between our wagon and Strongman's. He pulled on the rein again, turned his mount around and slowly walked his horse over towards us.

"Hold up there!" He yelled.

I drew in the reins, our horses responded as the wagon became motionless. We stared at each other for what seemed an eternity before I caught a glimpse from the corner of my eye of Circus Master approaching on his horse.

"So we meet again, circus riff raff! And you, the helpful, caring, dumb dwarf." I shivered slightly when I heard the vitriol of hatred in his tone. "Why did that Welsh churl, Glyndwr, take a shine to you, a dumb midget? You see Dwarf, I forget nothing."

He pulled at the reins to still his agitated mount whose nostrils flared, snorting forth breath which froze like mist around its majestic face. Just at that precise moment, Circus Master pulled his horse to a full stop between our wagon and Edmund.

"Hello. What is the problem here, Sir?" Circus Master stood up high, stretching the stirrup leathers from the saddle. He looked straight into the eyes of Edmund. "Do we know each other, Sir?"

His face, first quizzical and of concern, turned into a wry smile which began to stretch across his face as he recognised Edmund. Edmund glared at Circus Master contemptuously, his nose twitching as he snarled. "You know that we know each other and now our numbers are somewhat different, are they not?"

Edmund turned to look for the soldiers, but they had ridden on, unaware that he had stopped and oblivious to what was now happening. We had all seen them go. Edmund, of course, was so filled with bitterness, he was aware of nothing except the evil he was driven by to force pain and insult yet again to another, exacting vengeance on those weaker than he. Circus Master looked first at us sitting on our four wagons, before smiling and turning to face Edmund who sat alone. Circus Master said,

"I think not, Sir!" He waved his arm towards our company and repeated. "I think not Sir!"

"Have a care, churl!" Edmund fidgeted nervously in the saddle, his charge sensing anxiety shook its great head from side to side, stretching the reins and challenging his rider's command. "This is London, and I am the King's man! Your mouth should be respectful. Do you hear me?"

Well, Edmund had certainly become a little braver since Worcester, but nevertheless, he was still as foolhardy. He continued with blinding bravado.

"If you are here to perform, peasants," he spat on the ground. "Then you will have a paper of permission from the Gate Commander." He sneered. "Well?"

Edmund, the 'King's Man,' held out an open gauntleted hand in front of our Master. Circus Master smiled and without a word or a change in expression, his left arm, and gloved hand disappeared inside his tunic. He produced the paper, duly stamped by the Gate Commander with our permission to perform.

"I think this is what you are requesting, Sir?"

He handed it over to Edmund, retaining the lower portion between finger and thumb. Circus Master was wise enough to know Edmund may try to destroy our permission as part of his vengeance against us. He held it tight. Edmund saw the stamped seal then let go of the paper.

"Very well" he sneered. "Ride on, but have a care, you may not be as lucky next time we meet, and there will be a next time, churl, believe me!" As he turned his horse to leave, Edmund looked directly at me and said. "Until next time, Dwarf!"

He began to ride away as the soldiers returned, galloping towards him. Sadly for those concerned, but to our great amusement, the three collided side on, and Edmund fell to the ground in a less than graceful way. His mount bolted away as one of the dismounted soldiers helped the fallen 'King's Man' to his feet.

"Get off me!" Edmund screamed in embarrassment and anger, brushing away his helper with a sweep of an arm. "Where in thunder have you been?"

His torrent of abuse now turned on the two soldiers.

"My horse!" Edmund, the 'King's Man,' screamed. "Get my horse!" The other soldier galloped off and came back a few moments later with Edmund's horse tagging along behind. Edmund quickly re-mounted his steed and steadied his shaken self in the saddle. Sneering at me with one last look, digging spurs deep, he was gone in a cloud of water and mud that splattered upwards into the faces of the two soldiers, causing them to flinch. They looked at each other, sharing their contempt for Edmund, before riding on after him less than enthusiastically.

It was dark by the time we arrived at our site for the show. Fire torches blazed, casting eerie shadows, dancing wherever the eye may roam. We were all tired and fraught from the day's events, but we had to unload. It was time to set up for a performance here in London. I stood by the river, staring into reflections dancing on ripples in the water, swirling and turning. I pondered on the work ahead of me this night still to be done, of my meeting with Edmund and of Llwyd ap Crachan Llwyd's prophecy.

Tomorrow would be the time to say goodbye to my friends and new family, to Circus Master, Strong-Man, Blaze, Pale-Man, Crow, Wasp, Mermaid and the others. They did not know tomorrow would be our last day together, nor did they know of my Master's prophecy. Tomorrow would be my last show with the travelling circus as a 'performing dwarf.' In the reflections, shimmering on the surface of the river, I saw the smiling face of my Master, Llwyd ap Crachan Llwyd, and his aged, wrinkled features swirling in and out of vision. His voice echoed deep in my mind.

'All is as it should be, Crach! All is well!'

Chapter Thirteen

With the performance over, we sat to eat gathered around a huge blazing fire, wrapped in sheepskins to keep warm on this freezing night. It had been a good day, and I had managed to sleep for a few hours before my act. All had gone well. The huge audience this night had been very generous in both their applause and in the coin we collected from them. Circus Master had said there would be a few days of rest, there would be one more show, and the circus would move to another part of the City. It would soon be time to close for the winter. It was impossible to travel on tracks during heavy rain, snow and freezing temperatures that would take a man's life within a few hours. Everybody that had a fire stayed close to it during these cold months.

I had already decided that the show today would be my last as I now had to find the Apothecary to whom I was to deliver the scrolls which were still secreted at the bottom of my bag. It would soon be time to say goodbye but I had to choose the right moment, and I was still not sure how I was going to do it. They deserved an explanation. I felt sad to leave them as not a bad word had passed between any of us. Only hard work, laughter and loyalty had been shared. They had all been so kind to me. Everything else just seemed to happen quite effortlessly, and with added protection from Circus Master, all had been very safe for this little dwarf. I also enjoyed the company of such interesting and humble folk. It was the first time that I had lived and worked with anyone other than Llwyd ap Crachan Llwyd. I had enjoyed it tremendously, having learned much about so many things I had previously not known.

It was so cold. I huddled inside the sheepskin, draining the last of the pottage from a wooden bowl, savouring its taste while the remaining warmth filled my belly. I was not sure when I would get my next meal, but I knew this would be my last as a 'performing dwarf' in this circus. Looking around at my friends, seeing and hearing their nattering, I thought to myself that it would take me a long time to mime my goodbyes and to answer the many questions that, no doubt, would be asked. If I spoke in the voice they had never heard during all these months, they may be angry, they may misunderstand. On the other hand, they would understand because I would be able to explain and their anger, if it did exist, would surely dissolve into laughter due to the times we had enjoyed in each other's company. Was it safe to break my disguise now? Had it served me for long enough? I stared into the roaring flames, warmth and heat enveloped me, and I soon began to feel tired.

The flames danced in front of my eyes, my eyelids felt heavy, and my focus bleary. Flickering flames, moulding and winding round and around in the white smoke, began to form shapes. Shimmering images danced in my mind. Faces appeared then faded, melting into each other—my Mother and Father, Llwyd ap Crachan Llwyd, Fwynedd the Shepherd, the drunken man driving his wagon, unfriendly faces in windows hurling insults unheard, my friends here in the circus, Glyndwr and Edmund. As quickly as the spectres appeared, they were gone. Only Edmund's face seemed to hover in the fire for longer than the others, changing from hysterical laughter to awful sneering and grimaces that filled me with fear and trepidation. I could feel a trembling from deep within my being, but it was not physical. Edmund's face disappeared as the fire spluttered sparks in all directions. My ears buzzed as a bee gathering honey from a flower, my toes and fingers tingled. Llwyd ap Crachan Llwyd spoke.

"The time for no words is passed, Crach, it has served you well."

His image was gone, and the fire spluttered again, sending out grey and white puffs of smoke. A hot spark landed on my hand, making me flinch and jolting me back from daydreaming. I cried out in pain.

"You okay, Crach?" Looking surprised at hearing me scream, Crow shook my shoulder. "That was hot I bet!" He laughed.

I turned towards him, stared into his questioning face and whispered.

"It burned me, Crow!"

Crow sat looking at me, speechless, open-mouthed, and gaping in astonishment.

"You, you can speak!" He stuttered, finally finding words to express his surprise. "Wasp! Everybody! Crach can speak!

The dwarf talks!"

Crow jumped up and danced with his usual excitement when he was not sure what to do or say. I looked around quickly at the faces of my friends, unsure as to what their reaction might be. I had only been thinking about my plans to share my plight with them but had not reached a conclusion as to how and when would be best. The spark from the fire had changed all that. I wondered if Llwyd ap Crachan Llwyd was responsible for casting the ember to speed my journey. It certainly would not surprise me, not after all that had happened throughout recent months. I shivered with humility and a little trepidation as to what might happen next.

Wasp was the first to react by bursting into side-splitting laughter, immediately sensing the joke if indeed there was one at all. Strong-Man stood up and walked towards me, smiling and applauding, clapping his huge hands together, creating a sound like a long roll of thunder. Pale-Man sat rocking backwards and forwards like a manic pendulum, tears rolling down his face, unable to control his amusement. Strong-Man picked me up with his enormous fingers clutched under my arms before throwing me high up onto his broad shoulder. He was howling with laughter, and from behind one of the wagons, the wolves joined the chorus of merriment now echoing through the night. Blaze grabbed my hand and shook it furiously.

"Well done Crach, you fooled us all!"

He laughed again and shook my hand so firmly that I nearly fell off Strong-Man's shoulder and would have done so had his other hand not grabbed at my chest just in time to stop me plummeting head-first to the ground. Scrambling to his feet, Pale-Man clawed at the air to gain composure and joined the throng of circus performers now gathering around me, patting my back, which I must say was becoming a little sore. Circus Master, in his usual firm but very sensitive manner, urged his charges to calm.

"Come, friends, let us sit."

But he too started to laugh, accompanied by a repetitive snorting every time he tried to take a breath. On hearing this snorting cacophony of laughter, everybody fell apart again. Strong-Man gently lifted me from his huge shoulder and placed me on the ground. My legs were shaking, in fact, I was shaking from head to toe, not in a state of fear but in a place of shock. Shock from my friends' reaction and from the love and understanding that just happened. I was quivering.

Circus Master gathered himself and gestured, by waving his arms towards the ground, we should all sit down. Everybody sat around him as he stood, warming his rear against the flames of the fire. For some reason that I did not understand, I stayed standing firm. Well, I say 'firm,' my legs were still trembling. Circus Master opened his hand to me with his palm uppermost, wiggling his fingers backwards and forwards, begging me to join him by the fire. He was smiling warmly when he said quietly, so only those gathered should hear.

"Crach has a story to tell us, friends." He patted my shoulder as I stood next to him with my head only reaching his rather tubby waist. "Now, we will hear your voice, Crach." He lowered himself to the floor, tapping my back as his large frame flopped down. "We are listening, Crach!" He smiled.

Mutterings of agreement fluttered amongst my friends, my final audience, sitting and waiting. Unknown to them, of course, this would be my final performance and this time with no rehearsal. I looked at their smiling faces, light from the fire casting dancing shadows around us all. *'My time has come.'* I thought. My throat suddenly found a lump sitting where no lump should sit. I coughed loudly before swallowing hard and whispered.

"Friends, I thank you."

"Speak up Crach!" Crow shouted before he burst into laughter at his own joke. Circus Master interjected.

"Be still, Crow!" He tried to be firm but even he continued to smile as Crow still muttered and giggled.

"Crach, speak up! But not too loud methinks or we would not have enjoyed so much silence these months passed." Circus Master snorted with laughter at his own joke, and we all joined him. I now felt happy that whatever I may say, my friends would understand. I hoped this would include the respect for my disguise.

Shuffling from foot to foot, clearing my throat, I prepared to speak more words in a few moments than had passed my lips since joining the circus in Shrewsbury so many months ago.

"Friends!"

I had found my voice and spoke now above that of a whisper so that all near may hear but with eavesdroppers unwelcome to our truths. With my feet planted firmly on the ground and taking a deep breath, I continued.

"I am sorry that my disguise fooled you and I meant no harm, my friends. I never wished to be dishonest, but it is the best disguise that I may have. Now you hear my voice and my poor words in your language, you will know that I am not English."

"Are you a spy?" Wasp shouted, and everybody laughed. Circus Master quietened the murmurings.

"A spy would know what he is looking for and be giving information to someone about what had been seen, so I am no spy!" I replied.

I was feeling quietly confident now and full of surprise at how much of the language I could speak without difficulty. Perhaps it was because I had spent so many moons simply listening. I continued as silence fell over my friends.

"I have for many years been an apprentice, and one day, not long before the night I walked into your camp in Shrewsbury, I was told I must give up my duties and make my way to London. I have been learning how to heal the sick (I thought this was the wisest thing to say as I needed to be honest but I still had to be very careful about how much of my Master's prophecy I would share) and I have had to make my way to London to meet an apothecary so that my learning may continue."

Shadows danced across their faces, all quiet now, listening intently to my every word. Mind you, talking was a lot easier than miming, I had forgotten that.

"That is my story, my friends!"

I bowed to gentle clapping. Circus Master dragged his frame up from the floor, first on one knee and then the other. He stood in the bright light cast by the fire and for the first time, I thought he looked much older and tired.

"A fine story, Crach, and not one to disbelieve, I'll be bound." Quiet words of agreement sprung from all present. He continued. "So Crach, are you pressing on with your journey, or will you stay in your new profession as a performer?"

Everybody applauded, encouraging me to stay with them in the travelling circus.

"I must leave, my friends." I felt sad but had no choice

but to fulfil my destiny.

"So when will you leave, Crach?" Strong-Man looked sad. "I will miss you."

I was sure I could see tears in the corner of his big eyes. *'And I will miss you,'* I thought.

"I will leave in the morning, if I may?" I replied.

I looked around at the faces of my friends, guessing agreement which was confirmed by nods of their heads. Circus Master spoke softly but loud enough for all to hear.

"We have heard your story, Crach, and I think all here would agree it is a good one. You know from your time with us that we never judge and just try to get by as quietly as we can."

A hum of agreement sounded around the group.

"We all have a story of how we came to be here in the travelling circus. Some may be true, some may be within a hair's breadth. It matters not, Crach, as we are a family and you will always be a part of us."

A small cheer sounded from my friends. Now it was my turn to feel tears welling in my eyes. Crow jumped up and in his usual excitement, suggested we all have a party in honour of my leaving. Blaze wholeheartedly confirmed his agreement but added that it should also be a celebration in expectation of my return in order that I may do so without fear and at such time as I chose to. Now the tears were dripping, then rolling down my cheeks.

I need not have held any fear about telling them, it had all been so easy and all I said, accepted without question. This was part of my journey. I suddenly recognised feeling so much wiser, wiser than I had ever felt before.

Pale-Man and Blaze shared out wooden bowls between

us, whilst Crow, cavorting in his usual manner, poured wine into each from a flagon half his size. He balanced it precariously between shoulder and hip, skipping from one outstretched bowl, held in expectant hands, to the next. It was an accident waiting to happen as he spilled more than he poured. We did not have long to wait before he slipped, skidding in a pool of wine liberally shared with the ground earlier, landing on his backside in a most embarrassing fashion. He then sat scowling, much to the delight of our party, who once again descended into torrents of uncontrollable laughter.

Looking around at them, chatting, drinking and laughing, I thought 'I *am certain of today, but I do not know tomorrow.'* The party ended quietly as, one by one, everybody fell asleep around the fire. It was only I who still had open eyes. I looked around at them for the last time, sleeping and peaceful, my friends.

I thought of Llwyd ap Crachan Llwyd and how his wisdom was beginning to be truly passed to me. My apprenticeship was over and the events of the past seasons had proved that to me. The second part of my journey was now at an end, and in the morning, the security of the circus would stand behind me. I would be alone—alone in London. I snuggled under the sheepskin and before too long drifted off into a deep wine- infused sleep.

CHAPTER FOURTEEN

Shivering, I opened my eyes. Fire embers still shone in the half light, heralding the start of a new day. This day I would leave the safety of the travelling circus to continue my journey alone. I trembled slightly at the thought and sat up, pulling the sheepskin around me to stay warm. This night past had left a frost in its wake, glistening on the wagons, barrels, even on Strong-Man's nose which protruded over the top of the sheepskin. He was fast asleep and oblivious to the fact his bulbous nose, which snored most torturously indeed, was becoming blue and purple. Blaze was up and about already. Wide awake, he busied himself putting fresh wood, white with frost, on the embers. The fire spluttered into life as Blaze piled on more logs, whistling quietly, lost in his own dreams.

Crow was also awake, well almost. He leaned against the wagon, weary eyes, with lids still heavy, attempting to see, cutting thick slices of bread and cheese, piling it into the breakfast bowls which were still stained with wine from the festivities of last night. Circus Master must have woken up and returned to his wagon because he was not in a heap by the fire where I had last seen him before closing my eyes. Everybody else stayed fast asleep, chasing their dreams. Snoring of differing pitches, high and low, intermittent whistles and trumpets, rang through the cold dawn. Covered in sheepskins, they looked like a slumbering flock of sheep.

I rubbed the last of the sleep from my eyes and stood up slowly, taking care not to lose any protection given by the sheepskin hanging around my shoulders. My fingers were beginning to feel numb from the cold, so I made a beeline for the fire. Blaze was certainly true to his name as the fire roared. Its heat and warmth formed such an aura, I was forced to take a couple of paces back to avoid scorching myself. Crow came over, passing me a bowl of bread and cheese. He grunted acknowledgement but seemed unable to muster anything further as he sat down with a bump on the cold ground next to me.

"Ouch!"

He tried to yell, but it came out as more of a squeak. Poor Crow. He had landed on his rear a few times and not having a lot of padding in that region, like some dwarves I could mention, he must have felt quite sore. I held out my hand to steady his shakiness which he took before slowly falling into my arms. Crow squeezed my rib cage and whispered into my ear.

"I will miss you, my friend."

I heard a little snuffle and felt a dampness on my neck, but he pulled his hand away quickly to hide his tears. Both hands now covered his face, and he stared at me through fingers interlaced across his eyes.

"You are my brother, Crach, and I will …"

His sentence was interrupted as he coughed and I saw the tears drip through his fingers. I held him in my arms, forgetting my strength for a moment and poor Crow found himself crushed into my chest. He gasped and realising his breathlessness, I relaxed and kissed his forehead.

"Thank you, Crow!" I held his arms lightly, aware of such a strong feeling of family and love. "You are my brother, and I will miss you very much. Especially your lightness of spirit and joy!"

One hand disappeared from his face, and he smiled.

"Do you mean my silly emotions which are like the seasons that can change at any time and we never know when?" Crow paused.

I smiled at the wisdom of his words.

"No Crow, I mean your light spirit and the joy you bring to all of us. You have brought me so much happiness with your friendship since we first met in Shrewsbury."

His tears slowed, and he smiled.

"Will we ever meet again, Crach?" He scratched his cheek, rested his head on one hand and winked in anticipation.

"Only the heavens can give that answer Crow, but I hope we do.

We dwarves live for many years so there is a good chance we might." He laughed and replied.

"Well, we are young enough, it is true." He laughed again.

"Forgive me for my emotions, Crach."

But before he could continue, I held his arm and interrupted.

"There is nothing to forgive, Crow," I smiled and said. "I hope we do meet again and when we do, it will be as no time has passed before. It will be as if it was only yesterday that we were last together."

Strong-Man awoke with a start. Like a volcano spluttering, spitting and rumbling, he began to regain consciousness. When he opened his eyes and saw us watching, he rubbed his face vigorously between huge hands and with large chubby fingers, he massaged himself back to life.

"Oh my head!" he groaned as he gripped his brow. "Too much wine?" I queried.

"Too much indeed!" He groaned again.

"Pass me some cheese, Crow," Strong-Man grunted his request. "I will feel better after food." He held his throat and said. "Oh! I am as dry as a well in summer. Water, Crow, if you please?"

Crow struggled to his feet, complying in silence. Pale-Man stirred under the sheepskin protecting him from the cold and Wasp sat bolt upright, still half asleep, casting his sheepskin to one side. One of the wolves behind the wagon howled, and a dog in the distance replied with a gruff bark.

Everybody was waking now and issuing breakfast orders to Crow. He shrugged silently, passing bowls of bread and cheese to all. Strong- Man held a flagon of water high in the air, draining its contents which poured like a waterfall into a waiting cave. He gulped and swallowed furiously, his Adam's apple bouncing up and down, creating a vision in my mind of a small animal trying to escape from inside his neck.

Circus Master appeared carrying a sack, full and bulging,

tied shut with a firm knot, its contents unknown. Passing the wagon where bread and cheese waited, he stopped and helped himself, filling an emptybowl without the assistance of Crow. He walked over towards me, bidding his usual collective greeting that had been delivered daily at dawn since I joined the circus and to be honest, it did make sense in every way.

"You are alive today because you did not die last night!" He laughed loudly. "To work, my fine friends."

He stuffed bread into a waiting open mouth, chewing with gusto while forcing in a slab of cheese. His cheeks bellowed out as far as they were able to stretch and he chewed and chewed and chewed. He was still chewing when he sat down next to me. Swallowing hard on dry bread, he coughed, bringing it from the back of his throat into his mouth again to be chewed some more, only swallowing again when he was satisfied he would not choke. With his mouth now empty, his hand swept the crumbs from his lips.

"This is for you, Crach!" He passed the sack to me and patted its bumps and lumps. "Food here for you, Crach, as well as an extra sheepskin and some coins wrapped up in a cloth, hidden at the bottom to avert prying eyes, if you get my meaning?"

I did understand and nodded my thanks for such a kind gift.

"There is enough there to keep you going for a while if you are careful. I wish you well on your journey, Crach. It has been my pleasure to have known you. I doubt our paths will cross again but we never know, do we?"

He smiled and bit off another chunk of cheese. I thanked him graciously, bowing my head in respect.

"I will miss you all."

I felt tears in my eyes again as I shook his huge hand.

"Take care my fine dwarf. I must away to work and no doubt when I return, you will have left. I will bid you farewell now and wish you good fortune, no matter which way the wind blows."

I did like the way he expressed himself. He was always so clear and sharp but moreover, calm and in control. He stood to leave and now bowed to me.

"Until the next life, Crach!"

He laughed loudly while striding away to mount his stallion. Taking the reins in his gloved hands, he dug spurs into the stallion's sides and rode off, waving without turning his head. As I watched him go, I felt a strong slap on my back. Turning around, I saw Strong-Man standing in all his muscular glory, eyes shining and smiling warmly. Looking down at me, he ruffled his shaggy head with big fingers, saying,

"So we must part, Crach. It is the moment for leaving, is it not?"

For the last time, I would get this crick in the back of my neck from looking up at his enormity.

"Yes, I must go. I am not sure where to, but I must find the Apothecary. That is my mission."

Strong-Man smiled, replying to my quandary.

"Well, here in London you will probably find him on the street with others of the same trade, such as surgeons, barbers and the like."

I must have looked quizzical because he offered an explanation without my requesting it.

"Here in London you will find all the bakers in Baker Street and all the butchers in Slaughter Street, but you can always ask somebody now, can't you Crach?" He laughed.

"Your language and understanding are quite extraordinary for a dumb dwarf!" He laughed again.

He was right, even my accent had somehow magically changed. I did speak well and understood so much more. I now had no fear of the language or of being discovered on my quest. I felt strong and confident. I thanked him for his friendship, and he patted my head for the last time. All my friends, in turn, came to wish me luck, even the wolves came to say goodbye. White Wolf licked my face, surprising me so much that I jumped backwards, landing on Wasp's foot! Black Wolf whined loudly and seemed to be smiling through those enormous, sharp, white teeth. Dripping a little drool from his pink jowl, he barked deeply and so loudly that my ears vibrated. Everybody laughed.

I picked up my bag, together with the sack given to me by Circus Master, slinging both into position across my back, I secured them with a leather thong tied into a knot. Dressed to be as warm as it was possible to be in this biting cold and having more supplies for my onward journey than I ever envisaged, it was time for me to leave. I bade my final farewells and slowly walked away from the travelling circus for the last time. I turned around twice and saw they all still stood waving, but upon the third turn when I was almost out of sight, they had returned to work. I was on my way.

I walked through street after similar street with the same ramshackle houses and foul gutters, producing an intolerable stench. As sure as a 'dragon is a dragon,' I was convinced I had been walking round in ever-decreasing circles. Suddenly, through the stench lingering within my very sensitive nostrils, I smelt something familiar. I raised my head as high as it would go (which meant standing on the tips of my toes), flared my nostrils and sniffed deeply. I recognised a warm aroma, that of freshly baked bread. Remembering Strong-Man's words and in particular those about street names, I pondered. Perhaps I had found Bakers Street?

I followed my nose down the muddy track and round a corner where I came across an old woman plucking a chicken. She discarded the deceased fowl's feathers, the wind catching each as if a little flurry of snow, depositing them in the gutter, onto passing folks' clothes, mine included. I picked off the offending feathers, letting them float to the ground from between my fingers.

There was probably around twenty shops and stalls lining both sides of the street, all selling bread. For the first time since I had entered London, there was a sweet aroma to enjoy. Tables full of similar shaped, freshly baked loaves greeted my eyes.

One thing that did strike me as being different here in London was that not one person had yet shied away from my dwarfness, nor indeed had anyone hurled any abuse. Maybe they didn't see me. Or, if they did, perhaps they had no care, only being concerned with their own existence, as pitiful as many seemed to be. At the show last night, I had seen many people in finery but everyone I had seen today only bore the attire of nothing more than was needed to live from day to day.

Suddenly, a commotion at the end of the street brought me back from my dancing thoughts with a flash. Several soldiers on horseback galloped through the street. Old men, children, and women, seeking their daily bread, scattered in fear, screaming for mercy. I stood back taking refuge behind a cart which stood above my head. Feeling secure in the fact

I could not be seen, my eyes took in the action as it was unfurling.

Folk ran for cover to avoid heavy hooves stamping through the mud. An old lady in ragged clothes once made for a much bigger person, her back bent so much she appeared to be half of her actual height, staggered blindly into the path of the galloping horsemen. Bandy misshapen legs had neither the strength nor fortitude to speed her passage from the path of the oncoming riders. A sturdy mare caught the old lady fully on its powerful broad chest, knocking her sideways into the path of another horse and rider. From a dying mouth, she screamed a final insult at life. It was a pitiful sound. Flinging her through the air as if she was a rag doll, the horses galloped on, encouraged by their riders. The old lady crumpled to the ground, her face scarred with fear, surprised eyes fixed in a horrific death stare. The troupe of soldiers careered past my hiding place, turned the corner at the end of the track and vanished down another street. Not one rider turned their head nor saw the old lady sprawled across the street, her lifeless body seemingly invisible and unimportant to each of them.

Several folks appeared from their temporary havens of safety and saw the old lady lying dead in the gutter. A few walked over to her, staring at the lifeless body. A very thin man bent down on one knee, seeking signs of life but none were present. He turned his head, exclaiming to the onlookers.

"Old hag is gone to a better place!"

Rumblings of pity whispered when a hidden voice spoke above the hum of the crowd.

"Better take her to the barber surgeon."

Another voice agreed as its owner stepped forward, grabbing a small handcart standing idle near to a stall still full of bread, having avoided a collision during the recent mayhem. The stranger pulled the cart to where the old lady lay and the two men lifted her body, placing it gently on the damp wood. Hearing them say 'barber surgeon,' I recalled Strong-Man's words. It was possible I may find my Apothecary on the same street, so quietly and hopefully unseen, I followed the two men as they pushed the cart.

The old lady's body moved with a twitch or a jump at every rut in the track and over every stone that was laying forlorn without a wall. At times it seemed to me that she still breathed, but her lifeless eyes were devoid of all thought and sign of life.

I followed the cart through a number of streets, one full of blacksmiths busy at anvils, hammering hot metal into all forms of implements in varying shapes and sizes. Great big men with leather aprons and muscles like stallions, bodies scarred with many burns from sparks of past furnaces, lifted hammers larger than me, bringing them down with a crash upon the hot orange metal below. Sparks flew, some catching straw laying scattered here and there, but as soon as a smouldering began, a small boy appeared with a bucket and wooden ladle, spooning water to extinguish danger of fire igniting. Several small boys were kept very busy indeed and never seemed to draw breath between filling buckets from a trough and ladling water onto the offending sparks. One unfortunate urchin tripped over some large tongs and fell headlong into dirt and ashes, the contents of the large wooden bucket simply soaked into the ground around him. The blacksmith suitably aimed a large boot and dispatched the boy to his small feet after a short flight through the air! The boy landed in a heap, face scowling and eyes bulging, verging on the edge of tears. The blacksmith cursed, and the boy returned to his task, rubbing his bruised rear vigorously, muttering through gurgling breath.

Around the next corner, the racket of banging and crashing iron faded. It was much quieter and cleaner, although the track between the shop fronts and houses lining each side of the street was still foul and muddy where rain had gathered in pools. People jumped over or walked around the puddles, sometimes bumping into each other while doing so. It has always been like it when several pursue the same goal with no direction, catastrophe is in the stars. I then heard one of the men pushing the cart exclaim,

"Here is where she is then!"

Putting down the staves of the cart, he straightened his back and rubbed a rather large tummy that interestingly was the same shape as the huge, purple, bulbous nose on his face.

"Makes you hungry, this pushing!" He said.

"You can have her food if she has any in her pockets, Will! She don't need it no more!"

His partner laughed, and between them, they bundled the body of the old lady through a shop doorway. I heard one of them shout.

"We got one for you Barb!"

The cart stood forlornly outside the shop, staves dropped carelessly in the mud. Blood from the old lady's wounds stained the wood brown and red. A trickle dripped onto one of the wheels, bouncing in red drops like tears falling from a sad face, then on down to the ground to be lost in the mud. Sitting on a stool next-door to the barber's shop, a man stared silently into space as he was shaved by a smaller man with spindly legs and a very pointed nose, like the beak on a heron. Weaving swishes here and there with a very large sharp knife and fortunately a deft hand, he dispatched unwanted whiskers to the floor.

Across the street, a sign painted with pestle and mortar hung over a shop doorway. If my memory for detail, as given to me by Llwyd ap Crachan Llwyd, is correct, this is the sign of the Apothecary.

CHAPTER FIFTEEN

I stood for a moment and looked at the shop in front of me. It had a stable-door, and the top was open. Inside I could see an old man with very white hair bent over a table, mixing herbs in a large wooden bowl. He was pounding them, humming a tune under his breath. I deftly circled a large pool of rainwater on the street, climbed the step to the shop and peering over the bottom half of the door, I knocked firmly. The old man carried on breaking up the herbs in the bowl, oblivious to my knock. As I watched, I saw him lift his head, but he turned towards a table to the side of him, picking up more herbs. I knocked again, this time louder than my first attempt, so much so that my knuckles knew I had before the old man did!

This time the old man did hear me, and I was surprised to see how swiftly he turned on his heels, only to stare seemingly at nothing. He could not see me, probably because the top of my head was only just visible. He was looking out at the street through the empty space above the half-closed stable-door. The old man started to turn away, possibly thinking to himself that he was hearing things. I knocked again, and as he turned back to face the door, I jumped up, waved and bade him a forthright,

"Hello!"

Stepping back a little in utmost surprise, he raised one big bushy eyebrow on his thin, lined, craggy face. The one eye that I could see clearly, the one that was not in hiding under a bushy brow, was deep green, piercing and shiny, reminding me of the lush green forests of my homeland in the springtime. Lifting both of his arms in welcome and waving his long fingers gently towards me, he said.

"Come in friend, come in!"

Stepping enthusiastically towards me, he pulled the door open, smiling, both bushy eyebrows raised up like two foxes tails, revealing another deep green orb, both eyes now shining into my being. His eyes were as clear as pools on a mountain, reflecting all he could see and had ever seen. Before I could say a word, his face exploded into a huge smile, stretching aged wrinkles into momentary youth, beard and whiskers quivering.

"Delighted." He said, half under his breath and then out loud. "Yes! Yes! Of course!" Then he spoke very loudly. "I have been expecting you, Dwarf! Come, sit. Let us find out if you are who I think you are, shall we?"

He pointed to a small wooden chair, small to a normal sized person that is. For me, I still had to almost climb up onto it and sit with my legs dangling. Before I could say a word, he continued.

"I believe that you have come on a very long journey and

from another land."

He smiled a quizzical and yet knowing glance, staring eyes piercing mine, but not uncomfortably so. I was certainly amazed at his comments. Of course, I shouldn't have been because by now, after everything I have experienced, nothing should surprise me. I also acknowledged what was now becoming increasingly obvious, there was, and is, more at play in my life than merely what I thought I could see. The universe was working miracles as I was witnessing time after time after time.

"You are Master Healan?" I questioned.

"I am he." He said smiling again, he continued. "You are from Wales, my home, are you not?" I nodded in reply and said,

"Finding you has been so easy that I cannot believe it!"

"Believe it, my fine Dwarf." The old man said as he scratched his beard and raised a bushy eyebrow. "You have to believe it. It has happened. When our course is true, the heavens move with us."

He smiled again in the same fond way Llwyd ap Crachan Llwyd often did. Master Healan reminded me of my Master, not only because he was old and obviously wise but because he radiated an aura of peace, harmony, and love. I had never heard a word spoken in anger by Llwyd ap Crachan Llwyd in all the years we were together. That is, of course, until my final day with him, the day I left to make my journey here to the home of Master Healan, bearing sacred hidden scrolls. It was when my Master told me about the English and the ways in which they treated our countrymen, his passion against the taxes, abuse, and killing, which manifested into anger at the end of his story. Such was the hatred he felt. Perhaps Master

Healan felt the same.

Master Healan locked the door from the inside and closed the shutters across the open windows.

"I think it is time to talk and prying ears and eyes must, at all costs, be avoided."

He pulled the door to make sure it was secure. Satisfied it was so, he turned to me and suggested we should take some food and drink before we heard each other's story. He did not speak again until he had finished putting food on the table. It looked like a grand repast indeed, with trenchers of bread under a large chunk of cheese, together with cold rabbit and apples. It was far too much food for a dwarf and an old man. A wooden jug sat in the middle of a large wooden table covered in scrolls, bowls of herbs, liquids, and potions in varying forms of preparation. He cleared a space for the food, pushing everything that was laying on the table top with a gentle sweep of his arm, moving it all from one side to the other. A scroll fell onto the dusty earth floor and a lone bunch of herbs, tied together by a small piece of reed, landed on top of it. Master Healan laughed as he bent down to pick up the fallen items, clutching the small of his back and giving a little moan, I saw him wince in pain.

Turning quickly, wincing again but quickly replacing his look of discomfort with a wry smile, he said,

"Eat up my friend and make the most of it, the English have strange laws decreed by the church. We are forbidden to eat meat on Wednesdays, Fridays, and Saturdays."

I looked surprised as he continued with the same wry smile radiating across his face.

"I pay them no heed, of course. They are stupid laws with no foundation in anything a reasonable man could understand. All 'fire and brimstone,' idle incongruous rules made by men with no connection to the earth on which we live. It is a fantasy of reality, a religion they have written. It has nothing to do with the 'time of things.'"

He gestured that I should join him at the table and we sat down to eat. Not a word was uttered until our repast was almost done. I had not realised my hunger would take so much to satisfy and even more surprised at how much was eaten by Master Healan. He held a staunch appetite for an old man. I had noticed Llwyd ap Crachan Llwyd's appetite diminish over the years, to the point where he would peck at his food like a starling. Rarely had he cleared a plate I set for him in recent years.

Master Healan's home was a place of study and for practising the magical and mysterious pathways of the ancient. It was a testament to his art. A small grate burned with a fire large enough to heat the room. Logs were piled somewhat precariously next to the grate, seemingly dumped rather than stacked. In one corner of the large rectangular-shaped room stood a cot, covered with a sheepskin, which made me realise the old man slept where he worked. Bottles containing herbs and potions lined the walls, sitting on dusty shelves and underneath them, a hundred scrolls and more lay in boxes, stacked tidily against each other.

It was a warm space, and I felt comfortable and welcome, just as I had with my Master. Master Healan was just as Llwyd ap Crachan Llwyd had described him to be. With our appetites satisfied, Master Healan placed his elbows on the table where we sat and cradled long ancient fingers together before resting a bearded chin upon them. He looked at me with warm eyes and said, "Now it is time for proper introductions, my friend.

I do not need to ask you who you are because I already know but I do not know your name. You did not know me, but now you do. We have spoken little to this point, but perhaps you could start with your name?"

"My name is Crach," I said. "Crach Ffinnant."

"A good name, Crach, an ancient name. And Ffinnant is where you are from?"

He lifted his head for a moment, stretching an already long thin neck before returning his head to rest on cradled fingers. He gave a warm smile as I continued.

"It is where I was born and where my father, a woodcutter, and my Mother, a healer, brought me into this world."

He raised his eyebrows when I said my Mother was a healer. "A long time ago, or so it seems now, I was apprentice to...."

Before I could finish the sentence, he interjected by firstly, placing his hand gently on my arm and secondly, motioning me to silence with a finger held quietly to his lips.

"An apprentice to...."

He scratched his head with the silence-seeking finger and now sported a knowing smile, playing over wrinkled lips. He squeezed my arm with his other hand and spoke my Master's name for me.

"Llwyd ap Crachan Llwyd!" His tone changed, almost as if he were calling him to him. He then laughed out loudly. "It is he, is it not, Crach?...It is, ha!"

The old man slapped the palm of his hand down on the table in a demonstration of excitement and squeezed my arm again. I had uttered nothing but nodded my head, acknowledging the truth of his words. Before I had a chance to speak, he told me.

"It was a dream, Crach, I had nearly a year ago. A dream when my old friend Llwyd came to me and told me of what lay in front of us. I speak of our responsibility as the 'keepers of knowledge,' the ancient wisdom of those most wise, that which makes all things work."

He winked at me in a knowing way. He knew that my Master had taught me well.

"What I do not know is how you got here, or why. I only know that in my dream Llwyd said you would come. He did show me images I can recall, but I fail to understand their meaning. I do know that in all these matters there is a reason, a lesson, and a message. It has to be something very, very important for the magic of the universe to work with such synchronicity."

Suddenly his features changed and he looked serious, furrowing his brow to the point where his eyes were just slits from which the two green orbs searched for answers as yet not revealed.

"Scrolls, Master Healan. I have brought scrolls for you in the service of my Master, Llwyd ap Crachan Llwyd."

I reached for my bag which lay on the floor, nearly falling off the chair as I stretched down to pick it up, saved from an ungainly fall by Master Healan's aged, yet strong, grip. As he helped me right my posture to something a little more commensurate with comfort, not to mention keeping my dignity intact, he picked up my bag and passed it into my waiting hands. I thanked him with a polite nod of the head and dug deep into the bottom of the bag to seek the scrolls which had lain hidden there since my journey began. Feeling a thin strip of leather thong binding the parcel of written secrets, my fingers traced the surface of the cloth that held the scrolls. Wrapping my fingers around it, I pulled it from the bag.

"Here you are, Master Healan. My quest is now at an end!" I bowed my head politely as I passed him the parcel.

"I am grateful to you, Crach. The universe is grateful to you. Please wait for a moment whilst I take a quick look at that which you have risked your life to deliver. Then, with your permission, we may return to your story, and I will follow with mine. When our tales have been told, perhaps sleep and rest may be a good thing to consider. However, with your patience, I would now like to open this parcel of secrets."

Silently nodding my head, I begged him to continue, watching as his fingers undid the knotted thong, unfurling the cloth to reveal three scrolls, each tightly bound around a carved wand. Placing the wrappings of cloth, together with the thong, upon the table amongst the herbs and bottles and gently moving a few bits and bobs, he created a clear space to place the scrolls. For a moment or two, he sat staring at the three scrolls laying on the table in front of him before stretching a hand over them, dropping a finger at random. Picking up the selected scroll and gently unrolling it, he held it out further into the light of the fire to get a better sight. Gnarled hands with long fingers held top and bottom of the parchment, making it easier for him to read. The old man perused the scroll quietly, occasionally making tiny gasps under his breath. Once or twice he paused, relaxed the scroll from sight, and dropped his arms whilst pondering that just seen, before raising them again to read on.

The 'quick look' to which he earlier alluded, seemed to have become a thorough examination. I sat warming my feet by the fire, watching his features dance in the firelight as he read on and on. I know not how much time passed, but Master Healan read all three of the scrolls thoroughly and in silence. I stumbled from my perch twice to add more logs to the fire. He continued to read while the logs burned, radiating heat to my feet which were, I must say, lovely and warm. Rolling up the third and final scroll, he returned it to the table top alongside the other two, each back around its own wand again. Looking across the table at me, he said,

"Well, Crach!" He chuckled quietly and then said, "I am sorry I became so immersed in these writings, but I will reveal all I now know very soon. The rest will be up to you."

He coughed gently, accompanied by an almost indistinguishable sneeze, but a sneeze indeed it was.

"I will read more a little later, and I think we will discuss all another day."

I am not sure what he meant by *'the rest will be up to me,'* but I had a sneaky feeling that I would soon be finding out, and *'another day'* indicated that I may be here for a while. Well, considering I did not have any plans as my journey was in fact now over, I did not mind at all, especially as winter was here on the doorstep, there was a good fire in the hearth and food and ale on the table. Master Healan was so like my Master, my mentor, who I missed so much, even though he had visited me in dreams many times since I started this journey. Yes, stay I will. When he invites me, I will cordially accept. Perhaps I may learn from him also.

"So, Crach, your story, my friend, if you please?"

He beckoned to me with an outstretched hand, pouring himself a small ale from the jug with his other before doing the same for me. I thanked him before taking up my bowl, drinking deeply, feeling the warm ale slipping down, the hops tickling my senses. Clearing my throat with a gruff bark and taking a deep breath, I relayed my story and shared all the events which had passed throughout my journey, starting with my trek across the Marches with Fwynedd the Shepherd as my guide. I explained my decision to disguise myself as a 'dumb dwarf,' particularly my encounter with the drunken wagon driver, at which he guffawed with laughter, praising my ingenuity and sniggering at my naivety.

My story amused him as, I must admit, it also amused me, and in the telling, I felt enthused and passionate. I ended by sharing my sadness at leaving new friends and the circus, as well as my recent encounter of witnessing the tyranny and brutality of the King's soldiers when they had ridden into the old lady, knocking her to the ground while not giving a backward glance or care. I became very passionate when I described the synchronicity between events and how finding each other had been so easy. He did not seem in the least surprised by anything that I said but highly amused by the telling. By the time I had finished my story, we had drunk dry the jug of ale and placed several more logs on the fire. It was very late and had been dark for hours.

"You are a fine storyteller, Crach. Much of the telling will make more sense to you soon. But I think...." He stopped for a moment to clear his throat. "I think we should retire to our cots. In the morning we can talk more and decide what we should do with you!"

I thanked him for his hospitality and said that I was happy to stay for as long as he felt would be helpful.

Yawning uncontrollably while stretching my weary limbs, Master Healan helped me to make a cot out of two large boxes. The contents of scrolls, parchments and the like were tipped into a heap. He spread a sheepskin on top of the boxes and together with my own two for cover, I would be cosy, warm and dry this night.

"I bid you goodnight, my new friend, and I thank you for your visit. We will speak again in the morning." Master Healan said, rubbing his hands together.

With that, he mounted his cot, covered himself, turned under the sheepskin and within seconds was asleep. Tiny snores buzzed around the shadows reminding me of bees seeking honey. It had been a good day.

CHAPTER SIXTEEN

The hour was late this morning when my weary eyes slowly opened to the warmth and safety of Master Healan's home. Stretching my still sleeping legs as far as it was possible anatomically, I yawned and sat bolt upright, taking in my new surroundings. Master Healan's cot was empty, his sheepskin folded tidily in preparation for the next night. The fire still burned with a cooking pot steaming over it, suspended by a chain secured to the wall above the hearth. Master Healan was nowhere to be seen, so I decided to return to the warmth of my bed to snuggle beneath the sheepskins a while longer. My thoughts wandered to the mountains and valleys of my home, to the green pastures and impenetrable forests, vision after vision before my eyes. In no time at all, I was asleep again. I was awoken by a gentle tap on my forehead and to the sound of a very quiet voice speaking my name. I opened my eyes slowly to see the face of Master Healan smiling down at me.

"If your eyes are awake, then the rest of you will follow!"

He laughed, and I grinned at his humour. Throwing back the sheepskin, I hopped off the makeshift cot. My bare feet struck the cold floor and I hopped back up again, seemingly much quicker than was my descent. Once back on the cot, I quickly put on my boots, not wanting to repeat such an uncomfortable experience! Master Healan laughed again, inviting me to join him for breakfast. As I sat down at the table, he ladled steaming broth from the cauldron into a bowl, passing it over to me. I nodded my gratitude. Crusty bread helped soak up this delicious meal of broth made from herbs and vegetables. Not only was it tasty and filling but each mouthful seemed to invigorate every cell in my small body.

The supping of the broth brought back memories of how both Llwyd ap Crachan Llwyd and Fwynedd the Shepherd had secretly fed me wormwood. I especially remembered Fwynedd and his manic hilarity when I realised how our journey had seemingly been shortened. That was, of course, after he had shared the secret with me.

Not a word passed between us whilst we ate heartily, washing our repast to digestion with a jug of small ale. There was the occasional slurp, gulp, and burp, but words had no place at a table when a man was at food. "I have some work to do later, Crach, but I would like to carry on from where we left off last evening if that would sit well with you?" I nodded my agreement.

Later that day at evening-time, it was my turn to listen to

his story. Sitting on the chair, tilted back towards the table, I straddled my legs against the hearth and waited to listen. Master Healan began his story,

"First of all, I will tell you of my friendship with your Master, my friend of many decades, Llwyd ap Crachan Llwyd."

He scratched his forehead with a long fingernail sprouting from a spindly finger which was ingrained in the soil of his work. He then continued his tale.

"My name in Welsh is Myrddin Goch ap Cwnwrig. Many years ago, far too many for the counting but much in the remembering, Llwyd ap Crachan Llwyd and I were both apprentices to our Master, Gruffyd ap Morgan Gruffyd. From around our tenth year, we grew together. Although I had been an apprentice for some nine months before Llwyd ap Crachan Llwyd, we were equals in so many ways and mastered our crafts quickly and naturally." He glanced over at me, raising his eyebrows and said. "Mind you, we did not have the natural earth magic that flows through the veins of a dwarf!" Smiling, he continued.

"When our apprenticeships concluded, your Master was sent into the mountains of Gwynedd to further his knowledge and hone his skills in earth magic and healing, whereas I went to Bala and learned much of what I practice now, the making of potions to heal the sick. We both carried on with our work for a few years, but in March of 1349, a great plague swept across England and also penetrated every corner of Wales. Within a year, one in four people had died. Every family in Wales lost somebody to this Black Death."

I saw tears in his eyes, one rolled down his cheek. He rubbed it away with the back of his hand and continued his story.

"It was a time of great sadness and time that proved futile as we all tried in vain to find a cure. Welsh villages and towns rang with tolls of sadness from the rumble of the cart of death. Funeral pyres burned from one end of the land to the other, their dark smoke billowing skywards, darkening the light of day and choking our breath. If ever there was a time for magic that was it. The need for a cure was so great but all efforts to discover one had failed. From all over Wales came the healers, magicians, prophets, and seers to gather together at Bala Lake in March of 1350, exactly a year after the Black Death had arrived."

He leaned forward and asked me to pour him a bowl of water from the barrel in the corner. I passed it to him, and he reached out, took the bowl and drank thirstily. He wiped his mouth, using the back of his hand, and then sneezed very loudly before saying softly,

"I hope this story does not bore the heart of a young dwarf."

"On the contrary," I replied, motioning with my hand for him to carry on. "Please continue, Master Healan."

"Thank you, Crach." He settled back into his chair and taking a deep breath carried on speaking.

"Well, we all met as the moon was full. I remember the reflections on the lake as if it were yesterday. It was stunning in its natural beauty. A number of very important things happened over the following few days and nights. We shared our knowledge and ideas with each other while sitting around an enormous bonfire. Whilst we did not find a cure for the plague, we did discover various herbs that would slow down the infection and give some relief to the sufferer on their journey. A cure has never been found and, as you know, although it is not as prevalent, the disease is still with us today. There was also a most interesting phenomenon that occurred on our second night together. In the very early hours as we meditated, several of us saw the same visions."

He began to perspire, small beads of sweat forming across a wrinkled forehead. Adjusting his position and sweeping his hanging, long, grey hair behind both ears, he again continued.

"We saw great visions foretold across the sky in the shapes of many horsemen carrying English flags, galloping and splashing in foamy white waves, through the valleys and over the mountains of our country. It was as if the heavens had split wide open to reveal these visions. The wind began to pick up, and the clouds flew faster over our heads. Our feet felt stuck to the earth, we were unable to move or even to close our eyes. We had no option but to watch and see what the heavens insisted be revealed."

Master Healan coughed and looked up at the ceiling, his eyes remembering.

"Castles, huge and built of stone, drifted across the sky. We recognised most of them, a ring of impregnable castles from Builth in mid-Wales, to Caernarvon in the north-west and to Flint in the north-east. These ten castles were built one hundred years previously by the long- dead English King Edward and were the physical embodiment of the power of the English rule, designed to intimidate and subjugate our people of Wales. The visions of the night ended as the castles disappeared amongst the clouds and the dawn started to break over the horizon. We all fasted during our time together in order to focus our attentions on meditation. On the second night, more visions were revealed when the skies and heavens opened again." He stood up from his chair and leaned against the table, staring into my face with a look of concern and compassion etched across his features. Speaking quietly he said,

"We all agreed that the first night of visions was almost a historical reminder of the chains that bound our country in submission to the English Lords. On the second night, the heavens revealed the arrival of a man who would lead us all to freedom, a man now already born in this year of 1349, and twelve months on from the plague's arrival. Clouds turned dark and light sped across the skies, thunder echoed in the distance as lightning bolts flashing earthwards, illuminating the mountains surrounding the lake. One bolt lit up the skies above our heads, like a tree with roots spread. One shot into the centre of the lake, urging geysers of water towards the heavens. As the water fell back to the lake in a spray that completely filled our vision, golden crowns began to fall, one after the other appeared and disappeared. Then, emerging through the mist, came a knight on a white charger, clad in full armour. He bore the insignia of our ancient royal heritage on his shield. As his mount reared with steam emanating from flared nostrils, he held a huge battle sword above his head and then the vision was gone."

I watched him closely and could feel a great sense of sadness as the story further unfurled. He sat down again, leaning both elbows on the table while he cradled his chin on interlocked fingers.

"On the third and final night of our gathering, again the heavens opened. At first, it seemed as if the visions of the first night were reappearing. The skies above our heads were embraced by galloping horsemen in full armour, but this time it was not English flags fluttering above their heads but those of the Welsh Princes. Castles reappeared but no longer did the insignia of the English rule fly upon the turrets, it was the flag of the Welsh Princes. It became clear to us that a war with the English haunted the future. We did not know when but as the prophesied leader of our revolt was still a child, whatever was predicted lay in our distant future."

Master Healan leaned back from the table and folded his arms across his chest, tapping on his shoulder with gnarled fingers.

"The final part of my story ends with all the prophets, healers, seers and magicians returning to their homes across Wales, but not before it had been decided that we needed to know more and particularly the precise time when these events may take place. As you know, you're Master and my friend, Llwyd ap Crachan Llwyd, is skilled at reading the stars and back then our gathering relied upon him to define the events and their approximate moment of arrival in our future. That was twenty- five years ago and it is only he and I that still live, the remainder of our number are long gone. Thus it is only he and I who remember these nights of discovery, and we have been bound by the heavens to keep this knowledge sacred until the time the prophecy would come into being. Your Master recorded all the events on one of the scrolls you brought here to me. The contents of this are, of course, well known to me because I was there. The contents of the other two scrolls, I am not familiar with."

He scratched his bearded chin and wound loose wisps of long white hair behind his ears. He then smiled at me from across the table.

"There is one more thing I will tell you now, Crach, but I

will reveal all to you soon, that is when I think you are ready. Your visit wasforetold in my dreams on a number of occasions when your Master came to me, but he also told me that you would ride at the side of our new Prince."

I gasped in astonishment at what he just said and interjected. "Me! A dwarf! Ride alongside a Prince!" I sarcastically summarised his words.

"Yes, Crach!" He looked straight into my eyes repeating his words and telling me that perhaps my destiny would soon become clearer.

I stood up from my chair feeling rather confused, if not a little frightened, by his story. I nervously fiddled with a log stacked on the pile leaning against the wall before placing it in the grate, stepping back as sparks flew from the embers beneath. Master Healan raised himself from the chair and slowly stepped across to me, placing a warm aged arm around my shoulders. Squeezing me gently, he pulled me into his hold and said,

"You see, I told you I was expecting a dwarf, and it is you. Your path is decided by the heavens, Crach. All that remains now is for you to fulfil your part in that which is foretold. Will you do that, Crach?"

He examined my face quizzically while waiting for a response. I smiled at him, knowing my answer, as did he.

All through my life, and before, burdened with onerous taxation and restrictive land policies, the Welsh people, my people, were, and still are, chaffed under English domination. Our Welsh myths and legends, as sung and related by bards and minstrels, foretold of a 'national redeemer.' We had all prayed for a man who would rise up, and now it appeared, according to prophecy, I was to ride at his side! This was a bit much for a simple dwarf such as myself to believe, but believe it I must. There was no choice. My destiny had seemingly been written before my birth into this world.

CHAPTER SEVENTEEN

I woke early the next morning, having been visited in my
dreams by Llwyd ap Crachan Llwyd. He shared his delight
with me of how his work had come to fruition until this point.
I had been in awe of him during our dream-scape. His aura
blinded me, shining more brightly than I had ever witnessed
previously. He said that upon my waking today, I would
hear words to my advantage and insisted I listen carefully.
He concluded his visit by giving me a scroll but telling me I
would only be able to read it during my dream-time.

Leaning up on one elbow whilst still lying under my
sheepskin, I twisted my head around and saw Master Healan
sat at the table, busily writing on parchment, scrawling
with a quill between finger and thumb stained black with
ink. He looked up, and when he saw I was awake, he smiled
and put the quill down on the table, neatly placing it by the
parchment.

"So you return from your slumbers, Crach!" He laughed.

"I think you had a visitor during your dreams and I wager it was the same one that came to me too."

"My Master also visited you, Master Healan?" I asked. Surprised, I immediately sat upright, swinging my legs off the cot, letting them dangle above the floor below.

"He did indeed, Crach, he did indeed!" The old man smiled, a grin from ear to ear lighting up his face.

Master Healan stood up from the table and walked over to the fire, poked at the embers in the grate and placed a few pieces of kindling strategically before bending his head and blowing gently until the flames took hold. Adding a log, he turned to me and said.

"We have much to discuss again today, Crach, but first let us eat our breakfast."

He disappeared, leaving through a small doorway at the back of the room and returning a little while later, clasping bread and cheese in his hands.

"Let us break our fast, Crach!"

So much to talk about. I had no idea what may come but was astounded by the story as it unfurled. The hours of this day flew by as a murder of crows at dusk. I now knew all there was to know about what was happening and why. I understood, thanks to the patience of Master Healan in the explaining of the matters at hand. For over one hundred years and beyond, the English had terrorised Wales and waged unreasonable demands upon my countrymen. Master Healan said it was incongruous that Wales paid taxes to the English when Wales belonged to the Welsh who had their own Royal Heritage. He told me that the castles were built by the English without the permission of our Princes. This stands wrong within the scheme of things.

'*The heavens and the earth are as one in the soul of a Welshman.*' The words of Llwyd ap Crachan Llwyd shared with both Master Healan and myself when visiting us in our dreams during the previous night's slumber. His magic and ability within the 'dream-world' were indeed awesome to behold. I was already amazed he could talk to me in my dreams, but now to know that he also visited Master Healan on the very same night, staggered me beyond belief. But believe, I certainly did.

Master Healan explained how my Master had given him the guidance he needed us to know so that the unfurling prophecy may move on as the heavens declared and the heavens were well signed. All was in harmony, and we both felt this radiating passionately within our hearts. I had been in the company of Master Healan for only a matter of a few short days, and already the timelessness surrounding our every doing was reminiscent of all I had known in the past with my Master. I told Master Healan about the secret scroll given to me. He smiled before bursting into a mindless guffaw of insane laughter, clutching his sides to support an ageing frame. He had also been given one, together with the same instructions.... '*Only to be consulted during dream-time.*'

Following a momentary lapse into insanity, Master Healan gathered himself and once again became serious, telling me there was a similarity in our experiences as it was intended we walk the same pathway until the heavens posted a change in direction. He told me again of the prophecy, first seen on the night all those years ago on Bala Lake, where every healer, prophet, and seer from every corner of Wales had gathered. Now they understood all they had seen, confirmed by scrupulous examination over many years, it was the coming of a Prince. Master Healan said that my Master told him during dream-time that I had already met this Prince. He urged me to remember, but it was no use as I did not think anyone I had met during my travels may fit this description. I had met so many people on my journey from Shrewsbury to London, seen so many faces, but nobody jumped into my mind. However, it was something of a relief to my conscience and poor memory when he told me that I would meet this stranger again, and soon. There was talk of great battles, and he predicted the coming of comets to foretell confirmation of heavenly intercession, deceit, and betrayal.

I found the story fascinating in detail, if not somewhat perplexing as to what my role may be. Battles and comets are certainly not the like of which I have ever considered, and yet, here I was now having to contemplate such things. I was transfixed in their telling by the hypnotic tones of his voice and by his piercing, all-seeing eyes. The old man's face changed so many times as the storytelling unfurled, appearing to turn his features into that of another. Lines of age sat deeply in his forehead, seemingly like crow's feet engrained around those sparkling eyes, lurking below a furrowed brow. His sharp nose was accentuated by light, shimmering across his features in the dimness of the room. His face changed again and again. He concluded by reminding me *'to be in the now at all times, to be prepared for anything and to know that whatever happened, all would be well.'* I felt like an explorer with nothing more than the stars to guide me. This is the way of things.

This was acceptable to me as, in reality, what difference did I know? I had been living this way since leaving Wales and embarking upon this journey. A journey which had arrived at its destination, only to select another journey but with no station of arrival yet determined. We talked and talked, both lost in our chattering until a very firm 'rap-rap' upon the stable-door made us both nearly jump from our skins. Master Healan leaned across the table, a look of surprise in his eyes and said quietly.

"It is late for visitors, Crach, and I know not who stands at the other side of my door." He broke off from whispering and hailed. "One moment if you please, the hour is late!"

The old man stood, stooping more than usual and gathered a stick from the hearth to steady his now frail gait. He suddenly appeared very old, as he had done when I first saw him through the door on my arrival but during my time with him thus far, I could not determine his age as he changed so much in appearance. Mind you, not as much as he did when his face transformed into other folk. Perhaps this was his disguise, as dumbness had been mine.

Upon reaching the door, he opened the top half, gnarled fingers clasping at the bolt. Pulling the half door towards him, the silhouette of a man stood with the failing light of day cast behind him. Master Healan appeared to recognise the visitor instantly and bent to open the catch on the lower door. He did not change in appearance, still seemingly ancient in stature. He creaked the door ajar with a bidding of welcome upon his lips. A gust of icy cold air passed through the room, reminding me of the inclemency of the weather at this time of year. How pleased was I to be here in the warm, cosy and dry.

"Come in, Simon. Come in! I bid you a grand evening and hope that this day has been a good one for you." He stumbled backwards, allowing the unexpected visitor passage. The visitor quickly grabbed at Master Healan, taking him by the elbow to steady his stance.

"Take a care, Master Healan, you may fall."

Simon was a young man of perhaps equal years to me but, of course, he stood much taller. His voice was quiet and respectful. Once ensconced within, he bowed politely and upon seeing me, he bowed again.

"Thank you, young man. Thank you." Master Healan said, almost whispering, maintaining the vision of advanced age to our visitor.

"I hope I find you well, Sir. You are wise to be here in the warm as it is a perishing wind that blows outside and seeps deep into our bones. Winter is upon us now," said, Simon, as he glanced around the room and smiled when taking in my face but uttered not a word, his expression remaining pleasant but with a distance in his eyes.

"How may I help you? It must be urgent for you to venture out at such a late hour. Your Master keeps you late at your bond." The old man coughed and looked quizzically.

"He does indeed, Sir. My apprenticeship is a hard road, but as a clerk at Lincoln's Inn, I will secure a good future, as my father is certain." Simon smiled confidently and continued.

"My Master is unwell again, Sir, and is in need of your potions. He has sent me to you and says I am to tell you the pain is much greater than before. He cannot sleep, and concentration on tasks at hand is proving difficult for him. He greys in colour by the day."

I looked at Simon and noticed genuine concern for his Master's health etched across his face. His clothes had been clearly passed to him by another who must have been much larger than he. A thin cloak wrapped tightly, offered little protection against winter and his boots were worn, weathered, and damp and stained from the filth lurking in the gutters he had tramped through to get here. Master Healan beckoned Simon to be seated. Scratching his chin with a feeble shaking finger, he said,

"Your Master's illness, as you know, cannot be cured. We can only give him the relief from pain needed to continue with life as he wants it to be. I will give you a small clay pot wherein lays the potion to be taken now and will last him for a few days. Pray, be in patience whilst I attend to this need of urgency."

He turned crookedly and ambled slowly across the room, disappearing behind a sack curtain, concealing all that lay therein. Simon got up from his chair at the table and moved towards the blazing hearth in a few rather long strides. Deftly he turned on one foot and bending slightly, he warmed his rear by the heat of the flames. He clapped his hands together and then gleefully rubbed palm against palm. Sharp, well defined, young features, almost hawk-like, peered down at me. Smiling, he enquired,

"I bid you hello!" He bowed again. "You are a patient of Master Healan?"

I had thought to answer but decided against speech, shaking my head in a silent 'no,' my disguise of a 'dumb dwarf' again taking precedent. I cannot say I returned to the safety of dumbness for any other reason than intuition, flashing as lightening from the heavens into my very being.

"My apologies, my friend. I am sorry for your affliction." Simon said in recognition of my inability to speak.

He stared at me and seemed genuine in his remarks. I smiled and gesticulated my thanks for his compassion just as the sack curtain fluttered with the reappearance of Master Healan carrying a small clay pot in his hands. The old man coughed as he came through the door, distracting both our attentions. I felt both relieved and saved by his arrival. The old man proffered the pot in his outstretched hand towards Simon, saying,

"Here is the potion for your Master. It is a little stronger than the last due to the increase in pain and discomfort that you describe."

Simon stepped away from the warmth of the hearth and took the pot from Master Healan lightly in his hand, bowing with gratitude. The old man smiled, adding further instructions for Simon to pass on to the patient, his Master.

"Give him five drops in his drink when he awakes and five before sleep. If the pain worsens during the interim hours, he may take another five drops but no more than twenty in any one day."

Simon listened intently and checked he had correctly understood by repeating the instructions back to Master Healan. He counted out three coins taken from a leather purse hanging from his belt and passed them to the Apothecary. The old man nodded his thanks and fondled the coins in an aged hand before concealing them deep in the pocket of his cloak.

"That is correct, young man." The old man smiled.

Master Healan slowly ambled towards the door, silently informing our visitor that the consultation was at an end.

"Remember all I have said and know that the poppy seed may take the pain away, but if taken too often your Master will not awaken from his dreams!"

He opened the door, allowing a blast of freezing air to enter the room as a ghost unseen but known to be there. Simon, the young apprentice, bade farewell again, bowing to both of us. Master Healan called after him as he stepped out into the cold.

"Inform your Master that I will send more potion for him in a few days!"

Simon turned, acknowledging the old man's words with a quick wave of his hand before striding off into the night.

Master Healan firmly closed the stable-door, securing it above and below with wooden bolts. As he turned from the door, he suddenly looked younger again, years ebbing from his features, lines smoother, his disguise abandoned. Thus, since the earlier arrival of Simon, I too disarmed my disguise of dumbness.

"Well Crach, it seems we are alone again and time to dispense with disguises!"

He giggled into his long grey beard, eyes sparkling with amusement at the success of our mutual deceit, fooling our visitor into thinking that Master Healan was decrepit and me, dumb!

"Perhaps now is the time for me to tell you who I really am, Crach, and why I have been here in the bosom of the English for the last fifteen years."

The old man pulled a chair from under the table, scratching it over the floor before bringing it to rest aside the hearth. Sitting down comfortably, crossing his long aged legs and leaning into the warmth of the blaze, he rubbed his hands to invite good circulation of old blood before continuing.

"My name in Welsh is Myrddin Goch ap Cwnwrig, and I was born many years ago near Lleweni in the Vale of Clwyd. My brother, Iolo, and I were well schooled as Father believed we would both, in our own way, serve Wales well and insisted we work hard at our studies every day. This we did and learned much. Later, as you know, I became an apprentice, along with your Master. My brother is now a Bard and travels the length and breadth of our country. Mark my words, he has a name which will be immortalised throughout history."

He smiled knowingly and continued.

"After the gathering at Bala, we all decided upon a number of strategies in preparation for what was to come. You are aware of some as I have related them in our stories, but it was also decided that we needed to know what bubbled amongst the English Lords. The only way that this could be achieved would be for one of us to become an Englishman, if only by appearance. My schooling and command of the language had prepared me well for this role, and as there were no other contenders from amongst us, it was to be me. I have been here, within my disguise as an Apothecary, in this cruel, dark and forsaken land for nearly fifteen years." He paused and stared deeply into the fluttering orange flames dancing in the hearth. Looking up from the fire, scratching his forehead, he said,

"My job is simple. My ear is very close to those who make laws and rule this land because I make them well when they are sick. My reputation is built upon much hard work. My disguise, well you have seen that for yourself, as I indeed have known yours." He smiled. "Perhaps we should consider that to all who may come here whilst you are under this roof, our mutual disguises must hold fast?"

He paused, awaiting my response. Without thinking, I agreed.

"I think that would be a very good idea, Master Healan. It seemed to work well a moment ago with your visitor, and it has certainly served me well on my journey to your door."

He smiled again and interjected, his voice younger. "As

mine has served me this last fifteen years."

We both laughed, sharing our amusement of the plan to continue concealment of our true selves and purpose amongst the English. I rubbed my belly, feeling pangs of hunger gnawing deeply and it sounded its discontent by growling with emptiness. Master Healan laughed again, and I joined him when his gut echoed in a cacophony of rumbling. He leaned forward, again warming his hands at the hearth, before standing and placing a weighty hand on my shoulder, announcing we should tender to the needs of our bodies as they had, without doubt, requested a need for satisfaction. Our evening meal lay in wait.

Chapter Eighteen

Several days passed by and 'time' with Master Healan, as it had been with my old Master, was 'timeless.' I settled into assisting him in daily tasks without difficulty, shredding and pounding herbs and plants, boiling, steaming, mixing and stirring, all as instructed. During our labour, he would relate stories of old. It was as if he had so much to share with me but lacked sufficient time for the telling of all he felt he should. I sincerely hoped that my memory would serve to remind me of his words when the time required it. He had assured me that it would. I, of course, had my doubts.

I ran errands here and there and delivered prescriptions which enabled me to begin to see more of this place called London. Compared to all I have known thus far in my life, I must say that never have I seen so much filth and poverty, nor have my nostrils been so insulted by innocuous smells ushering unseen from buildings, gutters and the people themselves, such as those I experienced here. Streets were muddy and swamped with pools of dirty water, splashing all who stood near as carts, wagons, and riders passed through hidden depths.

I saw numerous accidents, like the one I had witnessed on Bakers Street that had led me to Master Healan. Old people and children, either too slow or too reckless, were trampled by riders on horseback or crushed under the wheels of heavy carts. The old man said that not a day came to night without some poor unsuspecting soul finding themselves unceremoniously dispatched from a life once lived. On one occasion, I witnessed a child's leg being severed by a wagon wheel as it ran blindly over the fallen body that had slipped in mud, now mutilated forever.

Today I was again to venture out into unknown dangers lurking in the streets in order to deliver prescriptions for Master Healan, one of which was to be taken to the Abbey of Saint Clare. I had already been sent here on a previous occasion. It was not too far from Bishopsgate where Master Healan lived, so I knew the route to take. I was also to collect a rabbit from Slaughter Street for our supper. Of interest is that today is Friday, being one of the days where meat and fish are banned from our plates. How they, the leaders of the English Church, could call them 'fast days' astounds me.

I have fasted many times as part of rituals my Master taught me. To spend a day or two in meditation without food of any type passing my lips is what I would call fasting. I could sense no logical reason for this law, where only abstinence from meat applied to these fast days and yet, a law it was.

However, it was a law that we two Welshmen did not adhere to within the confines of Master Healan's home. Rabbit stew for our evening meal sounded most appetising to this ever-hungry dwarf. I suspect we were not alone in keeping our affairs private behind closed doors. Master Healan also asked me to visit Lincoln's Inn to deliver a Tincture of Poppy for Sergeant Roger Mortimer, Simon's Master, the man who faced imminent death. This was a fair walk for a short dwarf. I would follow the river from Billingsgate to Westminster which would take me all day.

After our breakfast of bread and reheated pottage left over from last evening's meal, I cleaned away the wooden bowls and spoons, readying myself for the day's labour. The old man busied himself, ladling steaming, green, pungent liquid from the cauldron, suspended at the hearth, into waiting empty clay pots. He was humming quietly under his breath, as a bee may do whilst draining pollen from a flower, content and lost blissfully in work. I watched Master Healan closely, observing his every move as carefully he poured the potion, dark green liquid dripping slowly into each waiting vessel. When he completed decanting the medicines, a little plug was placed into each small clay pot, securing the contents from air and spillage. As I had done before, and as instructed, I gathered up the prepared pots and stacked them carefully on the shelves behind the sack curtain in the corner of the room. This small anteroom was lined from floor to rafters with shelves full of clay pots and jugs of differing sizes and shapes, containing medicines and potions to cure or aid all sorts of ailments passing through the lives of man. Collecting the bag of medicines that required delivery from the table and slinging the pack over my shoulder, I bade Master Healan farewell and ventured out into the cold.

As I walked through the streets of this hostile place, something struck me as lightening may a tree in the midst of a storm. It was the fear I saw etched across so many unknown faces as they bumbled about their business. They were often surprised and scared out of their wits when seized by soldiers, accosting them and demanding explanations for no apparent reason other than the aggressor's boredom. Soldiers loitered at every gate, checking folk as they passed through, some more alert and more committed to their duties than others.

I was trundling up one dirty, unkempt street and down another, carrying medicines in a leather shoulder bag given to me for such a task by Master Healan when the heavens opened and down lashed the rain, turning quickly to sleet as it fell. Pulling the hood up and wrapping my cloak tightly around me, I shielded my person as much as I could from this unprovoked assault by such sharp, vicious, freezing, tiny arrows pelting down. I bent my head and fearlessly trudged on. Walking slowly through Cornhill, I passed horses, heads down with eyes closed in an attempt to hide from such inclemency. They stood motionless between the staves of stationary wagons, overladen with heavy loads, their drivers sitting under covers of sacks, waiting for a let up in the current onslaught from a crack in the heavens.

Approaching the Abbey of Saint Clare, I had to enter through Aldgate as on my previous visit. It was guarded by armed soldiers, as were all of the gates in this place. It seemed that dwarves were low on their list of priorities as suspects of rebellion, misdeeds or otherwise, or perhaps our aura and reputation for magic made them think twice. I do not know why, but they did not bother me at all.

Two large men in front of me were harangued by one of the guards who took the largest by the arm and forcibly dragged him out of line whilst pointing directly at the other, telling him in no uncertain terms to stand still. Both of the men protested loudly, their faces turning crimson with guilt before turning deep purple with anger. Profanity thrown at the guards in both attack and defence, questioning their parentage, did not fare them well and only made the soldiers even more determined to strip both bare of everything they carried in their search for contraband. Baskets and sealed sacks were opened and unceremoniously scattered in the mud as the sleet thickened and came down in sheets. The soldiers, hardened to such attitudes from folk and the inclemency of the English climate, carried on with their duties regardless.

Suddenly, the man who the soldier had told to *'stand still,'* turned around quickly and bolted past with speed, his bulk almost knocking me off my feet. Pushing his way through the few who gathered behind me, he disappeared down a side street. The watching soldiers simply smiled and let him run as they probably knew who he was anyway, so he would not evade their grasp forever.

Seeing his colleague successful in his bid for escape, the huge man who was dressed in clothes made for a much smaller frame, with enormous hairy wrists hanging tightly below short sleeves, clenched his fists and swung wildly at his charge. He lunged in vain, striking fresh air as the soldier side-stepped, ducked and brought his stave firmly down on the prisoner's head with a skull-crushing blow. The big man crumbled lifelessly to the floor, a gaping wound across his head oozed blood like a crimson river flowing momentarily across the earth before disappearing, washed away by the rain and sleet.

I stood waiting, now next in line to pass through Aldgate, as the sleet began to turn to flutters of snow. The guard who had struck the big man was busy dragging his lifeless body away from the gate, whilst the other was kicking the emptied baskets and sacks to one side. They waved me through with ne'er a second glance but when an old lady, clad in rags, who had been standing behind me began to follow me through, she was stopped in her tracks as the soldier's strong hand flat-palmed her chest.

Without so much as a peek through the corner of my eye or a turn of my head to look behind, I walked on in apparent ignorance to all who may have been watching, glad to be a dwarf in this godforsaken place called London. After delivering several pots of medicine to the gatekeeper at the Abbey of Saint Clare, I headed out again, tramping through streets which were now becoming deep in slush. A thin layer of snow was beginning to spread across the rooftops. Turning towards Crutched Friars, I followed the streets to Billingsgate in search of the path along the river to Westminster. Master Healan told me earlier that I would find the rooms of Sergeant Roger Mortimer at Lincoln's Inn, a place for those engaged in administering and learning the laws of the land. My instructions were to deliver the potions whilst keeping myself in low profile to all who I may see or pass. The latter seemed rather amusing, given I am a dwarf!

The rain poured no more, and the sleet had turned to flurries of snow which were now a steady fall, covering all in a blanket of white wherever it fell. It was very cold, and the ground beneath my feet hardened to the frost. People were scurrying to and fro, seeking shelter as the snow became thicker all around, work and labour now forgotten. The river flowed fast and grey to my left, swollen by the rainfall. I passed by London Bridge, only to be accosted by another queue of huddled folk waiting to pass through Ebgate. Just one soldier guarded here, a tall, thin, gaunt, tired-looking chap. A long deep scar ran from his forehead down to a pointed chin, grey with stubble. His face, stained and weather-beaten, held a dark stare which penetrated all who passed as he waved us through, one by one. But that was all he did, 'stare fiercely,' as if this was enough to maintain law and order, challenging no-one. As I passed through the gate, he averted his stare heavenwards.

Snow continued to fall, and the wind picked up a pace, sweeping flurries like clouds in a storm, blinding my path. It was as Master Healan had said, *'a long walk.'* Pleasant in fine weather, no doubt, but in foul like this, it was a case of just getting on with it, a task to be done. It would, of course, have been quicker to take a ferryboat down the river from Billingsgate to Westminster but Master Healan thought it may draw undue attention to me, which he did not want. After many years of living a double life in this strange capital of the English, I bowed to his wisdom.

Dowgate and Black Friars were far behind me as I passed through Whitehall but the snow was giving no credence of relief. The streets in Westminster were now under my feet which, incidentally, were very cold and damp at this point. I sought Lincoln's Inn for my final delivery of the day, and from there I was to secure a rabbit for supper. But, by the way, this day had passed thus far, time taken as a breath, a blizzard blinding my path, hard of foot slowing my gait, it seemed to me I may return to Master Healan with one task unfulfilled.

Hoping that I may still complete my business at Lincoln's

Inn and collect a rabbit from Slaughter Street before the purveyor of our supper had found his cot for the night, I stepped out with purpose, my short legs slipping and sliding on the snow beneath my feet.

"Lincoln's Inn is not too difficult to find."

This feigning dumb dwarf, with ears that hear all, overheard a voice that attracted my attention. A group of young gentlemen gathered at a street corner, shuffling from foot to foot, and cloaks gathered around them, rejecting the cold. Some of them had scrolls of parchment held partially hidden under their cloaks in an attempt to safeguard the writings against being fouled by dampness. As I walked past unnoticed, one of the party remarked his intention to leave instantly for Lincoln's Inn. Stepping aside quickly, I concealed myself behind a very large barrel and waited. In a matter of moments, he bade his farewells and stepped out through the snow. Following behind in his shadow, I made my final steps towards Lincoln's Inn.

Torches blazed on both sides of the entrance to the Inn, shedding some light across the street as the day darkened into night. The stranger I had followed strode boldly through its doors. Lights from candles flickered at every window through vents in the shutters. In my mind, it seemed like a *'house with many eyes.'* Much later I was to learn that my impromptu christening of Lincoln's Inn was to hold much truth in its definition. A brazier stood blazing on the porch, and several men dressed in finery came and went as I looked on from the other side of the street. The huge door of oak opened and closed, shedding flashes of light cascading across the snow. Never had I seen so many comings and goings of such a variety of folk.

I crossed the street, slipping on slush while taking care not to be trampled by passing horsemen. Stepping through the enormous oak door, I found myself standing in a large hallway of polished wood where candles burned brightly, affording no corner or crevice where darkness could lurk. At a table near the door sat a small round-faced man with the reddest cheeks I had ever seen, they radiated warmth like coals in a brazier. Beads of sweat leaked from his shiny bald head. His tiny plump fingers plucked at a stack of parchments laying on the table in front of him. Raising his head, he peered enquiringly through sharp, beady, black eyes, this busy little man caught sight of me looking rather lost. He banged on the table with the flat of one of his tubby hands while pointing at me with the other.

"You have business here in the House of Lincoln's Inn, Dwarf?"

His voice was shrill, and it pierced my ears. I walked over to the table, smiling while raising a hand towards my lips, gesticulating an inability of speech. Fumbling deeply in the satchel hung across my chest, I produced the clay pots of medicine.

"These are for a gentleman who has rooms here at the Inn, Dwarf?" His voice squeaked as spit dribbled from the side of a small tight mouth. I nodded in agreement, so my voice need not be heard and passed him the parchment given to me by Master Healan. Taking it from me with his chubby fingers, he unrolled the scroll, raising it closer to his face in order to peer at the writing. He raised his eyes and without any expression crossing his face, announced recognition of the name on the parchment with a grunt, sharply accompanied by a tiny sneeze.

"Yes, yes." He stammered, placing the scroll on the table.

"I will make certain these medicines are passed to Sergeant Roger Mortimer who will be pleased as he is most at dis-ease."

He stacked the pots in an empty space near the scroll and told me again that he would ensure all was delivered as required. I nodded my thanks, but I do not think he saw as no sooner had he announced his intention, he returned to fumbling through the pile of papers upon the table, now oblivious to my presence.

Feeling as if I had been dismissed by the top of his bald sweaty head, I turned to leave when the heavy oak door was kicked open by an unseen man laden with scrolls in his arms, stacked precariously above his head. He staggered blindly into me with a crash. The scrolls tumbled from his arms, and within an instant he had fallen to his knees, frantically trying to gather them. Some scrolls, upon falling and hitting the floor, rolled open, frustrating the unknown carrier in the process of picking them up even more. He was now scrambling blindly, grumbling strange words under murmured breath. Feeling some responsibility for this accident as I had been in the way of this gentleman's blind path, I joined him on my knees and gathered several of the scrolls in my arms. When my arms were full, I turned around quickly on my haunches and cracked my head upon his forehead as we crashed into each other yet again. Bouncing off each other's skulls with a start, we both ended up sitting on our bottoms, looking into each other's startled faces.

This face I had seen somewhere before and noticing his expression of knowing as he saw mine, I could see that he remembered me too. His was the face of the 'defender' from the show in Worcester, the stranger who had stood by another when bullied, the gallant young man who had knocked Edmund to the ground, bloodying the bully's nose. He was as tall as I remembered, even though now sitting, and very handsome with fine sharp features of regal appeal. He radiated a quiet authority, despite the apparent mayhem surrounding him. His smile was familiar to me, as was his face. We sat on the ground amid the rushes, glancing at each other in familiarity. I sat in front of the Welshman, Owain Glyndwr.

CHAPTER NINETEEN

"Crach!"

He dropped the scrolls into his lap and grabbed me in strong hands at my shoulders. Smiling warmly, he said,

"You are here in London! What a grand surprise. Is the travelling circus here?"

I nodded and gesticulated that I had now left the circus. He started to lift himself from the floor and whilst balancing on one knee with an arm full of scrolls, he stared into my eyes and said, "Do you remember when we met in Worcester? I told you I suspected we would meet again and here we are!"

He laughed, standing erect, towering over my still-seated self. The plump bald caretaker stepped from behind the huge table and with little haste of action, hobbled over to us and began to assist in the picking up of the scrolls. I leapt to my feet and passed the scrolls that I held in my arms to Glyndwr, who in turn gave them to the fat man, who then stacked all upon his now over-filled table.

Glyndwr took my shoulder lightly in his hand and motioned that I should delay and wait for him. He turned to face the bald man, giving instructions that he was to ensure that the scrolls were returned to the Inn library from where he had taken them on loan. Nodding politely and acknowledging his understanding to Glyndwr, he returned to sit down behind the table, fumbling at papers again. Glyndwr shouldered his cloak and turned, raising one hand, placing a finger upon his lips to mime silence before smiling and saying

"Let us walk away together, Crach. Perhaps you would like to join me in a small ale aside a roaring fire on such a night as this?"

He smiled again. Bidding the bald man an evening of peace, he moved towards the door and waved for me to follow. The bald man, still oozing sweat like a horse well ridden and wheezing a sufficiency of labour, nodded his head in a servile bow, his eyes never leaving the papers upon the table. Walking outside under the shadow of this tall Welshman, the heavy oak door closed behind us, leaving the warmth of Lincoln's Inn behind to be replaced by icy cold air biting the back of my throat. Glyndwr turned around and explained that we had a brisk walk to share in order to secure refreshment and a large fire.

"We will talk on our way, Crach, and it would please me greatly if you would address me as Owain." Looking down at me, he took my shoulder with a polite squeeze. "We must not waste a breath of our time together as I feel my dreams are almost to fruition. I have an abundance of ideas and thoughts. There is magic afoot, Crach. Magic!"

I nodded as we stepped on through streets covered in snow

as far as the eye could see while a steady flurry continued to fall. Few people were out and about in this foul weather, preferring to stay inside by the warmth of fires blazing in grates. Those who were unfortunate enough still to be out, scurried through falling snow with heads down, cloaks pulled tightly cushioning them against the cold but in reality affording little protection.

It felt so good to shed my disguise and to be able to talk freely again. We spoke in Welsh when no ears could hear, returning in a flash to English when they might. Owain repeated the story previously shared in Worcester, detailing the recurring dreams that haunted his sleep. It was very clear to me this was the man Llwyd ap Crachan Llwyd prophesied was born to lead. *'But did Owain Glyndwr know this yet?'* I wondered. I thought not. Owain told me that his lodgings were to be found in Saint Botolph Street which, unbeknown to me, was but a long stone's throw from Bishopsgate where I was presently staying with Master Healan. It was indeed good fortune Owain knew the streets of London well. In ignorance, I probably did spend some time walking in circles, perhaps chasing my tail, but I always eventually found my way. We were to board a barge at Whitehall that would take us upriver to Billingsgate, whereupon we would decide where to eat and take warmth and shelter. The snow fell and fell and fell.

I explained to Owain that Master Healan held reservations about me using the ferry in case I drew unnecessary attention from unwanted eyes. Owain assured me that at this time of night, together with the bad weather, we would be unlikely to draw a glance. He urged we take the barge because it would not be long before the river became ice when all transport would cease. Trusting his words, I agreed to take my first trip somewhere without earth beneath my feet. Owain sensed anxiety, laughingly dispensing my fears as unfounded but then adding that all would be well unless the boat sank! He then asked me if I was able to swim, which I cannot! He laughed again. Well, if we had sunk and disappeared to the bottom of the river, I would not now be relaying my story. Thus it will be clear to you that we did not.

Snow continued to fall. The ferryman bent his head into the wind and rowed with all his might. Whilst we sat frozen at the rear of the barge, the ferryman perspired. His labour of endless backwards and forwards movements was clearly not of love but essential to preserve life and limb. This observation filled me with a feeling of some security as he was a very big man and the barge swept along the surface of the icy river at some pace under his oarsmanship. A sack covered his head, providing protection from the elements. The ferryman's shoulders, broad and muscular like flanks of a carthorse, strained at the oars. A firebrand burned on the bow, affording some light on the darkness of the river. The moon in the heavens hid behind clouds full of snow in readiness for its assault upon the land. Shadows occasionally danced across the ferryman's face, and his blankness of expression made him seem more like a ghost.

It was very cold and damp during our journey back up the river to Billingsgate. Owain and I were the only passengers, and we spoke in English, using whispered tones so the ferryman could not hear our conversation. The hue of grey radiating from the surface of the river cast darkness over the water lit only by reflections of hundreds of small lights shimmering from buildings along the bank. The ferryman continued to strain the oars against the tide, enormous shoulders stretched at his clothing as bulging muscles throbbed beneath. The barge passed under London Bridge. Above us folk scuttled to and fro, taking advantage of the brief respite in snowfall in search of destinations unknown to all but themselves.

I learned that Owain's father, an Officer to the Earl of Arundel, an English Lord, sadly passed to the heavens when Owain was only a boy, leaving him in the care of his mother. Owain did not talk about how his father died but was seemingly saddened by the memory as tears came to his eyes in the telling. He said his father was respected by the Earl, giving loyal service over many years. Owain spent some time in the Earl's company, and several years ago he had arranged for Owain to live with an Englishman, one David Hanmer. He said he had been studying Laws of the English in London for nearly a year now, dispatched into studentship by David Hanmer who had chosen to groom Owain in the affairs of the land.

His tale reminded me in some small way of my own beginnings. My Father had not passed to the heavens, but I had entered into an apprenticeship with my Master, Llwyd ap Crachan Llwyd, as Owain was now an apprentice to the Law. Enthusiasm for life emanated from his every pore in the telling of his story. Words danced from his mouth, embraced by honesty and truth. For a Welshman, he seemed to like the English, but he had spent some years in their company. Perhaps he understood them, unlike this dwarf who is a stranger to all things, not Welsh. Up to this point in his story, Owain certainly had not alluded to any connection to the ancient Princes or mentioned his heritage. In fact, he spoke nothing of his ancestry, other than briefly mentioning his parents.

The ferryman pulled at the oars one last time as the barge floated freely, coming to rest at the river landing. We had arrived, the sky above clearer now, stars beginning to glitter and twinkle high in the heavens. Our boatman grabbed a coiled rope of hemp from under his seat. Unfurling and holding the rope in a large muscular hand, with a flick of the wrist he tossed it to a thin, wiry man clothed in dirty rags who was standing on the riverbank. Catching the rope in skeletal hands, the thin man secured the barge to a wooden stave, stuck deep in the mud. Owain stepped from the barge with one long stride, avoiding the river below. I followed him, blindly leaping from barge to bank but losing my balance on landing. As I began to stagger backwards, a strong arm grabbed me by the scruff of my neck, hauling me to safety and preventing what would certainly have been an unwanted bath. Heaving a sigh of quiet relief, I thanked the ferryman silently with a polite bow for his speed of wit and strength. Owain passed some coins to my rescuer's waiting open palm and muscular fingers closed around the fee. The ferryman bade us a curt 'goodnight' before his huge legs strode towards a tavern across the street and disappeared behind its closed door with ne'er a backward glance.

No soldier guarded the gate tonight. We slipped and slid on the soft snow, our feet finding little solid earth to grip on to as we trudged through Billingsgate's dark streets, lit only by occasional candles blinking through cracks in shuttered windows. As we walked, I told Owain about Master Healan, and he expressed delight to meet him. He told me that as we had to pass through Bishopsgate to get to his own lodgings, perhaps it may be opportune to call on him this very evening, providing this was welcome. This reminded me of what Owain said earlier; *'we must not waste a breath of our time together.'* I agreed wholeheartedly with this suggestion, recognising that once again synchronicity prevailed.

I suddenly remembered the rabbit I was supposed to fetch for supper, or rather the absence thereof, and shared my anxiety of a table with no repast. Owain knew the streets well and assured me supper would be served. He knew just the place to purchase a good rabbit, and by chance, it just happened to be around the next corner. As good as his word, Owain stepped through a door, reappearing a few moments later holding a rabbit in one hand and an enormous loaf of bread in the other. So the tasks of the day were at last completed, even if the final one to secure sustenance may have seemed by default. I wondered as I walked with him, listening to stories as snow started to flutter through the air, how two such inexperienced young Welshmen as us, so different in class and stature, could possibly be sharing so much in this strange and confusing place. I felt I knew him well. In fact, it was as if I had known him before, perhaps in another time, but I only knew what he told me as he only knew that I had told him.

Snow began to fall heavily again as we rounded the corner into Bishopsgate. As expected, a soldier stood huddled inside the gate, concerned only with staying warm, stamping big feet on the ground almost rhythmically, slapping his sides with hands purple from cold. The soldier nodded acknowledgement of access in our direction. Turning, uninterested, he rubbed his hands together furiously in front of a brazier of dying embers. The snow fell in a curtain of white, shrouding all where it gathered. We arrived at Master Healan's powdery white from head to foot and frozen to our bones.

I knocked loudly on the door, announcing our arrival,

then waited for Master Healan's answer. Owain and I brushed away the snow from our clothes, creating a snow storm within a snow storm all around us, just like tiny clouds out of place so far from the sky. With a creak of rusty hinges, the door slowly opened. Master Healan appeared standing in the open doorway, shrouded in a warm glow of light.

CHAPTER TWENTY

Stepping over the threshold, I smiled warmly at seeing the familiar face of Master Healan and at my relief of the day's work satisfactorily completed and behind me. I was bubbling with excitement from the tips of my toes to the top of my head, through to deep inside, exploding with the fire of a dragon preparing to cast flame. Here was Glyndwr stood at my side, about to meet Master Healan, the only man alive other than my Master, Llwyd ap Crachan Llwyd, who was able to truly confirm my intuitions. Owain Glyndwr, the 'Son of Prophecy,' the long awaited 'Deliverer,' as prophesied at Bala in the mists of time... Or was he?

Master Healan ushered us both into the warmth of his home, closing and bolting the door behind our shadows.

"Well Crach, we have a visitor!" Addressing me though staring straight at Owain. Turning to me, he asked. "Did you manage to secure all as intended, Crach?"

Before I could answer him, he glanced from me to Owain and back again.

"You would not have brought a visitor here without good reason little friend, this I know to be true."

Owain stood quietly, thawing his bones at the hearth, respectfully waiting, no doubt, for a formal introduction.

"Master Healan, this day has been as most since I left my mountains and valleys, a day of magic but perhaps the most magical yet." I bowed to him, smiling, and continued. "I must tell you the story of the day, but first I will introduce you to Owain Glyndwr who is a student of law. We fell over each other at the Lincoln's Inn!"

I laughed in remembrance. Owain bowed to Master Healan, who returned the courtesy. I continued.

"Owain is the young gentleman I told you about in my tale of Worcester. He is the 'defender of the offended.'"

The old man, remembering my story, raised thick bushy eyebrows in acknowledgement, revealing eyes that sparkled like stars in the night sky. Gesturing us both to be seated at the table, he said.

"So you are the Welshman who brought a bully to justice?"

Glyndwr silently pulled out a chair with one hand, placing the rabbit and loaf of bread at the edge of the table with the other, taking care not to disturb the clutter of the old man's work of the day. Master Healan laughed loudly and slapped his thighs in delight.

"Supper!" He cried.

"Courtesy of Owain, Master Healan," I said. Owain sat quietly and with a nod of his head said.

"It is an honour to meet you, Master Healan. Crach has

told me much about you, and it seemed fortuitous that as my lodgings are not far from here, I must seize the opportunity as presented and meet you."

Master Healan curled his beard around long fingers as he sat down. "As the clouds sweep a sky blown by winds unknown, we must never ignore synchronicity, Owain. Must we, Crach?" He said, turning to me with a knowing grin.

"I know not why I felt the need to come, Sir!" Owain leaned over the table and turning from the old man to me, he said. "There is something about this fellow. I knew this when our paths crossed in Worcester, didn't I Crach?"

He squeezed my arm gently, and I smiled silently, nodding agreement before excitingly bursting out.

"The dreams, Owain! I told you about them, did me not Master Healan? Remember; Owain, how you said we would meet again after Worcester."

"I did, Crach, and was I not right?" Owain said, squeezing my arm again.

Master Healan clapped his hands, snapping our attention.

"A very busy night is ahead of us, young friends. I would wager there is much we must discover on this day. We will see why it is you had the need to come here Owain and, perhaps, why there may be something about Crach that draws you to him. But first we must eat, and this looks like a fine rabbit— with fresh bread too! Are we agreed?"

Master Healan leaned across the table and squeezed the rabbit.

"A grand meal for which we must thank you." He nodded appreciation to Owain and smiled at me. "Let us prepare this splendid meal. We will first eat and then we will talk, my friends."

Whilst the rabbit roasted on the spit, the three of us exchanged pleasantries. Owain and I thawed ourselves through to our bones and were now warm and dry. Master Healan gave us both a hot drink made from herbs and related its hidden potency and magic, telling us that it would portend nothing but honesty to spring through our words later this evening. His words echoed in our minds.

"The importance of events occurring thus far require interpretation. During interpretation this evening, we will discover whether or not there will be a secure lifelong friendship between you. What I can assure you is that both your destinies were written in the heavens many years ago." The old man paused and leaned across the hearth, picking at rabbit meat as it turned on the spit, roasting slowly over licking flames. His old fingers seemed oblivious to burning extreme heat, the sizzling rabbit presenting little defence against the purging of a slither of its onceliving flesh. Stepping back from the hearth, licking his fingers of dripping fat while chewing a morsel, tasting its progress to the platter, his face took on the appearance of a noonday sun in summer.

"Our feast is ready and awaits." He muttered with contentment, a half-eaten slice of rabbit moving from cheek to cheek. Swallowing hard, he coughed and spluttered. "To the table, my friends!"

Before we had a chance to respond, the old man filled his own platter from the crackling spit and pulled a chair from under the table for the sitting. After seating an aged body, he did not look up until his platter was almost cleared. Mouthfuls of the spit-roasted rabbit, in turn with chunks of fresh bread, all washed down with small ale, maintained his total attention. Ne'er a word passed his lips, apart from an odd grunt of satisfaction 'betwixt gulps. Owain and I did likewise, respecting Master Healan's need for silence whilst eating. The old man told me many times how he was capable of doing numerous tasks at the same time, but eating was always done as a sole activity. A pastime essential to life should be achieved without disturbance. Even thinking should be disregarded whilst eating, he said it disturbed the digestion.

The vacant spit, now only coated with the residue of its past inhabitant burnt into iron, platters empty on the table and bones, licked clean, was the only evidence of a repast now done. Master Healan sucked noisily on a final bone held in one hand, ensuring nothing remained attached, whilst in the other a final lump of bread skirted his platter, soaking up any remaining juices. Taking a last look at the bone in his fingers and popping the bread into his mouth, Master Healan pushed the empty platter across the table thus concluding the feast. Sitting back on the chair, rubbing a full stomach with both hands, exclaiming silent satisfaction, the old man sighed in fullness, belching rather loudly.

"That was a fine meal, I am stuffed!" I said, loosening my belt to aid comfort and digestion.

Owain pushed his platter to one side, replying,

"I agree, Crach. A fine rabbit, roasted to perfection and as a testament to its tenderness is a platter full of bare bones."

He laughed as he picked up a jug and gulped, draining the remainder of his small ale. Master Healan turned his chair, scraping the floor to face us, suggesting our discussions should begin.

"Now is the time!" He said, twisting his long beard around long fingers.

"It is possible we have much to discuss. Good use must

be made of our time for we know not how many hours or minutes we may need."

I leaned forward, wondering what he might mean and said.

"Do you doubt the synchronicity, Master Healan, the sequence of events?"

I turned to look at Owain but, of course, in reality, he did not actually know what I was referring to. I had not shared too many of the prophetic considerations that had flown through my mind. Owain interjected in an assertive but quiet manner.

"I know only that I should be here, Crach. I know not why, but all feels as if it should be as it is."

Smiling, he leaned across the table to fill his jug from the flagon, pouring the ale to the brim. As he replaced the flagon lightly back on the table, he looked directly at Master Healan and said,

"I feel a certain sense of magic, Sir, a sense of something much bigger than me. I feel like a man waiting in the wings of my life. A life yet to be revealed. But it may be the ale!" He laughed and quaffed more, gulping and draining the jug to half measure.

"Those are wise words, young Glyndwr. You show a freedom of spirit and a distinct lack of fear."

The old man smiled and tapped his forehead knowingly. I nodded agreement, remembering how I witnessed his lack of fear when standing up to the bully, Edmund, in Worcester. However, I couldn't help feeling, after bumping into Edmund's ego again when arriving in London, we had made an enemy of this man. Glyndwr looked much older in candlelight, his features changing as flickering shadows danced across the wall behind him, brought to life by flames burning brightly in the hearth. In fact, the walls were moving with dancing shadows in every corner. They floated amongst the clutter of scrolls and jars on shelves and on the rafters where hung bunches of herbs in various stages of drying.

All felt warm and comfortable and with a full belly, I was a contented dwarf who was excited by the prospect of what may lay ahead at the conclusion of our discussions tonight. Then I remembered Master's words, echoing across my thoughts. *'One stepping stone at a time, Crach, and the crossing is assured to safety on your journey.'*

I took a deep breath, recognising the need for nature to take its natural course, then I would not miss anything by thinking about what might be, instead of what is. I silently thanked my Master for this intercession. Perhaps I should assist myself in this quest by clearing the table of greasy platters and bones, now of no use to either the rabbit or us, thus doing something menial which my Master told me always assisted an active mind to quieten into the now.

I did as I thought, moving speedily from my chair to gather platters, bones and all else no longer needed that remained from our superb feast. I stacked the platters and tossed the bones into a wooden bucket kept for waste. The old man would turn this into compost for later use in the herb garden. Striding purposefully on my short legs towards the hearth, I collected a few logs stacked by the wall, placing each one strategically into the flames. Master Healan and Owain looked on in amazement as I silently returned to the table. My intention successful, my mind in the now, I smiled to myself.

"A sudden burst of energy, Crach!" The old man laughed. "You dance around the room as do the shadows on the walls!"

He laughed again.

Owain smiled and patted me on the back, saying,

"You move with the swiftness of an arrow my friend."

Master Healan leaned across the table, smiling warmly at Owain, he said,

"This is a dwarf who has a mind of the same pace as an arrow, my friend and knows and sees far more than most. Sometimes he surprises himself, don't you Crach?"

His features aged momentarily in light from the candles, although his eyes, sharp and clear as a mountain stream in springtime, suddenly seemed as two bright suns, shining into our hearts.

"I try my best Master Healan and with as much good humour as my heart will allow." Bowing to the old man and turning my head politely, I repeated the silent courtesy to Owain.

"I would wager your 'worst' is better than most folk's 'best,' Crach. Given I don't know any other dwarves, I, of course, compare you with taller folk!" Owain laughed and continued. "I must add though, Master Healan, Crach has impressed me in many ways, not least of which in his ability to relate a grand tale."

Master Healan casually interjected, raising his hand and pointing a finger directly at Owain Glyndwr, saying,

"Not one of his stories does not conceal words within words, hidden tales to tell. He is a prophet, or rather will be a prophet!" The old man laughed and reached across to pat my knee. "Crach, you will be one of the greatest of all time. As was Merlin to Arthur, you will be to Glyndwr!"

He looked directly into Owain's startled face. Well, who would not look startled upon hearing a statement of this nature? I mean to say, to the initiated it is a trifle shocking when a seer sees and then tells you what they see. I am used to it but poor Glyndwr, my new friend, is not. The startled gaze in his eyes now shone with curiosity. Filling his jug from the flagon once more, Owain sipped at its contents, slowly, perhaps savouring flavours or, more likely, buying time to think. He gently positioned it in front of himself on the table, staring at the liquid.

"I think it is time to move on in earnest. Let us begin."

Said the old man, who was looking not so old at the moment in the candlelight (yet something else I am becoming very familiar with). He clapped his hands lightly, palm to palm, slowly. Each clap echoed around the room, bouncing off wall to wall, to rafters and back again, resounding in my ears. Glyndwr looked up from the jug, abandoning all thoughts. Master Healan had our attention.

The magical atmosphere vibrating around the room reminded me of many times in the past. Now this old man was creating a portal between fluttering dimensions, flirting with each other in front of my eyes or, more correctly, as if I was in the midst of it all. My perceptions were sharper, and all that I saw with my eyes was well defined and bright in shimmering colour. I recognised that we had all been busy at something since the moment both Glyndwr and I had walked over the threshold and all that required concentration had been, and is, in the now, without effort.

'*Wormwood!*' I thought in a flash—'*Wormwood!*'

The old man must have put it in the steaming concoction drunk by us earlier when we stood thawing out by the hearth. Still, all was appropriate as we needed time but knew not how much, so what better than to slow it down, or suspend it altogether, than wormwood. This was, after all, one of the finest qualities this herb possessed, a fact well known by magicians, prophets and seers, even as far back and beyond the ancestors of Merlin. I admired this old man, he had filled a guiding role in my life which had been absent since leaving my Master, and I was not ready for flying as a dragon on my own just yet. This evening was going to be interesting.

Master Healan sat cocooned within a bright purple glow emanating from deep inside him, shimmering in a flickering blue hue. Voice, deep and hypnotic, echoed as it would in a cavern, bouncing from chamber to chamber. Eyes, shining and piercing, stared into the ether overcome by trance. He shuddered slightly, smiled briefly, before seemingly levitating slightly from his chair. He was in a trance. Glyndwr silently looked on, astounded, not knowing what was happening. I could see the confusion in his eyes, but I did not recognise fear hiding there. Catching his glance, I motioned with a finger to my lips, gesticulating silence. He nodded in acknowledgement and looked determined and serious as his eyes focussed again on the old man. Deep in a trance, Master Healan spoke with authority.

"On the night of your birth, Glyndwr, the heavens spoke loudly, thundering your arrival to this life. Lightning bolts shot through the sky. Horses, stabled for the night, were found the next morning by your father's groom, standing up to their fetlocks in blood, Owain, blood!"

The old man paused for breath, glancing towards the flames roaring in the hearth. He continued.

"Your father witnessed a vision of an enormous battle sword, shimmering above the cradle where you lay, newly born, in the early hours of your birth day. You have heard the story, Owain?" He asked.

"I have Sir. But pray, it is simply the ranting of joy, no doubt, at my birth. Folk do love to create mystery, do they not?"

Owain awaited an answer. Master Healan smiled wryly, his eyes twinkled like stars in the night sky, candle flames mirrored in pupils, jet black and dilated to the size of saucers. He leaned forward and said to Owain.

"It has been known for mystery to be born in many ways, often through, and by, uneducated men with idle minds. But in your case, what you have heard is true and does not belong in the dreams of a 'make- believer.' You, Owain Glyndwr, are of a great and powerful beginning. There is much for you to do before you take your rightful place as the true Prince of Wales."

He paused, staring into the shadows dancing across the wall around the hearth to the rhythm of flashing flame. Smoke, grey and white, rose from the fire in small puffs, like clouds floating towards the chimney, searching for the sky. Glyndwr looked astonished and gasping said,

"Me, a Prince?"

But that was all he said. I remember saying much more when the old man told me I would ride at the side of a Prince. Owain became silent, reflecting, and transfixed, almost suspended in time. Wormwood helps, of course! I had heard of this prophecy before, on three occasions now. Firstly from my Master, secondly from this old man and thirdly, from the scrolls I carried to London from Wales. Glyndwr still sat motionless, eyes widening, growing bright. Flames from candles reflected as may flickers of new life radiating through the heavens. The old man turned from the dancing shadows, voice deeper now as if heralded from the depths of the earth, he continued.

"Studying the Laws of the English and living amongst them, as you have done thus far in your life and will continue to do for some years yet, is indeed a sound foundation for grasping the ways people of this land think. You will need to know all these things as the years turn into decades, of which there are many that lay in wait for your journey. All is as it should be within the scheme of things."

The old man bowed his head and sighed in resignation to the unfurling prophecy he was witnessing now. He also reflected on his part, along with many others, all those years ago at Bala. He remembered the night when the heavens opened and revealed all to watching eyes. Now, after so many years, Master Healan and Llwyd ap Crachan Llwyd are the only ones still alive, the only two men who have both the wisdom and the skill to truly interpret the ancient map of prophecy. I watched on, mesmerised by Glyndwr's face, his concentration intense, not a muscle twitching, not a blink.

Master Healan coughed from deep down inside his chest and wheezed, lifting aged hands towards the rafters, almost touching the hanging herbs. Tightly closed eyes snapped open as the old man returned to deep trance again, his body rigid, motionless, almost vibrating in stillness. We waited, feeling the room brimming with unknown energy, the silence deafening. His breath became shallower and shallower and with quivering lips, he spoke again, voice firm and methodical, slowly delivering each word, so all were clearly heard.

"Soon you will be done with studying English Law, and in the next chapter of your life, you will take a wife, inherit lands and learn the Englishman's ways of battle and war. You will also learn the ways of the warrior, and you will excel in battle, fighting alongside the English King and you, Crach, will be at his side."

I winced at the very idea of battle, not something anywhere near a thought to be considered in my mind, I can tell you. Battle means anger, bloodshed, and death. I have never been angry and know not how it feels to be so out of control, I hate the sight of chicken blood, ne'er mind a living man, and I love life so sincerely and hope that my death will come many years into the future. I remember well, back at the start of this adventure, having difficulty in accepting the idea I was to become a performing dwarf in a travelling circus. Never had I left Wales but my Master told me I would, as did he predict much of what had happened already, and now Master Healan was fleshing the skeleton. There seemed much more to come in the future than I had first thought. The adventure continues! This did perplex me somewhat. Everything seemed to be moving at the speed of a dragon in flight, but then that is the way of a prophecy given from the heavens. A prophecy that, in reality, was shaping the lives of Glyndwr and myself, not just for a couple of years, but forever!

Master Healan, deep in trance, haunting deep voice filling the room, every word echoing as a shepherd hailing a flock in the valleys of my homeland.

"Your fight will be just as you are a just man. You, at this point in your life, do not believe the English are an evil self-seeking people who have little conscience for their actions. Yes, you may feel the King you will serve to be a good man. Know he is the best of a bad crop, and he will face betrayal. His golden crown will be knocked from his proud head and stolen by a bully who will then pronounce himself King. You will witness lies and deceit, and you will be passed over, rewards for your service will never be given. Your words of protest will fall on deaf ears. All that truly is yours will be taken, and you will return to a cold hearth." The old man began to tremble, and his eyes sparkled brighter and brighter. His sunken cheeks were shallow yet flushed and beads of sweat ran from a wrinkled forehead, dripping and disappearing into his beard. With lips quivering, the voice echoed again.

"Your eyes will open to the injustice done to all Welshmen. Even their rights will be plucked from them as feathers from a chicken. Then will come the time when every scrap of knowledge held from your experiences will be as arrows in a quiver. You will unite your countrymen and rise as one against the transgressions forced upon the people of Wales by the English."

The voice paused, and the old man stared into a space that we could not see. Glyndwr sat on the edge of his chair, silently listening to every word spoken, intent on missing not one breath of sound echoing all around us. He sat motionlessly, bent in submission to concentration; astounded possibly, shocked possibly, but it did not show on his face.

"A great comet illuminating the skies above your armies will herald victory in all you do. It must be known that such victory brings deceit to your door once again, words will be false, and promises will be broken. All you love will be taken from you, except for one thing, my Prince, one thing. Your life will always be yours and never will it be taken from you, never! Know this! It is finished!"

The old man gasped, the voice fell silent, eyelids closing as if to sleep. His head slumped forward, coming to rest as bearded chin met chest. The trance was over and so much had been said by the voice speaking through the old man. So much that, to be honest, in this dwarf's mind, I was scared at the very thought of everything I had heard. If I was to be at Glyndwr's side, I would need to be mounted, and I had never even been upon a horse! But perhaps this would be the very least of my worries yet to be considered.

Chapter Twenty-One

It had been a very long day which had been so full of the unexpected. This morning, when I trudged through foul weather and even fouler streets, I knew little of the future, excepting sketches in the sands of time. For the most part, it was yet to be told. Master Healan, or rather the voice speaking through him, had now given a map for the prophecy, signposting the lives of Glyndwr and me, Crach Ffinnant, a dwarf. So my future was decided, irrespective of what I may feel or want. This seemed certain, and I wondered if I really had much of a choice within the scheme of things.

The old man gently snored, each rasp of breath encouraging his whiskers to dance, bearded chin still resting on his chest. Owain sat in silence, as did I, listening to the old man's slumbers. I leaned across the table and gently tapped Glyndwr's arm lightly with my pointed finger. He jumped, a little startled by my intrusion of his thoughts. He looked weary now, and dark rings encircled his tired eyes, but still, they sparkled like stars in the heavens.

"I'm sorry, Crach." Smiling and returning from deep thought, he said. "I was lost in the visions that our 'sleeping prophet's' words still conjured across my eyes."

Bringing both hands up from his lap, Owain massaged numbness from his face with long fingers, sporting the cleanest fingernails I have ever seen. *'Hands of a clerk'* I thought. *'How could these hands wield a sword?'* I pondered a moment in silence, wondering what he thought of the words heard this night.

He looked extremely preoccupied, eyes staring into a place only he could see. But who wouldn't, after hearing the map of their future life unfurled in front of them before they had even lived it. My predicament was equal to his in many ways, but with one exception, in that, I am a dwarf. Glyndwr turned his vision from that secret, unknown, private space within his mind's eye and looking directly at me, said,

"You will remember when we first met in Worcester, Crach, that I alluded to dreams haunting me where I became friends with a dwarf. Well I now know, you are he."

I nodded in agreement and replied.

"It would seem to be that the heavens direct it but I can't help wondering if all this is but a dream that I will wake up from soon, only to find myself back in the safety of my mountains."

Glyndwr cautioned me to silence, finger pursing his lips.

"It is much the same for me too Crach, but there are things I have not told you. In the dreams that haunt me, and have done since I was old enough to remember them, I have been plagued by visions of battles and felt myself, nay seen myself, as a reflection in a lake, wearing a crown. Nights for me are not particularly a time of rest as they are for many because when my eyes drift towards sleep, the doors of hell unleash visions of so many horrors."

He looked anxious for the first time since I had known him. I held his arm in compassion, and he smiled.

"Now!" He said. "After the synchronicity of events between us since our first meeting and now hearing Master Healan unfurl the prophecy, I know my dreams are more than that, they are prophetic. All of this is something far bigger than me. I feel like an ant below a mountain, overwhelmed with respect to what I have witnessed tonight. Master Healan has described my dreams with words that I understand; the pictures of dreams that were so confusing and frightening, now have formed." His smile disappeared to be replaced by a look of resignation. "The more thought I give to what I have heard, the more I know my choice is a simple one." A smile returned to his face. "I have a destiny to fulfil, Crach and the heavens say you are to be to me, as Merlin was to Arthur. I will need my 'Merlin,' Crach. What do you say?" He leaned across the table and picked up the flagon, refilling his jug to the brim before filling mine also. "Are you with me, Crach?"

Without hesitation, I found myself saying.

"As the heavens direct, so it is. I am with you, my Lord, and will stand by your side at your pleasure."

"It is my pleasure, Crach! Let us drink to the prophecy."

He raised his jug, and I did likewise. We cracked them together, waking the old man who began to stir from slumber. We toasted to the prophecy and to our agreement. As we drank deeply, the old man opened his ancient eyes, coughing and spluttering himself back to full consciousness. Glyndwr picked up the flagon from the table and drained its contents into Master Healan's jug.

"A toast, Sir!" he raised his jug and faced the old man, smiling politely. "To you, Master Healan, to you Sir!"

We all drank. Master Healan yawned and placed his jug on the table to free his aged arms for the process of stretching tired limbs, attracting circulation of blood, bringing back life.

"It has been a long night my friends, and there are more things we need to achieve, but weariness overtakes these tired old bones of mine and the call to bed urges me to say no more today." The old man smiled but looked worn out.

"I will prepare your cot for you, Master Healan!" I leapt to the task at hand, wishing this old man, this gifted, wise, old sage, nothing but a rest worthy of his spirit.

"Thank you, Crach. I am most grateful to you!" The old man said as he turned and stood motionless, facing Glyndwr. "I have no doubt that you have many questions, Owain, but perhaps it would be opportune to consider all on a new day."

"That would suit me, Master Healan," Glyndwr replied, standing up and shifting his chair away from the table. "I will return to my lodgings now. I bow with dignity and great thanks for the hospitality shared with me but, moreover, for things I need not mention." He smiled knowingly and proceeded to bow. Glyndwr continued. "I have work in the Courts of Justice that will take my time for a few days. A Will that is disputed by greedy relatives!"

Taking his cloak from the box where it had lain all evening, now dry and warm, he slung it around his broad shoulders, pulling the cloth tight to his body.

"May I call again in seven days' time? I am free on this day and can come at a time that suits you, Sir." Owain smiled expectantly at the old man.

Owain warmed himself in front of the blazing hearth one last time before venturing out into the icy cold of the night. Master Healan extended his hand towards Glyndwr, affording a seal of mutual gratitude and agreement.

"This will be most convenient for us, and we look forward to seeing you in the early evening, seven days from today. Don't we Crach?" Master Healan smiled at me knowingly, a twinkle in his eyes.

Glyndwr took the old man's wrist in his hand, gripping gently and Master Healan reciprocated as he held Owain's wrist in his old hand. The two men sealed the evening. Owain bade me farewell by warmly taking my small hand in his, telling me that our future together was an honour he looked forward to. An icy blast of wind, accompanied by a flurry of snowflakes, whirled into the room as Owain stepped out into the dark streets, closing the door behind him. The old man rubbed his gnarled old hands together in front of the hearth, soaking the radiating heat into his every pore.

"Time to sleep, Crach!" Master Healan yawned.

He shuffled across the room and climbed onto his waiting cot, smothered with sheepskins. Within the flutter of an eyelid, the old man fell asleep, and the room was soon filled with the quiet buzz of his snoring. It prompted me to think of bees flying in and out of their hive at the height of summer. Sleep also came quickly to this tired little dwarf, snuggled in the warmth of a cosy cot, and it was not long before my dream-scape was invaded by an old friend.

My Master, Llwyd ap Crachan Llwyd, appeared at my side as dreams took me again to Llyn Tegid. I was standing looking into

*the lake with the mountains looming all around me. As I stared
at my reflection, a fish jumped from the depths, spiralled in the air
and splashed the surface of the water with a flapping tail, before
diving deep again. As the fish disappeared, circles of ripples spun,
stirring my reflection into shadows beneath tiny waves. Then my
image began to reappear, shimmering into clarity as the ripples
flowed away and the usual stillness of the lake returned, but I also
saw, reflecting on the surface, my teacher and companion for over
ten years, Llwyd ap Crachan Llwyd, standing at my side.*

*Such majesty was held within this landscape. Its great
beauty overwhelmed me; towering mountains, green with forest,
reflecting around the edges of the lake's surface. There on the
water shimmered a hot noon day sun at its highest in the sky. I felt
the old man's arm around my shoulder as I watched him in the
reflection, smiling. His voice, warm and friendly, whispered—a
whisper within a resounding echo.*

*"Hello, Crach! Well, well, well!" His reflection wavered. "All
goes as well as it should, and a new apprenticeship begins, Crach.
My old friend will continue to help you to prepare for your future,
and I see that you get along with each other exceedingly well."
His eyes twinkled across the image in front of me, like two tiny
suns, spreading flickering golden shards over the surface of the
lake. His voice echoed again with a haunting whisper. "You have
met our Prince. It is he who you will serve. This is your destiny,
as you now know. For a little while, you will both continue on
your separate journeys, gathering knowledge, skills and gaining
confidence, until your paths cross again. When you meet again at
the crossroads, you will both take the same road and thus journey
together for the remainder of your given years. All is as it should
be."*

His smile reflected back at me from the mirrored surface of the lake. Another fish leapt from the depths, somersaulted and splashed, returning to its underwater world as ripples rolled towards the shore. Calmness came again to the water and my Master, Llwyd ap Crachan Llwyd, had gone.

I awoke to a now all too familiar tap on my forehead as Master Healan raised me from slumber. Looking up at his kind face, smiling down at me through my still weary eyes, I sat up on my cot and stretched limbs back into life in preparation for this new day. I nodded and grunted my *'good morning.'* The aroma of steaming pottage, freshly prepared, filled the room. All was warm and cosy from the roaring fire in the hearth. The old man had been busy since waking, and as I swung my legs to the floor, I thought what a nice change this was for me. Every day of my time with Llwyd ap Crachan Llwyd, over so many years, come rain, snow or shine, I had been the first one to rise, the one to make preparations for the start of each new day. But with Master Healan, there were no such expectations.

He busied himself, stirring breakfast.

"Are you hungry, Crach?" The old man asked through the back of his head as he poked the fire. "I would have thought after all your dream travels and nattering to my old friend, you will have worked up quite an appetite!" He laughed.

I realised, once again, Master Healan had also received a visitor in his dreams. The old man spoke again through the back of his head as he ladled steaming pottage into waiting bowls.

"Yes Crach, he did." He laughed loudly this time.

Now the old man was doing it too! Now he was reading my thoughts! *'Is there no privacy when with magicians? Should not thoughts be sacred to their beholder?'* But this was the way of things, I was resigned to that.

"Then I need not tell you what he told me!" I replied sarcastically while laughing at my own joke. "And yes, I am hungry and I am grateful to you, as is my grumbling tummy."

I sat down at the table in front of a steaming bowl of vegetables, floating in a dark soup. It looked so tasty that I burnt my mouth in haste to eat, which did slow my appetite somewhat, but I eventually scraped my bowl clean. As at all meal times, not a word passed between us, all thoughts absent, eating was a divine meditation to embrace.

Seven days later, as the sun fell from the dark overladen sky, a sharp knock came on the stable-door which startled me and rousing my attention from the scroll I was immersed in. Master Healan, who was busy preparing herbs, put down the chopping blade on the table and shuffled over to the door. Opening it to our caller, who stood on the threshold and to the freezing cold air, the old man bade a silent welcome.

Owain Glyndwr stepped inside, bidding *'good evening,'* firstly to the old man, and then to me.

"Such inclemency, friends. Can it become any colder, I wonder? My toes are ice, and there is so much dampness all around." He declared as he stamped his feet.

I pulled a chair closer to the hearth for him, while the old man invited him to remove wet clothes and warm his frozen bones. Owain took his seat with much pleasure.

"Good evening, My Lord!" I said bowing.

He laughed, returning my bow sarcastically, whilst tipping his forelock.

"You make me laugh, Crach! You make me laugh until my sides split from my body!" Glyndwr chortled.

The old man joined in the hilarity, filling the room with much mirth. "Humour is one of his gifts, Owain. Crach sees the funny side in all things. I never find him in the slightest bereft of a quirky remark in order to bring light. I have laughed more in the short time this dwarf has been in my company than I have for many a year. There is not much to smile about in these dark times. He lightens my soul." Master Healan laughed again.

"And mine!" added Glyndwr smiling.

Owain did not come to call on us empty handed this cold winter evening, with his generosity extending to a roast chicken and fresh bread, together with a flagon of red wine. The wine was booty from a French ship that had been impounded by the courts, its contents seized as a fine for some impropriety committed against the King. The three of us dined well at the table that evening within the warmth of Master Healan's home. The wine was sweet and fruity, which aided my digestion very nicely, and the repast was, as always, conducted in silence.

After feasting, we exchanged a multitude of words. The old man answered the many questions asked by our young 'Prince in Waiting.' It became very clear Owain had spent much time over the last seven days preparing these questions as each one was methodical in nature. By the time he had exhausted the prepared list, read from a roll of parchment secreted from within his shirt, hours had passed. I sat listening intently to everything that was said, knowing full well it all concerned me. If I was to spend many years following this prophecy, what concerned Glyndwr and his path, equally involved me.

CHAPTER TWENTY-TWO

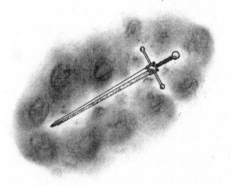

Minutes turned into hours and yet for all of the words passing between us on that night, all seemed to take just a few winks of an eye. Whenever there is great magic at hand, time stands still. It always has and always will, that is the way of magic—timeless. Everything around us became surreal. Normally solid walls, floors, rafters, even the physical being of the old man, appeared permeable. Dimensional portals, flickering boundaries, and unseen doorways—such is this thing called magic.

The three of us were deeply engrossed in the whys and wherefores of the prophecy. Master Healan, as animated as ever, seemingly losing decades from his face as he spoke. The hearth blazed, and yet a draft of cold air materialised from nowhere, sweeping across the table in front of us, fluttering leaves of parchment, as a breeze through an open window but none was ajar. Suddenly the flames in the hearth flew into a rage, leaping to and fro. Outside, in the dark of a cold night, thunder clattered overhead, rattling the rafters as it roared angrily across black skies. As the thunder sang into the distance, assisted by flying winds sweeping it away, the hearth resettled into a steady flame. At that precise moment, there was a tap on the stable-door, quickly followed by another and then another. Master Healan rose to his aged feet and chuckled. I noticed a wry smile creep across his face as he turned and stepped towards the door, grabbing the bolt firmly with rheumatic fingers.

"I think I know who this is, my friends!" He remarked, turning quickly to address us before returning to the bolts.

As the old man pulled the door open, great swathes of purple and white smoke appeared from nowhere, akin to rolling clouds midst a storm. There, through the haze, was Llwyd ap Crachan Llwyd, stepping through the doorway! *'Am I asleep? Is this a dream?'* My old Master stood shimmering within a golden aura, sparkling all around him. Shafts of pure light illuminated the darkest corners of the room. I pinched myself, nipping my leg between thumb and forefinger, and it hurt! I was definitely not asleep! Owain sat in a state of shocked, yet seemingly respectful, silence. He was staring at the spectre of Llwyd ap Crachan Llwyd, but again I saw no fear rooted in those dark, intelligent eyes. Master Healan was beaming from ear to ear, his grin engulfing an aged face. It was a most infectious smile and, needless to say, he looked years younger as is always the case when magic is at hand.

"My old friend, Llwyd! How good to see you!" The old man giggled, almost uncontrollably, like a toddler in the wake of a tickling from a loving, playful parent. "So the door opened, old friend!" He gained control, giggling subsiding now as he turned to face Owain and me, who were still seated at the table. "The very manifestation of magic is proven to you this day, My Lord."

He bowed in respect to Owain, our 'Prince in Waiting.' *'And the prophecy continues to unfurl'* I thought, excited by the prospect of all my years as an apprentice now truly coming to fruition. Almost as an echo, the voices of the old man and my Master responded in unison to my thought.

"It does indeed, Crach, it does indeed!" Both laughed, having now achieved in unison the effective reading of my thoughts—and the joke at my expense continues!

But by now you will realise I am a good-humoured fellow, thus the expression *'taking it on the chin'* springs to mind. Hopefully, a thought that will be allowed to stay inside my own head! The two old men sat together opposite us. Master Healan, in all his glory and splendour, as I have come to know him to be, and my Master, who I had not seen (except in dreams) for nearly nine months, a shimmering spectre in solid form. Owain sat in silence, but I noticed a look of expectancy on his face and wondered if he thought this was a dream he might awaken from soon. So much had happened to this man in the last seven days. *'He is only human after all.'* I thought. Master Healan leaned across the table, taking the flagon of wine, which had been kindly donated by Owain, and poured the sweet red liquid into waiting jugs.

My Master beamed at me with an enormous smile. His aura shimmered, vibrating like the wings of a bird assuming flight, shining as bright as a noonday sun, reaching a crescendo so bright that I was momentarily blinded. Suddenly the shimmering turned to a still bright, but dimmer, glow surrounding him. Llwyd ap Crachan Llwyd had truly taken solid form. He was really here in front of me, this was no dream.

"This is a pleasure, old friend!" Master Healan said as he raised the jug, brimming with wine. "Welcome to you, my friend! Welcome! So many years have passed. We are old men now. How the seasons have treated us!"

I saw tears in the corners of the old man's eyes. So full was he of emotion upon meeting my Master again after so many moons. My Master collected his jug from the table in those familiar gnarled old fingers I knew so well. For a moment, it was as if they were oblivious to us sitting in the same space, drowning themselves in the pleasure and joy of their long-standing friendship. We joined them, raising our jugs in readiness to toast the celebration of their reunion. I drank in anticipation of what was to come next and in wonderment at the way Llwyd ap Crachan Llwyd had travelled so far from our homeland.

I knew there had been no walking along muddy tracks in the pouring rain for my old Master. I also knew that he would not have joined a circus to perform in all weathers, nor would he have taken nearly eight months to reach his destination. No! He had made an ancient incantation, summoned misty gateways from the distant past to open, stepped across the threshold and now, here he was. It crossed my mind that it had probably taken him no time at all. I could hear echoes of his teachings ringing in my ears. *There is no such thing as time, Crach!*

Of course, this is true for magicians, alchemists and the like. We understand and manipulate energy accordingly in such ways, studying and learning over many years. Even then, not all of us can achieve it! Often I have thought that this is because of the power of the universe, creating all things will only allow those with a true heart and with heavenly intention to use the gateways. For a farmer, it is the seasons that govern abundance. For all of us, it is the sun and moon which create day and night. We work and play under the sun, sleep and dream under the moon – the rhythm of life.

Master Healan gently placed his well-drained jug on the table. As he leaned forward to rest upon lumpy elbows, the sleeves of his gown fell from his wrists, gathering in folds, giving his thin arms an appearance of having no attachment to him at all. It was as if they sprung, spectre-like, from the table. He leaned across the table, staring at us with eyes intense and shining. Peering over the rim of his jug, his eyes brightened as his look bore deeper.

"And so, Crach, here we are again, but this time you are awake!" Smiling and gently replacing the half-drained jug on the table. His look then turned towards Owain. "My Lord!" The old magician bowed his head in respect. "It is as the heavens decreed, but before I continue with my part in this greatest and most heavenly of tasks, I have a question for you, Owain Glyndwr. We have spent many years preparing for your coming, and we know who you are."

Master Healan nodded his head in silent agreement, knowing both question and answer methinks. Owain nodded too, saying, "I would hear your question, Sir, although I suspect I know its nature already."

"Yes," My old wise Master agreed as he fiddled and twirled his beard between long fingers. "I am sure you do. But you will permit me the question, as ask it I must."

Smiling sarcastically, with that wry grin I knew so well, he continued to twirl his beard. Glyndwr winked at me before nodding in agreement.

"Master Healan has explained the prophecy to you, My Lord, as I have to Crach. Your life has thus far given visions of sleep and opportunities in waking. You have taken everything that has come to you in good spirit at all times. You do know who you are, we know that. So, all that remains is for you to swear allegiance to your destiny. Will this be your choice?" Llwyd ap Crachan Llwyd paused in wait for an answer.

Owain Glyndwr, 'Prince in Waiting,' pushed his seat backwards away from the table and rose to his feet. A serious stare shone from his hypnotic inquisitive eyes. Standing perfectly still, he spoke in a voice I had not heard since we were in Worcester on the evening that Edmund became our enemy. The evening that Owain showed to me for the first time his passion and stance towards the injustices of man to man. His voice echoed around the room, as had my Master's, bouncing from corner to rafter.

"Gentlemen!" Owain lowered his head respectfully, although his eyes did not leave us. "I know without any fear of doubt in my heart that my destiny is as you say it will be. I know all was written before my birth. I trust in the heavens and in your words, gentlemen. I will follow my journey in life as so decreed, and I swear to give my life willingly to the fulfilment of this prophecy, as is laid down in the scrolls. I will take my rightful place when the heavens so dictate. Master Healan, Master Llwyd ap Crachan Llwyd, Crach Ffinnant." With arms outstretched, Owain opened his hands, palms uppermost, raising them to the heavens and said. "It is done!"

Owain bowed one last time before pulling the chair back beneath him and sitting down. Master Healan burst into one of his fleeting fits of uncontrollable coughing and spluttering and reached for the jug in need of the momentary relief he knew the red wine would bring. Drinking deeply, the old man gulped at the temporary cure. The coughing ceased, but only until the next time he would be overtaken by frailty that even magic could not stem.

My Master smiled and raised his hands towards the rafters as his body began to shimmer again, taking on a purple hue. Throwing back his head, Llwyd ap Crachan Llwyd spoke in a haunting deep voice, erupting from within and yet sounding as if it came from everywhere.

"My Lord, may we remind you, although you have pledged your life, it will never be taken from you by a human hand. There are gifts demanded by the prophecy which will, in time, be given to both you and Crach." He lowered his arms and sat back on the seat, appearing to float in and out of our vision, his form splintering, then reforming. The voice continued. "Crach Ffinnant, you will ride at the side of our Prince as prophet, seer, and healer but firstly you will both return to your studies. When your paths again cross, it is then that your journey will truly begin." His aura vibrated, and the colours deepened.

"You will need eyes that see where no man can, to enable visions of truth and to receive messages on wings of the wind. A raven will join you on your journey and will be your constant companion, Crach. You already know and understand their language and magic, in time you will also know their friendship." The old man paused for breath.

The silence was deafening and prolonged—but I was sure I could hear the sound of wings beating! He gasped and continued.

"Your skill with runes, Crach, will guide decisions."

He clapped his hands together, and white smoke swirled in clouds all around him. He clapped again. A well-worn, tanned leather pouch ported from within the smoke and fell to the table, making not a sound as it landed.

"Your runes, Crach!" Llwyd ap Crachan Llwyd motioned silent fingers, pointing towards the pouch that was now laying with its loosened drawstring open on the table. The rune stones scattered, each face down with not an image to be seen. Thus no reading or consultation appropriate as no 'casting' had been made.

My Master clapped again, three times. Short, sharp, surprisingly loud claps. Wisps of smoke swirled from between his hands, rising upwards and becoming dense, getting thicker the higher it rose. His body shimmered blindingly. He clapped again. The clouds of smoke dissipated a little, revealing a glorious battle sword floating above the table as if held by invisible hands. An amber stone decorated its hilt, resonating magic from the heavens. Its handle was bound well with a thong for a strong grip. Its broad blade glistened with edges honed to perfection for the delivery of justice. A sword which was truly fit for a Prince. The old man spoke again.

"My Lord, take your sword and guard it well until the call for battle is heard. Keep your sword, 'The Blade of Justice'!"

Owain stood up from the table, taking the sword from invisible hands. Holding the hilt firmly in his grip, he raised it towards the heavens, as would a knight before a battle charge. It sat well in his hands and though I know little of swords, or any other kind of weapon if I am honest, I know balance when I see it. This wondrous heaven-gifted blade would extend the reach of his intent throughout the mists of time yet to come.

Master Healan passed a bundle of sacking to Owain, suggesting it be used to secret the sword from inquisitive eyes on his later return to his lodgings.

My Master sat quietly, his form beginning to fade away in front of my eyes. He spoke for the final time.

"My deed is done, friends. My time here is up, but we will meet again." His voice became fainter, shimmering harmoniously with his disappearing form—fainter and fainter. "We will meet again!"

Vibrations gyrated throughout the room, shimmering, lessening from a wholesome intensity into a betwixt night and day feel, a between space, a something and yet a nothing. Llwyd ap Crachan Llwyd was gone!

Llwyd ap Crachan Llwyd, by travelling through portals between the dimensions, had delivered not only clarity but also heavenly gifts that were written within the prophecy. Runes for me, a 'blade of justice' for Owain, together with notice of much to come. I cannot speak for My Lord, Owain, but for me, it was refreshing the prophecy decreed no human would ever take his life away from him, or my life from me.

I looked forward in great anticipation to those years yet to come as foretold, when 'Raven Magic' would share my steps. Their language was both ancient and mystical. Few could converse with them nowadays, except those such as I. Oh of the wonders to come! A raven on my shoulder! He would see all that I did not. All would be within my reach due to the Raven's friendship. But this lay in the future. I suspect there will be many more footsteps to be taken to who knows where before such time. So many paths lay outstretched in front of me, so many moons before all foretold thus far would spring into flight.

Master Healan sat quietly, glancing at Owain and myself with eyes twinkling and grinning from ear to ear and said,

"I think that is enough magic for one night, my young friends, don't you?"

A belly laugh followed, and we joined him in good humour. Owain picked up a jug from the table and what lay left therein, he drained with gusto before refilling it to the brim from the flagon. He held the jug between interlocked fingers, raising it slowly to sip its sweetness.

"It has indeed been a night I will never ever forget, not for as long as I walk on this earth!" Owain sipped again and continued. "Believe me, my friends, when I say I have pondered much over the events that led me here today. It is good for a man to know his destiny, thus enabling one to strive like a warrior to its conclusion. I know my ancestors, and yours, Crach." He turned and gently touched my shoulder.

"I am bound to do as the heavens say, and from this night, I know there will be some seasons to pass before we meet again. But when we do, things will be very different." He laughed and continued. "We will both be much older!"

I joined him in the joke when Master Healan interjected.

"And I, my friends, may be helping you from elsewhere. My time, like my oldest friend, will not be for too much longer on this earth."

I saw a tear in his twinkling eyes as he pulled a rag from his cloak pocket, blowing his nose loudly. Clearing his gruff throat, the old man replaced the rag, found a smile and bade us quiet with a wave of his hand. Little did he know it would be some years hence before he received that final call from the heavens?

"You have confirmed for two old men, plus the many who

were part of translating this prophecy through time, we were right, My Lord." He bent his head in a light bow of respect whilst speaking. "Know it will be a decade before your paths re-join after this night, my friends. For some this is a lifetime, but for you, Lord, and for your Wizard…." His eyes exploded with light as he spoke. "… But for you, it is the beginning of your journey to becoming a Prince, with your seer at your side. Together you will ride with justice. The people of Wales will rise behind you against the English. But first, you will know their betrayal, as we know it now. You will beware, Edmund, who will be a thorn in your flanks for many a year. There will be others, but you will know who they are. Alas, my dear friend, our time together now is over, and this matter must never be discussed again with any other person, be they, King or common man."

Owain leaned across the table, took the old man's hands into his own and squeezed them gently in friendship.

"Master Healan, all is as it should be and until the day I meet my friend, Crach, again, I will not think on this. I will allow all to unfurl, as indeed it must until the time is right. After that? Well, we will see!"

He smiled, relaxing his grip on the old man's hands and patted them affectionately, before picking up his jug, raising it skywards.

"To Wales, my friends! To my destiny and to our friendship! To you, Crach!"

He drank deeply as Master Healan raised his jug in reply to the toast. "To 'The Land of the Free.' To you, my Prince. To you, who our bards and minstrels will still be singing about and praising for hundreds of years to come. Never will the mists of time conceal your heritage and deeds, nor the brave warriors who will ride at your side." He suddenly smiled, with a knowing sarcasm flashing momentarily across his face, and added. "It would not surprise me if my brother, Iolo, does not scribe a ditty or two." He laughed again.

"Crach, you will stay with me for a while as we still have work to do and I must take you to meet your allies soon. But for now, my dear friends, this night is done, and we must draw all to a close, just as sleep closes my weary old eyes." He drained the jug.

Owain stood from the table, gathered up his cloak and wrapped it closely around him in preparation for the cold early morning walk which lay in wait, he said, "Crach, I will see you at 'the crossroads'!" He laughed. I stood, bowed my head, and replied.

"May the Gods watch over you until that day, my Lord?" I bowed again.

The old man passed Owain his new sword, now tightly concealed in sacking, hidden from eyes that may pry where none should do so.

Owain thanked us both several times before the cold air of early dawn invaded our warmth as he disappeared through the door into the half-light of dawn.

It would be ten years before I would see him again.

CHAPTER TWENTY-THREE

Days turned into weeks, weeks into months, seasons passed, and years behind me were clouded in mists of hard labour and study. I learned much from Master Healan, having almost served another apprenticeship, but he had grown very old now, and frailty pervaded his every breath. The old man's back had become considerably more arched as the years went by. His features had become thinner, almost emaciated. However, the twinkle still shone in those aged eyes! Whenever work took his attention, which was more often than not, silence was accompanied by the odd cough, disturbing concentration.

I had spent many days, weeks, months and years reading ancient scrolls, pounding herbs, boiling potions, delivering medicines to every conceivable corner of London, casting runes, interpreting dreams and learning magical keys and phrases to manipulate dimensional portals. I was a very industrious dwarf and well versed in all I may need on my journey through life. I knew London well now and was accustomed to its strange smells, filth and odd customs. My command of the language was now second nature. My time here was well spent, although in my dreams, sometimes not, I longed for the mountains and valleys of my home.

Llwyd ap Crachan Llwyd, still a regular 'dream visitor,' used the portal often and the two old men spent many hours examining and interpreting ancient scrolls.

I had become a familiar sight around the streets of London. It was true that being a dwarf had advantages, folk either avoided me or applauded great respect for the mystical heritage of dwarves.

Over the last few years, I completed much of the heavy work for Master Healan that his advancing years prevented him from achieving. Competence and knowledge, couched within my calm persona, invited respect from many of the old man's patients and some days I was kept so busy that my attention was taken until the early hours. Stories and tales, drawn from Master Healan's long life, entertained me until sleep summoned when my dreams busied me with learning from the 'magic scroll' my old Master had given to me.

Rising early this day while leaving the old man to sleep on as he needed to do nowadays, I walked down to the river just as the summer sun began to shimmer, rising far away where the earth fell from the sky. Deep, long, thin, ochre-stained clouds swept across the waking sun's face, encircled by a deep blue sky. It would be a hot day, as was yesterday, and as it had been this last few weeks. The prolonged warm months heralded an even greater stink than usual in this large city. Disease was rife in the streets, be it of the body or of the mind. Beggars haunted every corner. Cut-purses and thieves wandered around, taking advantage of any weakness seen in another. Harlots teased drunkards into parting with a few coins for a moment of pleasure. Orphans ran in gangs, avoiding the helping hands of the countless monks that strolled here and there.

Soldiers guarded all gates in and out of the city, but never was I stopped or searched as I struggled by them, laden with packages for our patients. I kept myself to my own thoughts for the most part, and although I was now familiar to many people in this midden, it was only Master Healan whom I would describe as a friend. I had not seen Owain since that night, almost ten years ago. But last winter, as every year since I had said goodbye to them, the Travelling Circus ended its season here. It had become an annual highlight for me and the only time when I felt truly surrounded by friends. Not that I am complaining. I have learned how to enjoy my own self.

The annual visit of Wasp, Crow, Strong-Man, Circus Master and all the others was an event that I always looked forward to, but it was quite possible that last winter may well have been our last joyous meeting here in England. Master Healan had decided that he would like to spend his remaining years, if indeed he felt he had that long left, at home in Wales with his lifelong friend, my old Master. Often he had told me how he longed just to sit around a fire, sharing their old tales, sipping ale together and relaxing in retirement. Sadly though, we could not make this journey through the portals of time, which would have made life a lot easier. We would need to travel by small wagon and horse, a journey which would take a few weeks, and he wanted to leave soon.

What could I be doing, you may ask yourself, stretching my short legs, striding towards the river at such an early hour? Well, we heard that a man called Cornpiece had a horse to sell. The old man asked me to seek him out as perhaps the horse would serve our purpose for the long journey back home to Wales.

Walking through the streets of Billingsgate leading down to the river, I saw folk starting to go about their day, flitting and rushing here and there. Smoke billowed from rooftops as last night's embers were rekindled. As I followed the pathway to St Peter's, the early morning sun rose higher, now lighting the river brightly, reflecting the buildings sited on the banks from its depths.

Cornpiece, the horse trader, was said to own a stable verging the Thames so he should be easy to find. It was a fair walk though, further than I had expected, but enjoyable on such a fine morning. I did not have a care in the world with my head full of my possible return to Wales. Perhaps Cornpiece may have a horse for us, but maybe he won't. It did not matter to me because I knew that we would find one. I had consulted my 'runes,' and all was well posted for my little wander into commerce, which was a valley apart from my usual tasks. Smiling at the thoughts dribbling through my daydreaming, I rounded a corner and there, next door to an inn, stood a large stable.

It was, in part, ramshackle but provided sufficient shelter for the horses. A small mud and daub dwelling, with a thatched roof well in need of repair, leaned precariously against the buildings. A very fat man with not one hair on his head, clad in a huge leather apron that stretched across bulging muscles, busied himself, scattering hay on the hard, dry earth of the corral. Several horses, with heads, bent eating breakfast, shuffled slowly behind him, taking their share with gentle mouths in silent contentment. I climbed up onto the fence and leaned over, the fat man being totally oblivious to my presence.

"A good morning Sir!" I shouted, "It will be hot later, I'll be bound!"

He stopped spreading hay and turned to see where my voice had come from.

"Hello!" He said, catching sight of me in front of him as I sat on the fence. "A dwarf!" He exclaimed as he threw the remaining hay to the floor. Dusting enormous big-boned hands across the leather apron which was strapped around his huge frame, he stepped towards me, smiling. "What can I do for you, little friend? I hope that you are not here to curse me!"

He laughed loudly at his own joke, slapping a mountainous belly. I returned a quiet, polite smile while slowly shaking my head from side to side to reassure him that this was not my purpose.

"Jolly good!" He said. "I would not like to upset one of you fellows.

I knew a man who did once, you know."

He scratched an unshaven chin while searching for the story.

"Stole from a dwarf, he did, and it was after he had been helped by magic too. Turned around on him though, I can tell you. Should not have done it, he really shouldn't have. You would have thought that he'd have known better than to try and get one over on one of your people. Bloody idiot, he was."

He spoke as quickly as one of his horses may gallop, except

he did not seem to need to take a breath.

"Came out in boils, he did half the size of a chicken's egg, all over his body. Great, oozing, smelly boils. Not a one would go near him for fear of the curse."

He did then pause momentarily for breath, so I took the opportunity to try and get him to end this tale. I was bored with it already.

"What happened to this unfortunate creature?" I said. "Disappeared, he did. One day he was here, and in the morning gone!" He scratched his bald head. "Whisked off by demons, no doubt!"

The quizzical look on his bulbous face changed to a smile, and his tale was over.

I did not comment, and he did not seem to wish to hear if I had.

Seemingly content with the earlier shaking of my head, he continued. "So what can I do for you?"

He seemed less excited now, having got the story off his chest and allayed any anxieties he may have had about the fact a dwarf stood in front of him, but fortunately, not a dwarf who had come to lay a curse! It did cross my mind that he would certainly not try to steal from me if he believed his own story. I laughed quietly to myself and took my eyes from him to scan the horses.

"A horse you want, is it? Well, you have come to the right place!" He rubbed his hands together, sensing a sale.

"It is indeed, Sir. Tell me, are you the man they call Cornpiece?" I asked.

"I am indeed, Dwarf. I am indeed. Samuel Cornpiece is my name, and I sell horses to them that wants them." He rubbed his hands again, before spreading them in the direction of the horses. "Take your pick, if you have a mind."

He pulled at the rope securing the gate, opening it just wide enough to let me in but not so much as to allow the horses out. I jumped down and walked in to examine his stock. With my feet on the ground, this man towered above me, hiding all daylight in his shadow. It was like I was in the midst of an eclipse. But then, most folks did!

All of the horses looked cared for, healthy, groomed and well fed. Not a rib to see, a most unusual sight. Considering he cared for his charges in this way, he must be a sound man. Although, and I know more than most, appearances can be deceptive!

One stood out from the rest. A small dappled-grey mare who was standing quietly, savouring final mouthfuls of hay, her chops grinding from side to side. Eyes, large and dark-brown, almost black, focused in my direction. I could have sworn I saw her wink at me, or perhaps it was an irritating fly. Hundreds of the winged pests flew in clouds around the horses' rears, whose swishing tails fiercely fought off the invaders, and the day had only just begun. By 'dragons breathe,' it must be intolerable when the sun is at its zenith. There were flies everywhere, but where there is horse dung, well I will leave the rest to your own imagination!

She looked a strong mare, even though small. No more than a pony but still she stood well above me! I slowly walked towards her, extending my arm with an empty hand, palm uppermost. Our eyes met in a mutual gaze, and as I neared, she slowly ambled towards me, snuffling a moist, whiskered, soft mouth across my palm. She tickled my fingers with her breath and then stood looking at me as if waiting for a tit bit. I patted her gently and whispered in my dwarfish tongue, unheard by Cornpiece. Her ears pricked up and she snorted excitedly upon hearing my ancient language. She understood. I needed not to ask more of Cornpiece, only a price for this fine animal. I patted her again, and I think I saw a smile on her face. She and I had decided. Cornpiece coughed and said.

"She is not for sale, why don't you look at these others? Be it for the riding or the pulling?"

The mare stamped a hoof, scattering clouds of dust, choking and blinding the ever-swarming flies. She stamped again as if affronted by Cornpiece's words. I am a creature of nature, and when 'She' speaks to me in whatever language chosen by 'Her,' I hear and understand. We had chosen each other. All was unspoken, yet alive and understood between us. Our bargain was struck, but I had yet to persuade Cornpiece the choice was made.

"I want to buy this mare. Even though you say she is not for sale, you have a price for everything, you are a trader. I ask you your price, Sir?" My fingers caressed the mare's shoulder as I awaited his response. "I don't know, she is my best beast and a valuable piece of merchandise!" He parted his legs, huge hands and fingers eagerly seeking a place on his body where his hips should have been. "I don't know," he repeated.

Again, the mare stamped as soon as he finished speaking. Three times she pounded, making the ground shake. In my opinion, she was stating her answer clearly, leaving no doubt in my mind we would leave here together. I decided it was time for me to take the reins! I remembered his earlier words, not to mention his story. He had a fear of dwarf magic and perhaps I could make this work for me.

"Is there anything you need from me, Master Cornpiece? Perhaps you need to know the future."

As I awaited his response, the mare snuggled her nose into the space between my neck and shoulder and snuffled. It did tickle! Cornpiece's belly rumbled loudly, and then he responded.

"I might not like what you say, so I would rather not know. No, my future does not interest me. I am far too busy scratching a crust, and this heat does not help." He wiped a sweaty forehead with the back of a chubby hand, painting it with beads of sweat, mingled with dust. "But I do have a problem with my leg. Can your dwarf magic help with that?"

Moving the leather apron over his fat belly to reveal a fat thigh, he pointed to a large purple swelling. It was very raw and the size of a goose egg. I had seen bigger and more ferocious swellings but usually, and somewhat surprisingly, upon horses.

"I have tried all sorts of potions but the surgeon barber says it must be cut out but I cannot stand the pain, nor can I afford their extortion. Take advantage of us poor, they do!" He rubbed at the swelling.

"Come the time when the sun is at its highest every day, I can hardly walk, and that means I cannot do my job properly. If I don't do something soon, they might chop off my leg, then I will starve and become a beggar. So if you can cure my leg, dwarf, you can have the pony. I need my leg more than money. Well?"

He dropped the apron and straddled his stance again. Now that I had seen the swelling on his thigh, I understood. By spreading his legs, he was distributing enormous weight, thus easing discomfort and pain. I could treat this swelling by poultice rather than a knife. A knife, if used in this case, would probably lead to infection and this was definitely a strong possibility with all the flies around.

"I can cure your leg, my friend. No blade will be needed!" I assured him.

"You can?" His big face lit up like a brazier in the snow, a grin spreading from ear to ear. "My word is my bond, Dwarf. Cure this abomination and the pony is yours."

"Then I will return tomorrow with some herb poultice," I said. "I will do the same for the following six days. I tell you, my friend, by the end of the treatment, all will be done, and I will not take the pony until it is. But when it is, your word will be honoured!"

"It will be Dwarf, it will be. I will see you in the morning." He smiled as he spoke.

I waved as I turned to leave and left him with a few words. "I will be here and mind you take good care of that mare!"

Each day I rose early to visit Cornpiece and change the poultice I had prepared from my own special concoction to draw out the poison. I also gave him a small dose of poppy juice to take every day for the pain, but he seemed to drink more than I suggested as some mornings he was quite silly, talking in riddles. Nevertheless, here we were on the seventh morning and the swelling had gone, taking with it all the ill humour that had poisoned him, just as I told him would be so.

"Dwarf, you are truly magical! My leg is now well, if not better than before!" He laughed loudly and slapped his huge paunch underneath the leather apron.

"I am pleased to have been of service to you, Master Cornpiece." I paused and smiled knowingly, waiting for him to honour his word. "Your pony, my friend!"

Cornpiece strode purposefully towards the fence where

the mare stood quietly tethered. He was whistling a jolly ditty as he returned towards me, holding the bridle and presenting his part of our bargain.

"She has had a good wash down and has been groomed, as you can see." He told me while scratching his chin furiously.

The mare certainly looked healthy and well.

"She has a good appetite and is as good with a saddle as between the staves of a wagon. You will not be disappointed. And remember I told you when we first met that I believe in the magic of your people so I would not be stupid enough to lie to you now, would I?"

His colour changed and he went quite ashen, as would a morning grate cooled after a night of blazing.

"Worry not my friend, calm yourself. You must have no fear. I can see that all is as you say. You will have no further problems with that leg."

He passed me the reins before helping me to mount. Her back was soft and comfortable for a small fellow such as myself. Cornpiece opened the gate to the corral and I rode out with my new pony beneath me. I bade him good fortune as I left him standing easily, staring at me.

I would call her Merlina, after Merlin, a most befitting name for such a wonderful creature.

CHAPTER TWENTY-FOUR

It has been almost ten years since I last saw my homeland, other than in dream-scape when I would usually be joined by my old Master, Llwyd ap Crachan Llwyd. Now here I was, sat on a wagon with Master Healan by my side and Merlina between the staves. London was two weeks behind us and Shrewsbury but a few days away. From Shrewsbury, we would journey through the Welsh Marches and on into Powys. The stench of London was now merely a memory, but not one that I would forget easily. How could I, it was ingrained in my every pore but fortunately, as I said, only as a memory. The old man had travelled quite well, although he did spend a great deal of time fast asleep in the back of the wagon. Despite the decrepitude racking his aged body, he was in fair health and spirit. The wagon provided good shelter when we could find no inn. However, it was the height of summer with warm nights, and we were fortunate in that it had not rained for weeks. Day after day, there was nothing but blue skies above our heads. A hot blazing sun warmed us and kept the deep ruts which raked across the tracks below us dry, jarring the wagon often and in turn, rattling our bones.

I still remember well my journey to London, wandering aside Fwynedd the Shepherd through rain and storm from my mountains to the Welsh Marches, before becoming a performing dwarf in a travelling circus. Yes, I had many fond memories of that journey, also of my time with the circus and of my years of learning and work with the old man who now sat next to me, lost in his thoughts, staring at the passing scenery. Twenty years ago, I was a young dwarf. Now I am a magician, seer, and healer. I have become well versed in the ancient arts taught to me by my masters. I had come a long way and gained much knowledge and skill to aid me through my journey in this life, which is far from over. These thoughts took me to the moment that I would meet Owain Glyndwr again, a moment that was drawing near.

Merlina had served us well. Our long journey was complete, and we had, at last, safely reached our homeland. Master Healan and my old Master, Llwyd ap Crachan Llwyd, were now reunited. As he was now home, Master Healan had returned to using his Welsh name, he was again Myrddin Goch ap Cwnwrig. He sat comfortably with his old friend, relaxing on sheepskins draped across large chairs, warming their ancient toes together in front of the burning grate. Autumn now heralded colder nights, warranting a fire not just for cooking but to heat the cottage too. No longer did I need to cook and serve for either of the old men as my old Master now employed a widow from a hamlet in the next valley. She had been with him for several years and had seemingly settled into a good routine that suited them both. Our arrival, a few weeks earlier, had not rustled her feathers at all, in fact just the opposite.

Llinnar appeared to be around fifty years of age. A slight woman with a very strong back, as the huge heaps of firewood stacked and ready for burning under the lean-to testified. Although slender with features of a younger woman, tell-tale crow's feet lurked in the corners of her deep-brown eyes, giving evidence that more years had been lived than at first appeared. Her hair was in the midst of turning from black to grey, with silver streaks from crown to tip. She wore it braided tightly into a long pigtail which hung down to well below her thin waist. She spoke little but smiled a lot, two qualities my old Master embraced in others. He was very frail now, more so than his old friend and often required a little more help than his dignity was comfortable with but irrespective of this, Llinnar attended to his needs well and now she had two of them to cope with! They appreciated her kind spirit and were always good natured to her which, in turn, invited her to be likewise.

It pleased me that they would be well cared for as my travels loomed nearer. At least I knew they had all they needed, apart from youth, of course. They had both lived for a lot longer than they had led me to believe they would. And they were not ready for the 'other world' just yet.

Sitting by the fire blazing in the grate, I listened to the old men nattering. Another tale of magic would soon spring from one of their mouths. I did not have long to wait.

Llinnar served mulled wine by heating the poker until white hot in the fire in the grate, then immersing it into each goblet. It tasted good, and I drank deeply, feeling a tangy fruity warmth seeping down my throat after each swallow.

Llwyd ap Crachan Llwyd sipped his slowly before lowering the goblet to rest on his lap. His thin cracked lips quivered slightly as he began to speak.

"I was just thinking about my last encounter with dragons." He said, turning his head to look at me before staring back into the flames.

"Yes, and I also remember the last time that I was among them, old friend!" Chirped up Myrddin Goch ap Cwnwrig, who was known as Master Healan no more. There was no longer any need for disguise amongst the English, he was now home after many years in servitude to the Prophecy.

"You see, Crach!" Both old men exclaimed in unity of voice, followed by laughter at their own joke.

"Dragons are fiery friends to magicians, providing, of course, you happen to know one." Continued Llwyd ap Crachan Llwyd. "And you do, don't you Crach?"

They both laughed again.

"And a particularly bad tempered dragon he is too!" Interjected Myrddin Goch ap Cwnwrig, to which they both belly laughed.

"Tan-y-Mynedd is not bad tempered!" I protested. "Merely a sensitive soul who has lived for hundreds of years, many of them alone, deep underground."

"It is true that he does not suffer fools, ignorance, and cowardice but then what dragon does?" Said, my old Master. "But he is still bad tempered."

They both chuckled again.

"Perhaps Crach should relate a tale for us this night, old friend?"

Myrddin Goch ap Cwnwrig leaned across the space between their chairs and poked his old friend's arm playfully with a pointed finger.

"A grand design for this night."

"Agreed!" Llwyd ap Crachan Llwyd said smiling. "Will you tell us a tale of Tan-y-Mynedd, Crach?"

The two old men sat back in silence, expectancy etched across their faces in the waiting of my tale. Llinnar sat cross-legged on a thick sheepskin, her back straight against the wall, head bent in concentration with her vision focussed intently on stitching and repairing holes in an old cloak. Deft slim fingers pushed a needle through the thick cloth, drawing thread in and out across threadbare patches. Llinnar smiled to herself, hearing all and saying nothing as the needle pierced the cloth once more.

"Very well!" I said. "I will tell you a tale of Tan-y-Mynedd the Fire- Dragon. Perhaps the one about the greatest lesson he taught me if that would please you?"

The old men nodded in silent recognition, sipped more wine and adjusted their posture, seeking comfort for their aged bones in readiness for my story. I sat nearer the grate for warmth and peered deep into the flames as I recalled the tale.

"Tan-y-Mynedd the Fire-Dragon is a teacher and is of a great age unknown, whereas his reputation for wisdom precedes all."

"As does that bad temper of his!" Myrddin Goch ap Cwnwrig muttered under his breath, smirking.

Llwyd ap Crachan Llwyd sniggered in agreement. I continued, regardless of their sarcasm, be it in good humour or not.

"It was springtime, with new buds and new life wherever and upon whatever one's eyes fell. Trees and saplings sprouted new growth, rivers and streams flowed furiously bringing the melted snows from mountaintops to valleys below. The days were growing longer, and I had been dispatched by order of my Master to seek out Tan-y-Mynedd the Fire-Dragon. I was to go alone for the first time, without any supervision or company. During such a lengthy hike up mountains, across their tops and then down through luscious green valleys, dotted by thick forest, in solitude, I lost myself to fleeting thoughts and daydreams, as is often my way."

The old men laughed again, but I continued regardless.

"I slid down endless mountainsides, teeming in scree, small stones splintering in all directions. Pointed shards pierced through the soles of my boots each time my feet struck the ground. But Merioneth in springtime is most beautiful. Despite the cold nights and often wet days, I trudged purposefully through the valleys under the shadows of Mount Snowdon, the grandest of all mountains. Ffestiniog lay in front of me. The deep caves found in this place are hidden far below ground, spreading endlessly. Tunnels linking deep chambers, leading to more endless tunnels, seemingly always going deeper and steeper. Underground rivers flowed, disappearing into rock walls as tall as the mountains above. Here lay the home of dragons and other strange and wonderful creatures who are rarely seen above ground. Down there, the magic of the underworld hung in the air. A special place, hidden from the sun. A place where darkness provided light of its own.

Leaving the noon day sun far behind above the ground, my eyes became slowly accustomed to the darkness. I clambered over rocks, crawled on my belly through spaces that were tight, even for a dwarf! After several hours below ground, I quickly forgot about the earth above me, concentrating solely on where my feet fell in order to avoid my body doing similar! The tunnel I walked along grew larger on all sides. Dripping water formed solid spectres, frozen in time, yet always growing, sprouting from the tunnel floor and suspending above, hanging from the roof. In some places they formed a maze, interlocking their upward and downward spirals thus blocking my path. But there was always a way through, even though some of my movements could be described as acrobatic! As I made my way through this underground world, a strange yet familiar aroma drifted under my nostrils, making me falter in my steps. Such a pungent stink, so strong it stung the inside of my nose as would a wasp. I knew this smell—dragon's pee!

This was the home of my friend, Tan-y-Mynedd the Fire-Dragon. That foul smell definitely came from him! They do say dragon's pee contains magical properties, but I have to admit, I cannot get my thoughts past its foul aroma. But, on balance, it had a perfume that resembled a carpet of bluebells when I compare it to the stench of London. The tunnel opened into a gigantic cavern, glistening with speckles of light shining from the rock. Enormous crystals protruded here and there, giving some natural light.

Suddenly, I stood on the edge of a wide ravine, seemingly bottomless. How would I get around such an abyss? I knew that climbing down would be impossible and even if it was possible, how would I get back up?"

"Just an illusion, dwarf!"

A bellowing deep voice rang throughout the chamber. It was Tan-y-Mynedd, my dragon friend.

"Hello, Crach! I have been expecting you!" The voice resounded again and again. "Dip the tip of your boot over the edge of the ravine. Have no fear, Crach, as none is necessary.

As I just told you, this is an illusion."

I did as Tan-y-Mynedd asked and to my utmost surprise, my boot did not dangle over the edge, which at first appeared to lead to a bottomless void, but splashed into the shallow water, creating ripples which destroyed the image of the deep ravine.

"Now pull your boot out!" Tan-y-Mynedd's voice boomed.

I did as instructed. The ripples the toe of my boot had created, settled and the ravine returned to my vision in all of its former frightening glory. I knew now this was nothing but a huge puddle spreading across the cave floor. The ravine was, in fact, a mirage created by the reflections from the cave roof above. When the water lay undisturbed, the magical ravine reappeared thus protecting those living beyond its reaches.

"Come forth, Crach. Step with diligence my small friend. You will not plummet down to the depths of a bottomless gorge!" A dragon's mountainous voice, followed by uncontrollable laughter, is something to behold when it is resounding endlessly in one's ears, long after the real echo is gone.

Splashing my way through this huge puddle which, incidentally, my friends, was no more than a fingernail's depth in any place, I finally stood in front of Tan-y-Mynedd the Fire-Dragon.

In magnificent splendour, this great ancient dragon reclined on a deep ledge lodged between two huge boulders of granite. As I stepped closer, Tan-y-Mynedd began to stir from rest, and his huge scaled tail suddenly materialised from behind the boulders, swishing three times from left to right which resulted in such an underground funnel of wind that nearly blew me over, while creating massive ripples across the enormous puddle behind me. The ravine's existence was momentarily obliterated until calmness across the waters hailed its presence once more. A hind leg appeared from under his tail and stretched as far as its muscles would allow, knocking rocks and boulders from their resting place in its wake. Then, without any warning at all, Tan-y-Mynedd the Fire-Dragon sneezed, blowing me right off my feet and into the air, where I travelled quite some distance before landing in a rather ungainly heap. He sneezed again, and this time I landed bottom-first in the puddle I had earlier walked through. By 'dragons breathe,' there is goodness in small mercies. If this had really been a ravine and not a mirage, I would now be laying in several pieces at the bottom of who knows where!

"Are you hurt or broken, Crach?" The 'sneeze of sneezes' enquired. "Only my pride and bruised back end are damaged!" I replied, picking myself up slowly and wiping my now very wet breeches with equally damp hands.

Tan-y-Mynedd now stood fully erect in striking splendour, with wings outstretched. He held the colour of fading embers, smouldering in a grate. Three sharp talons upon huge webbed huge feet supported great muscular legs which were firmly set on the rocks beneath him. A row of bony spikes ran along his spine, from the top of a regal head to the tip of his long swishing tail. It was tipped by three bony protuberances, giving it the appearance of a trident. This would be a weapon to contend with if his temper frayed! His very large head was crowned by two great horns. At the end of his long snout lay flared nostrils, both secreting glands able to create enough fire to destroy an entire village with just one gruff snort. The gills in front of his ears flashed forward to reveal four bony sharp nodules. His huge wings now folded loosely against a large scaled body, sat upon chunky haunches. He snorted, coughed and shook his huge head from side to side while staring directly at me. I could see my reflection in his large, fiery, golden eyes, together with the mystical ravine surrounding me.

"So here you are again, Crach Ffinnant. I have been expecting you." Tan-y-Mynedd the Fire-Dragon snorted, with steam appearing from his snout. "Hang on to that rock, Crach! Now!!"

He sneezed forcibly and were it not for the urgent call to secure my grip on the suggested rock, I would have been flung into the air again. As it was my legs and body took off, but my grip on the rock stayed strong, avoiding any possibility of further flight.

"Thank you for the warning!" I said, smoothing down my clothes, for which I was grateful to still be in possession of after them nearly departing my body from the full force of a dragon's sneeze! "I am pleased that you were expecting me and if that is the case, perhaps you already know why I am here?" I questioned.

If dragons could smile, I am sure I witnessed it in those huge golden eyes when he replied.

"Of course I know why you are here, little man. I am Tan-y-Mynedd who knows everything there is to know, and that includes why you are here and why you have been here before, and why you will come again. Magicians need dragons!" He grunted, turning his head to one side as if listening to something I had failed to notice. "But I do often wonder if we dragons need magicians!" Another grunt followed. "And I know that Llwyd ap Crachan Llwyd does not come on this visit as he feels it is time you made the journey alone. Am I correct, per chance?" I nodded my head in agreement.

I told my small audience that I did not wish to interrupt a dragon in full flow, especially not this one! The old men laughed, and Llinnar giggled under her breath, but she did not look up from her sewing as I continued with my tale.

Tan-y-Mynedd playfully asked. "Was he not afraid that you would be eaten by wolves or, worse still, provide a tasty little snack for a dragon?" His throat erupted and the sound that ushered forth, I took to be a dragon's laugh.

"I jest with you dwarf, worry not a hair on your head!" That laugh again. "I see few folk from your world these days and speak little, excepting the thoughts in my own head. I do leave here, of course, but only at night and only when the moon in our heavens is at its fullest. Few speak our ancient language but for a young fellow, Crach, you do well with our words, your Master is a good tutor."

I nodded my thanks but bit my tongue to avoid speech. I was in awe of this magnificent ancient creature. The greatest lesson one can learn is that there is beauty in all things. This is especially true of dragons, even though they may be fearsome to look at and quite deadly if upset. Once upon a time, there were many dragons but man hunted them through fear, and now those that were left chose to hide deep down in the caves where only a fool such as myself may venture.

"Jump upon my back, Crach, the moon is full tonight. I will save you from the long walk home and pay my respects to your Master at the same time. We have prophecies and dwarves to discuss. Come along, be not afraid. Climb up."

Tan-y-Mynedd lowered his gigantic head, bending one of his front legs, then flushed out a gill. I scrambled up his leg and used the bony nodules on the gill as a ladder, enabling me to climb with ease up onto his back, where I sat 'betwixt huge scaled shoulders.

"Are you as comfortable as you can be upon a dragon?" His voice boomed.

"I am ready, I think!" I replied with some trepidation, my feet never having been so high in the air before, let alone on top of a dragon!

As an honest dwarf, I must tell you that I was petrified. I shook from my toes to the tips of my fingers, but he knew that!

"Hold on tight, Crach!"

Suddenly, great wings stretched slowly outwards before his whole body tensed as muscles prepared to spring into action, then with one great flap, his enormous body swept upwards, swirling and turning as we flew higher and higher up through the tunnel above his lair. Hanging on to his gills, a hand on each, my knuckles white with fear, gripping on for my very life. I looked up and could see the full moon in a clear night sky looming in front of us and within the wink of an eye, the entrance to the cave tunnel was far below. We flew higher and higher across the face of the moon. With my fear now gone, I felt the wind blowing through my hair and clothes as if I hung upon a line to dry. I now dared to look down and could see so much. Looking at the beauty of our mountains from such a height was magical.

In no time at all, Tan-y-Mynedd began to swerve and dive, then stilled his wings and stretched them out to their limits while keeping quite rigid. Then, with a twist of his great body and a flick of a flap, we began our descent. His strong wings slowed our drop to almost a standstill, as huge powerful feet felt the solid ground beneath them once more. I was home."

"My tale is now at an end, my friends," I said and bent

my head in recognition. Llinnar dropped the cloak, together with the needle and thread into to her lap, and giggled a little under her breath while giving quiet applause.

"A wonderful story, Crach. Thank you so much. What a grand tale!" She clapped again, enthusiastically this time.

Llwyd ap Crachan Llwyd slapped his knees and laughed.

"It is a grand tale, Crach. I remember that night well. Tan-y-Mynedd and I talked for many hours about what was to come. You, Crach— well you fell asleep and did not wake for three days!" He laughed again, slapping his lap once more.

"Yes, Crach, I also agree it is a grand tale and the lesson you learned, though not sought, was...?" Myrddin Goch ap Cwnwrig leaned forward, smiling quizzically in my direction, his unfinished question hanging in the air.

"It was to know the reality of 'illusion,' was it not Crach? If he had not dipped that small toe of his into the puddle, he would never have ridden on the back of a dragon!" Llwyd ap Crachan Llwyd burst into the loudest of belly laughs his ancient being could muster.

Myrddin Goch ap Cwnwrig, though a little more restrained, giggled, whilst Llinnar clapped her applause again.

"Time for some more mulled wine and then it will be the time for two old men to dream!" Llinnar stated softly with quiet authority.

They both smiled, grunted and nodded in expectation. She gathered up her mending, placed it gently on the sheepskin and taking the poker from the grate, thrust it deep into the flames.

CHAPTER TWENTY-FIVE

Merlina stumbled. I was daydreaming while sitting astride her comfortable wide back and her stumble would have sent me flying into the mud had she not lifted her head just at the moment I was about to plummet over. Instead, my head crashed into the back of hers, waking me very quickly indeed. Merlina, who was none the worse for wear, trotted on whilst I rubbed my sore head with one hand and held the reins tightly with the other. A strong wind blustered from the north, bending the trees far above my head as we rode on through the forest. It was late October, and only evergreen trees and shrubs were holding on to their leaves, staying always green, irrespective of the season. The ground beneath Merlina's hooves scrunched upon discarded foliage as the season demanded and so ordained by the Gods.

A sheepskin jacket tied around my waist, with the collar pulled tight to my ears, prevented the biting wind from gnawing at my flesh. In just a few weeks, this bite would become icy, and even such a coat as this would give little protection. A mid-morning sun offered little warmth on the forest floor, but the occasional breaks in the treeline allowed her great rays to strike my face, cheering my forehead and cheeks. I kept my thick beard tucked inside the sheepskin jacket to afford a further layer of warmth.

My old masters, no doubt, sat beside their grate with their every need catered for by Llinnar. This pleased me, as they could not be in better hands. I had left them a few weeks ago to set out once again to meet my old friend, Tan-y-Mynedd, at his home in the deep caverns of Ffestiniog.

We arrived at the caverns quite early in the afternoon. My journey had not been unpleasant or too harsh, eased greatly by my faithful mare, Merlina. The next challenge was to negotiate the underground chambers in search of Tan-y-Mynedd. I left Merlina, content with a nosebag and a well-earned rest, in the shelter of an outer cave whilst I trudged down and down, around and around, through the tunnels and caverns, until finally reaching his lair.

For the following two days, we discussed endlessly the time that was to come as defined by the ancient prophecy. Tan-y-Mynedd reminded me of the greatest fears of which I had not forgotten—'*our rivers will run red from battle in victory and defeat.*' Not a very comforting thought, I think you may agree!

He gave me a horn carved from bone. Magical ancient inscriptions etched in geometric patterns, adorned its curved shape. It had a small gold ring hooked at the hilt with a loop of knotted leather so that it could be slung over the shoulder. He instructed me to blow it three times if I was in need of him and reminded me that no other would hear the call except him. *'The call is silent to the ears of man, only can it be heard by me and thus I will answer to be at your side.'*

After a suitable and appropriate farewell, I left him reclining across the boulders of rock that formed his bed. Dragon snores resounding from the lair followed me back up through the tunnels, creating haunting echoes from chamber to cavern, becoming fainter and fainter with my every step towards the earth above, and then silence.

The night after our meeting, the strangest of dreams began to unfurl as I slumbered beneath sheepskins under an old oak tree, deep in the forest: *Flying landscapes and shapes flashed through my mind as images of the last twenty years - my apprenticeship with Llwyd ap Crachan Llwyd, my journey to London, Wasp, Pale-Man and Circus Master were all there in full glory. Edmund appeared, his blue plume fluttering in the wind. His helmet cast reflections from an unseen sun, creating a face that was black down one side and white down the other. He tightly held the reins of a black charger who suddenly reared and the vision was gone. The evil darkness of Edmund's presence stained my memory as blood seeping through a bandage. I could not shake the image of a coin spinning slowly in mid-air which was tarnished and stained, and although each side could be seen clearly as it spun, both faces were the same but every few spins the face would change. Edmund's face I instantly recognised but the others I did not. On one side a crown was worn, but there was no crown on the other.*

I awoke with a start, feeling shocked but instantly fully conscious. My eyes were bulging, beads of sweat seeping from every pore, dripping from my forehead. But I knew I had been given a lesson that would serve me well in the future. Even in my dream, I knew this vision was a prediction of betrayal. It could be nothing else.

Later in the day as I rode through the forest with dimness yielding as trees thinned, enabling sunlight to leak through, a glade opened in front of us. Thick moss adorned the ground and was sprinkled with crispy foliage, golden and bronzed, having been discarded by branches and blown into piles by the wind. The glade appeared circular. Tall, aged oaks protected its boundaries with their twisted branches, like the arms of gnarled warriors, challenging access to all who may enter. In the centre of the glade stood a stone pillar and even from where I stood, I could see rune symbols carved around the middle. Sitting silently on top of the stone, as if a carving itself with no discernible movement, not even the flicker of a feather, black as the night and bright as the moon, perched a raven. I pulled gently on the reins, and the bit in Merlina's mouth reminded her of my need to stop. As always, she complied immediately, shaking her beautiful head, long shaggy mane swishing in time with her bushy tail. She bent her head, searching for a juicy blade of grass to munch, nose snuffling through the fallen leaves. I climbed down from her back and jumped to the ground, patting her shoulder affectionately, leaving her to graze as I walked slowly towards the raven.

There was no doubt in my mind. Here was the raven predicted by Llwyd ap Crachan Llwyd all those years ago when he visited us at the apothecary in London, the night Glyndwr had been given the 'blade of justice' and I, the runes. It was also the last time I had seen Owain Glyndwr but I knew all too well, in the depths of my soul, it would not be long until we met again. The raven stirred, coal-black feathers fluttered, and large, brown, all-seeing eyes twitched back and forth. Extending a thick neck with its great black wings outstretched, the raven leaned forward and screeched, its huge sharp beak warning me to stop in my tracks and stand still. I did! Waiting several paces in front of the raven, I saw my image reflected in its dark eyes and felt its gaze penetrate into every pore of my being. Flapping wings and moving from foot to foot, its long claws scratching the stone below, the raven spoke its ancient language in a gruff voice which rasped from its huge beak.

"A dwarf comes riding on a pony into my forest glade! What nerve is this?" Feathers fluttered, with those forming a collar around its thick neck extending in protest as he cackled loudly.

"I am Crach Ffinnant, a dwarf!" I announced, taking a step forward. "I can see you are a dwarf! Do you think my eyes, though old, do not see such an obvious thing?" Wings flapped. "But wait!" The wings settled and folded. "This name is familiar to me." The raven bent its head, scraping its beak along the stone, first right and then left, before looking straight into my eyes. "Your coming has been long awaited and yet it has been no time at all since the call came. I think you are the dwarf who I will serve. Is this not true?" Its tone less harsh and brittle now, in fact almost friendly. The raven turned its head to one side, listening in wait for my answer.

"I am he!" I said firmly but kindly, bowing my head in respect.

Suddenly the raven took off in flight from the ancient stone and circled three times above my head before landing gently on my shoulder, balancing its huge feet as its wings folded tightly. He placed his beak close to my ear and quietly said.

"My name is Carron, son of Ether. I am to be your

companion, Crach Ffinnant. I think you knew you would come across me one day. Raven magic is your key through the doors of all worlds, Crach. From now on, no door will ever be closed to you."

Carron, son of Ether, spread his wings and gently tugged at my beard, as if in jest. A thought then crossed my mind - *'what a lucky dwarf was I to have befriended such creatures! A bad tempered dragon and a raven with a wicked sense of humour. At least I knew where I was with Merlina, her loyalty, strength and quiet fortitude being her grandest qualities'.*

Carron flew from my shoulder, somersaulted in the air, gathering himself again before landing on top of my saddle, much to the annoyance of Merlina. She turned her head quizzically at the precise moment Carron stuck his beak into her ear. I have no idea what the raven said to my pony on this day but from that moment on a friendship was born that lasted for many years between them.

Merlina strolled out of the forest glade, leaving the ancient stone that was carved with runes behind us. I sat astride her in my saddle with Carron perched upon my shoulder. Taking the reins firmly between my fingers, I pressed my heels gently into Merlina's belly, and she trotted willingly onwards. Carron took off from my shoulder, choosing to fly at our side.

How long it would be before we would reach the edge of the forest, I had no idea, but it was dusk and travel would prove difficult as the darkness of night fast approached. It was time I looked for shelter to rest until the dawn.

CHAPTER TWENTY-SIX

The following morning, after a good night's rest, I took the time to stand on the top ridge of a grand mountain, losing myself in the beauty that lay before me. With Merioneth Forest behind me, I could see for miles down into the valley below. A river wound its way around the contours of the valley, with streams trickling down mountainsides to meet it. Even at this time of year, with winter just around the corner, the valley was lush and green. I could see a field way in the distance, looking like plaited hair, deep brown earth, ploughed over from the last harvest in preparation for the next. A light drizzle filled the air, clouds swept high above, and the sky darkened. We were in for a storm, and if those clouds were anything to go by, it was going to be a big one. Merlina quietly grazed on short stubbles of grass, sprouting here and there amongst the rocks. Carron was nowhere to be seen. The raven often disappeared, sometimes for hours, but he always came back. It is probably a stroke of good fortune that while on the return journey from my visit to Tan-y-Mynedd, I had not encountered one person. Anyone, other than a magician of course, who might see me deep in conversation with a raven sat on my shoulder, would be forgiven for thinking that I had taken leave of my senses. Carron, son of Ether, chatted and chirped all the time he was near, sometimes putting his sharp beak so close to my ear, I feared he may nip it off from the side of my head. He was teaching me so much about how to use the ancient incantations that were the keys to dimensional portals. I am able to access such great magic, both with my eyes open and conscious to the world and also when deep in my dreams, but Carron could fly, whereas I could not, he was able to see that which I was not able to see and his ancient wisdom seeped from his every small breath. Carron was also a joker, often plucking at my sleeves and beard and there is nothing that creates greater glee for him than hiding my spoon at mealtimes!

The clouds grew darker. Still, drizzle turning into a fine rain, and it was becoming colder as the wind picked up, spinning, twisting leaves and twigs, scattering them here and there. Merlina, now bored of searching for tasty shoots that did not exist at this time of year, lifted her head and ambled over towards me. Unfurling the little rope ladder from the saddle, I climbed onto her back then gathered it up behind me and secured it with a thong, finished in a bow for ease of release when next needed. I could jump off Merlina without difficulty. However, mounting did present issues for one so short as me. Pulling my collar tight and hiding my head under the hood from the increasing inclemency, I was just about to encourage Merlina to trot on when out of the sky, apparently from nowhere, Carron son of Ether swooped down onto my shoulder. With our happy trio united once more, we set off down the mountainside.

We were almost at the bottom and onto the track leading through the valley when the sky cleared of grey, the sun burst through the clouds, and the rain ceased. Pushing my hood back, I shook my head and looked up, enjoying the temporary warmth, which cooled almost instantly as the keen wind reminded me of the season.

Carron twitched his tail, and within a blink of an eye, he was gone again, soaring in ever-increasing circles, up and up, climbing higher and higher towards the heavens.

Merlina trotted along with purpose, holding her head high, her long mane flowing in the wind. It was turning into a very pleasant day. Although the track beneath Merlina's hooves was muddy, it did not slow her. Each time a hoof hit the ground, splashes and clouds of watery mud splattered in our wake.

Suddenly and without warning, Merlina reared, screaming, as an enormous boar crashed through the undergrowth in front of us, savagely roaring. Its eyes were red with fear and anger, tusks flashing white. Seeing Merlina blocking its path, the boar side-stepped its huge bulk, narrowly missing an imminent collision and disappeared, bursting its way through bushes and gorse. Gathering the reins, I tugged the bit tight in Merlina's mouth, she steadied a little but before she or I could catch a breath, several salivating hounds, baying and snarling, passed us like the wind without so much as a backward glance. Merlina, already startled by the boar and now spooked from flying hounds, trotted uneasily on the spot, twisting and turning her body in fear and trepidation of what may, or may not, come at her next. Her well-honed senses were suggesting that something was! She was not wrong. Moments later, crashing like thunder, came four horsemen following the hounds in pursuit of the boar. They skidded to a halt in front of us. Merlina reared again, and it was all I could do to hang on. Her hooves crashed down into the mud, and she twisted before rearing again. This time I lost my grip and fell unceremoniously to the ground, landing with a grand splash on the muddy track. The four riders steadied their mounts, and an elderly man stepped out of his stirrups, passing his reins to one of the others.

I sat in the mud, feeling rather foolish, as the elderly man walked towards me. Bending down, he took me firmly in strong hands and hauled my momentarily crumpled frame to its feet. Merlina now calmed, knowing all immediate danger had passed and nosed the ground for anything she might find to eat, with the reins hanging loosely over her neck. Carron perched on the saddle and pecked at something held between his claws.

I heard one of the riders say something but the mud lodged in my ears prevented me from understanding a word. Two of the party, on hearing the words that I did not, dug their spurs and galloped off after the hounds who, no doubt, still tracked the boar. Hounds were merciless in their pursuit of such large prey, the boar would slow, collapse even, from lack of breath and exhaustion long before they did.

The elderly man brushed me down and as a poacher may manifest a pheasant, produced a large rag for me from the huge pocket in his coat. He wore breeches and boots and a thick leather jerkin over a hessian smock. Although his middle years were clearly far behind him, he looked well-fed and healthy. Shoulder-length grey hair hung down a broad, once muscular, back. His face was kind. Large green eyes stared out from under bushy eyebrows, a forehead creased in deep lines, cheekbones slender and prominent. A well-trimmed moustache sat under a sharp nose, the colour of beetroot, and a short beard disguised an even sharper chin. I took the rag from him and vigorously wiped my face clean of mud, before clearing my ears, enabling my hearing to return.

"We are sorry for this mishap and hope there is no injury to your person." The elderly man said.

He turned and bent down, picking up Merlina's reins from the mud, handing them to me. I nodded my appreciation while taking them in my hand. We exchanged a smile. The remaining rider sat a short distance away, quietly watching events. His mount, a great black stallion, pawed at the earth, snorting its impatience to continue with the chase. The man spoke loudly in a firm but calm voice, enquiring after my health following such a shock as this must have been to my person. The elderly man turned to address the other and said.

"It is a dwarf, My Lord, and other than the shock of it all, he seems well in body." He turned back, slapping me heartily on my shoulder. "Am I right, Master Dwarf?"

"I am in good health, Sir, and only a little shaken from the fall. I will be fine, and no harm is done. I thank you for your kindness."

I bowed to him and as I raised my head, the other rider who had been addressed as 'My Lord,' trotted over to where we stood. I thought that his voice was familiar to me but when I looked up at him clad in hunting leathers, sat on such a majestic beast, I knew instantly who he was. It was Owain Glyndwr who stared down at me, grinning from ear to ear!

"Crach! My dear friend. Oh, Crach!" He said as the biggest

of smiles engulfed his handsome features.

Jumping down from the stallion, passing the reins to his aide, Owain Glyndwr stepped over a great puddle, bent down, picked me up in a squeeze so tight that it halted my breath, and said.

"It is so good to see you, my friend! How did you know that this was the crossroads we would meet? My home in Syncharth is half a day's ride from where we stand."

Releasing the squeeze, he put me down, and as my feet touched the ground beneath, my breath returned with a gasp. The elderly man looked on bemused.

"My Lord!" I said and bowed in respect.

Then, looking up at him, I burst into uncontrollable laughter. He did the same, slapping his thighs, laughing loudly. Suddenly I stopped and asked him.

"What crossroads do we meet at? I see nothing but a track!"

"If the boar had not surprised you, Crach, you would see it. There!"

Turning around, he pointed in front of where we stood and at not twenty paces distant, four tracks met and criss-crossed.

Carron, son of Ether, spread his wings, fluttered his tail, leapt into the air from the saddle across Merlina's back and flew skywards to the heavens. Owain Glyndwr and I watched as Carron, now only a black speck, flew in great circles high above our heads.

CHAPTER TWENTY-SEVEN

We returned to Owain's home at Syncharth that same day, arriving late in the evening. It was a pleasure to meet his beautiful wife, Margaret. When I first saw her, she was sat with a baby cradled in her arms and their eldest son, Gruffyd, on a sheepskin by her side, playing quietly with a toy horse. He was just two years old but very tall for his age. In my honour, Margaret summoned a feast and ordered the great boar to be put on the spit and roasted immediately. It had been eventually brought to ground by the hounds and finished off with a spear to its heart. We dined on the roast boar and celebrated our reunion by raising goblets, brimming with sweet wine, giving praise to the heavens. During the feasting, Owain told me tales of his adventures, his travels and of how life had changed since our last meeting at Master Healan's home in London, now ten years past in the mists of time. The grand feast lasted for three days, as did our storytelling.

Margaret sat astonished as the tales unfurled, fascinated by my friendship with Owain, who was now known to all around as Squire of Syncharth. I remember her comments well as if just spoken.

"My husband's 'protector and seer' has arrived, all will be well!"

Owain had said nothing of the prophecy to anyone, other than his wife and brother, Tudur, both having sworn allegiance to silence. Becoming likewise to us, bound by chivalry, loyalty, and love, as indeed our ancestors would have us be.

Owain and his brother had only returned to Syncharth a few weeks previously and were still battle-weary. The long ride back from Scotland had taken weeks through bad weather. Hunting boar had relaxed their minds and maintained physical prowess, an ideal recuperation after dodging, weaving and ducking confrontations with fearsome Scots.

Owain and Tudur had ridden under the Banners of Earl Richard Fitzalan and the English King, Richard II. It must have been frightening for the Scots when Tudur and Owain, mounted on great chargers, galloped towards them, brandishing lances and shields. A man could be forgiven for thinking that the chivalrous warriors were twins, or even some ghostly manifestation thereof. They were identical in so many ways. Both had the same hair colour, both were tall, strong and muscular, with the same coloured eyes set above high cheekbones, slender faced and handsome. The only difference between the two was a wart sitting on one side of Tudur's nose.

This made me feel a certain kinship with him as I also had a wart on my face, but mine was on my cheek.

─୦

Many years had passed since I first met Owain and I was now riding at his side upon my faithful steed Merlina, sitting at his table, casting runes, manifesting magic and protection. We were very close and as his personal seer and prophet, my days, and often nights, were kept busy. Sadly by this time both of my old Masters had passed into the next life and although I would never again see them on this earth, they frequently invaded my sleep with lessons, teachings, and guidance. Even in death, Llwyd ap Crachan Llwyd and Myrddin Goch ap Cwnwrig were as committed to ensuring the fulfilment of the prophecy as they had been whilst on this earth.

Llwyd ap Crachan Llwyd had become very ill. It was almost two years after I first came to Syncharth when Llinnar sent a message by rider to the great house, saying the old man was close to death but was holding on until I could come. She did not think he would live for more than a few days.

I stood in the stable, saddling Merlina, knowing we had no time to ride over the mountains to be at my Master's side. I now needed to draw upon my learnings, so I conjured and summoned lightening-like energy. It came, shimmering faster and faster, first as a ball of white light, then growing larger in the blink of an eye. The magical doorway appeared, mist and flashing colours manifested as the portal opened. I mounted Merlina by climbing up the rope ladder, hauling it up and folding it back into the saddle, before taking the reins in my hands and gently encouraging her to go through the mystical doorway. Merlina trotted into the light which was now flashing and flickering as a thousand rainbows. The portal closed behind us, and we saw images of mountains and valleys, clouds and stars, and felt a warm wind filling the 'tunnel of no time.'

Merlina trotted on through air with no ground beneath her hooves but, unlike Pegasus, she flew without wings. Suddenly, the tunnel disappeared behind us, and Merlina was trotting up the path to the old men's cottage. It was early evening, and dusk was falling, dark shadows formed as the sun said goodbye to the day and the moon rose, saying hello to the night. This was the 'time between times' when portals worked much more efficiently as the space between the dimensions becomes thinner, helping us to journey with more pace.

Llinnar stood on the porch, waving at me as we rode towards her. Carron, son of Ether, flew in circles above my head then twisted into a slow swoop before alighting on a fence surrounding the herb garden. He fluttered his wings and picked at his feet for a moment, then became perfectly motionless, staring intently at the cottage. Wisps of smoke rose from the chimney, barely visible now through the evening mist falling in the half light, gathering in wispy clouds, swirling towards the ground. Llinnar stepped off the porch and walked towards us, rubbing her hands together anxiously.

"Crach, you are here! Thank heavens! Your old Master is still alive but failing fast. He is in and out of sleep, and his breathing is laboured. For all we have on hand to help him, nothing has."

She took Merlina's bridle in her hand and led us to the fence. Passing the reins to Llinnar, I jumped from Merlina's back, landing less than firmly on my feet, staggering for a wink of an eye before losing my balance. Bumping into the fence with a crash and bouncing off it, as may a blind acrobat, I landed on my rear. Llinnar, amused by my clumsiness, giggled under her breath as Myrddin Goch ap Cwnwrig appeared through the open cottage door. Whilst he looked frail, he moved quite quickly, nimble of step for his years.

"Crach, you are here!" He clapped his hands joyfully and with a look of great concern, urged me to rise and enter quickly, while frantically waving his arms in welcome. "Our old friend waits to depart this world, Crach. You will delight his heart. Come! Come!"

Entering the familiar surroundings of the cottage that had been my home with Llwyd ap Crachan Llwyd for many years, I was struck by nostalgia, remembering my youth.

My old Master lay on his cot. Llinnar had moved it to the wall nearest the hearth in order to keep him warm. Llwyd ap Crachan Llwyd was propped up by pillows and seemed so still, only his chest moving up and down slowly, hardly breathing. His hair, swept back, lay on the pillow, framing his head like a white aura falling down to his thin shoulders. The familiar face that I knew so well lay still and grey, skin stretched, tired, wrinkled and worn, eyes fluttering in and out of sleep.

Myrddin Goch ap Cwnwrig gently took my arm and silently walked me over to where my Master lay, whilst Llinnar took a chair from beside the table and put it next to the old man's cot. Sitting down, I took his old hand in mine and stroked it slowly and gently. It felt cold and clammy, and although I could feel his heart echoing its beat in his wrist, all was faint, seemingly distant. I quietly called out his name, but Llwyd ap Crachan Llwyd did not stir from his dreams. I continued to stroke the back of his hand, remembering so many years shared with this wise old magician, thinking nobody, with the exception of Myrddin Goch ap Cwnwrig, knew how old Llwyd ap Crachan Llwyd really was. I certainly did not. As I said at the beginning of my tale, he has been ancient for as long as I have known him. But here he lay with the end of his time on this earth only breaths away. I loved this old man so much and sitting next to his prone still body, knowing the inevitable hovered in the wings, haunted my reality. There was no magic able to prevent his demise, he had used so much to get to this point.

Myrddin Goch ap Cwnwrig stood behind me, his own frailty now so obvious and, like me, tears welled in his eyes which were still so full of light, life, and wisdom. He gently squeezed my shoulder and relaxingly and lovingly caressed the back of my neck. Feeling the warmth and energy from his hand, my tears burst uncontrollably, their flow blinding sight as if standing behind a waterfall, dripping down, disappearing into droplets, dampening my beard.

The old man stirred, his hand twitched, closed eyes flickered, opening with a stare penetrating my every pore. I squeezed the familiar old hand with delight at seeing his open eyes, and he smiled, recognising me. His lips quivered as if to speak. Llinnar stretched across the cot, moistening the old man's cracked lips with a damp cloth. Grief and death have a smell all of their own. It resembles that of fear manifesting through a great loss. I smelt this on Llinnar as she reached across and when I looked into her face, the sadness etched upon it overwhelmed my sanity, and I cried again.

Llwyd ap Crachan Llwyd twisted his arm slowly, taking my hand in his with a touch so light, like a butterfly. His lips ceased quivering as a smile stretched them into stillness. He spoke in a quiet voice, just above a whisper, with his eyes firmly fixed on mine.

"Dear Crach, you have come." His eyes gently closed.

He took a shallow breath, straining with effort and winced in discomfort. Lips quivering again, he continued to speak, every word delivered so slowly but with determination, as with everything he had ever done in such a long life, now nearly at an end.

"I am so proud of you Crach. All that I asked, you have achieved, plus much more. Never could I leave this world for the next until my obligations to the prophecy were completed. There is no more I can do in this world, Crach, but I am sad to leave you, sad to leave you all."

Turning his head with difficulty, re-opening his tired eyes to search for his old friend, Myrddin Goch ap Cwnwrig, who came forward and leaned over the cot.

"I will miss you, my old friend, but feel we will be together again before too many seasons have passed." The old man patted his friend's face gently. "There will be much for me to do in the next world but first I will rest after my death." He smiled. "In your dreams, Crach, I will be with you. I told you I would never leave you, and I will not."

He gasped, taking a breath, his eyes opening and closing with more and more difficulty. Llinnar sobbed, standing next to the hearth with her face buried in the folds of her apron. Myrddin Goch ap Cwnwrig stood motionless, leaning against the cot, head hung in sorrow.

"Goodbye Crach...." His voice quietened into silence.

Llwyd ap Crachan Llwyd coughed, shuddered for the last time as his body stilled, his eyes now staring blankly up at the rafters. A stillness that only death can bring flooded over my old friend and Master. He was dead.

We buried Llwyd ap Crachan Llwyd under an old oak tree at the edge of the forest the next morning. It took me a long time to dig through the hard ground, but dig I did. Myrddin Goch ap Cwnwrig sat on a tree stump, his head bent in silent prayer. With a sheepskin wrapped around his shoulders to keep out the cold and damp that still hung in the forest through the morning mist, he cried quietly, tears streaming down his pale cheeks. The sun hid behind unseen clouds in a sky so grey and overcast. Llinnar had cleaned and covered his body, and when I had finished digging the grave, she helped me to lower him into this final resting place.   His headstone, the oak tree, now bore ancient rune carvings to protect his earthly remains buried in the ground and his spirit in the next life. The three of us stood silently, looking down at the earth where he lay beneath, now returned to how it was yesterday, a forest floor, moss and leaves scattered around the foot of the old oak tree. The only evidence of his presence were the ancient carvings adorning the trunk. This was the grave of a wizard, sacred until the end of time which, as we know, does not really exist and thus, forever in eternity.

Myrddin Goch ap Cwnwrig stooped in prayer and chanted ancient blessings to the life of his old friend. Llinnar sobbed softly while I held her tiny hand to give comfort. The sun found a way to break through a dark sky, clouds parted, and a bright shaft of golden light spread through the branches of the oak tree, cascading across the old man's grave. A good omen.

Myrddin Goch ap Cwnwrig lived on for another seven years and was cared for by an ageing Llinnar until his end came. I visited when I was able, but my services to Owain meant it was not very often. We were in the service of the

English King, and our expeditions were frequent. I missed Myrddin Goch ap Cwnwrig and Llinnar just as my Lord also missed his family, but this was the way of things. It was whilst we were away from Syncharth on one such expedition to Ireland under the Banners of King Richard II that Myrddin Goch ap Cwnwrig passed quietly in his sleep to the next life. I might not have been at his side at his final moment alive on earth, but by 'dragon's breath,' both he and Llwyd ap Crachan Llwyd, as promised in life, were frequent visitors to my dreams and always at my side.

CHAPTER TWENTY-EIGHT

As clouds fly through the sky, tragedy and joy flew through Owain's days but Owain Glyndwr, Squire of Syncharth, faithful husband to Margaret, father to sons and daughters, strode through season after season onwards, ever onwards towards his destiny. Ten years had passed since our paths had not only crossed again, as predicted but since we had literally crashed into one another. From that day on I rode by his side. Neither of us was getting any younger and I, for one, was wearisome from so many days and weeks in the saddle and Merlina, like the rest of us, was somewhat slower than she used to be. But, for all this, I awoke every morning feeling younger, rather than older. Perhaps this was a legacy passed to me from my Masters, Llwyd ap Crachan Llwyd and Myrddin Goch ap Cwnwrig, perhaps I was beginning to understand their longevity. The more I used my skills in magic, as I had done almost daily since coming to Syncharth, it seemed fewer years passed, rather than more.

_6_

We sat in the great hall, debating. I was counselling Owain and consulting the runes as he had requested. Once again, great concern echoed throughout valleys, towns, and hamlets across Wales, as English Lords played power games in the name of the King and often without a royal seal upon the matter. Tudur paced up and down, cracking footsteps upon the wooden floor, ringing his hands and anxiously slapping muscular thighs.

"Brother, are you as happy as you think you should be?" Tudor asked. "King Richard is using us. Like Crach pulls a sheepskin around him to stay warm, they have pulled the wool over your eyes. You have served in battle, fought for them, given years of your life with a foot in both camps. I know, and you know this!" Tudur raised his voice, rattling the rafters in the great hall.

"You must make a choice!" Tudur bellowed as he dragged a chair from under the table, sitting down with a thump just before it stopped sliding across the floor. "You are Prince of Wales! Don't you want to take your rightful place? For pity's sake!"

He picked up a goblet from the table with one hand and a jug of wine with the other. Pouring the wine, he stared first at Owain before turning to me, slamming his fist hard on the table.

"Crach! What do you think? The prophecy and all it means is known to you better than it is known to any of us!"

I did not feel a response was needed at this time, so I watched as Tudur drank deeply, looking at me over the brim of the goblet quizzically, and waiting for my answer. Owain shuffled parchments, fiddled with a quill and dipped it into the inkwell, then paused, smiled at us and winked amusingly before he bent his head and scrawled some words. He looked up again and spoke.

"Tudur, you know I do! You know I will!" Putting the quill down gently, he smiled again. "The time is not yet though."

I, meanwhile, was chalking out three circles on the table top, one inside the other at a thumb's width apart. I shook the leather pouch wherein lay my magic runes. Concentrating my mind carefully, the runes rattled against each other inside the pouch, rubbing and moving mystically between my fingers, fiddling and fondling.

"Not yet!" cried Tudur "How much more do our people have to put up with? The English Lords treat us as serfs, worthy of nothing except the back of their hand if we disagree." Tudur muttered the remainder of his comments with bated breath.

As I untied the drawstring of the pouch, three runes fell onto the table, each falling perfectly into one of the chalked circles. Owain and Tudur leaned across the table, staring intently at the runes spread in front of us. Tudur raised his head, looking directly at me.

"Well, Crach?" He asked impatiently.

"Our first rune sits in the outer circle, telling us reasons behind the 'question' asked," I answered, whilst pointing at the magically marked stone. "It is Wynn, who is the 'Wind,' speaking of 'harmony,' bringing great blessings, joy, and affection, fulfilling desire. But she appears to us reversed within the circle and portends the opposite of harmony. All is grounded in the earth, Wynn is of the earth, and she speaks only truth. Dissatisfaction is like a disease, creating misery and fear, also impatience, leading to ill-thought-out headstrong actions, thus inevitably resulting in more misery. And so the cycle will continue unbroken unless we act upon the guidance as given from within the inner circle."

I paused for questions or comment, which is my usual way when consulting the ancient runes. Owain smiled in recognition, gripping his brother playfully by the shoulder and gently patting him on the arm, saying.

"Do you understand, Tudur? This speaks not only of all the concerns we have always had about being ruled by the English, but it also speaks of that which the prophecy is, of its reasons, of its very foundations. Whenever we have acted without great thought, all has failed. You are being headstrong, my brother, in urging action from frustration rather than caution and good sense."

Owain picked up a goblet, raising it in acknowledgement of his honour to Tudur. Tudur, now a little calmer, replied with speech slightly slurred.

"As usual, you are right, Owain. Wise council of course, but I make no apology for my frustrations. My words are only those repeated so many times by so many from every corner of our country." Tudur returned the silent toast, draining his goblet to the last drop.

"Gentlemen!" I interjected. "Shall I proceed?"

"Yes, yes! Please do Crach." Owain replied sitting back, tilting the chair.

He crossed his legs with one foot perched on the table's edge to maintain balance. Tudur refilled the empty goblet.

"Your interpretation is correct, My Lord!" I said.

I turned my eyes to Tudur and sympathised with all he said, knowing this to be true but it was not the way of the prophecy. Tudur was very like Owain in so many ways, as I have already said, but as one lacked a wart on his nose, the other lacked patience.

I stared at the inner circle chalked on the table top, concentrating on the rune that would give the guidance needed.

Carron, son of Ether, was dozing, perched on a chair back, when suddenly he awoke from his slumbers, squawked and flew onto my shoulder, alighting in a most ungainly manner, digging his claws deep into my sheepskin waistcoat. Owain and Tudur laughed. Carron, son of Ether, squawked loudly in protest. He was a raven who loved to play jokes on others. He often did with me, by hiding my spoon whenever I needed it, but he did not like to be the joke, and it was funny, so he had no choice. 'Such is the way of the Raven,' I laughed inwardly and continued with my reading, interpreting the magical symbol etched on the ancient stone.

"Rad is the 'wheel.' The journey continues as the wheel turns towards full circle. Rad sits on its side, giving us insight into meanings from both sides, positive and negative. Thus all said is worthy of more than polite conversation, it is crucial that any action considered must first attribute the interpretation as its foundation in reason."

I paused, taking a long deep breath, staring with intent at the rune, seeing and feeling power reflected from within the symbol. Carron, son of Ether, sat comfortably on my shoulder, pecking at the gold ring in my ear lobe.

"This is unusual for a stone to land on its side but also a great omen that the runes give to us." I continued. "There are messages that will come to you from both sides in many important things. It is for you to consider the right action, maintaining control of both sides through skill and ingenuity. But we must also consider the other side of this guidance as Rad asks us to do. Have contingency plans in place for all options that you may consider as unwanted interruptions that will delay the journey. You must always see deep in the shadows as not all light reveals truth when it hides from view, especially when it secrets behind truth and friendship."

Tudur interrupted my flow.

"So we are to be betrayed by those who would tell us they have love for us!" He said sneeringly, perhaps rightly, with contempt for any against us.

A look of anger and rage twisted across his face. He turned from the table, spitting on the floor in distaste at the very idea of betrayal. Owain leaned forward, playfully chastising Tudur.

"Perhaps not so much wine would make your tongue flap less, brother, and do have a care, Crach is not only my prophet, but he is also our good friend. Remember that, if you please, Tudur!"

He stretched for the jug sitting on the table in front of Tudur, removing it from his brother's reach. Tudur bent his head in shame, eyes full of remorse, remaining fixed on his brother. He spoke softly to me.

"I mean no disrespect, Crach. I give you my apology and offer it with sincerity."

I smiled at Tudur, telling him that I understood his frustration but I failed to understand his impatience as the heavens protected all. I suggested he needed to find faith in himself, then he would have less anger because the heavens would give him understanding. Tudur took a piece of cheese from a platter on the table with the point of his dagger.

"I should eat!" Tudur said, laughing.

We joined him in the joke, joyfully bearing no malice from his words now passed. Knowing you could rely on Owain's brother to be the first to accept the errors of his impatience, always helped to defuse confrontations. But he did enjoy a jug of wine, and like everybody else seeking such pleasures, he also had to accept the dark side created by excess. Tudur chewed on the cheese, spitting crumbs in all directions as he spoke, and called for the aide to bring water. Owain smiled. I continued with my interpretation of the runes, moving to the inner circle. "In this circle, dear friends, we can see the outcome, but only if the guidance has been considered and acted upon."

Tudur became silent, returning his interest to the reading. Owain sipped his wine, glancing first at Tudur and then fixed his eyes on me.

"This is Tyr the Arrow!"

I glanced from one circle to the other chalked upon the table top, feeling vibrations from each rune as they connected like the web of a spider, filling my head with colours. I saw images and heard voices echoing from worlds I could not see. I stepped aside, becoming a voice from deep within me and yet far outside, from an unknown place in the heavens. The voice spoke.

"A crown will change heads, murder will be done to a King. Promises made to a Prince will be broken by a new King. A dagger in your back will not draw blood, but he who thrusts the blade does so to steal that which is rightfully yours. A royal seal will be smashed. That which will come to you in this way will unite your people, your countrymen, as all is done to them, in the same way, a thousand fold."

The voice departed as quickly as it had emerged, abruptly

and without warning. I slumped into temporary sleep, my head hanging limply on my chest, the voice in my head gone. While I dozed, Owain noted every word I had spoken, scribing with great artistry in black ink, dripped skilfully from a quill upon parchment. I awoke tired and weary, my eyes fluttering, slowly becoming accustomed to the light in the great hall. An aide kindly brought me water to quench dryness. I drank deeply, feeling my 'self' returning to me.

"You are back, Crach?" Owain enquired. "Perhaps food would be a good idea. Are you hungry?"

"I am, My Lord!" I replied.

"Then food you shall have, my friend."

Owain hailed his aide to bring food to the table. The hour was now late in the evening, but still, quite a feast was served. I ate far too much for a dwarf and was bloated from such an excellent repast of venison stew, bread, and fruit, all washed down with sweet wine. It had been a long night, and I felt the need for fresh air in my lungs and wind on my face.

CHAPTER TWENTY-NINE

The moon this night was full, floating in dark heavens dotted with thousands of stars and far off worlds that are unknown to us. So clear, bright and mystical. A night such as this is when anything can happen and usually does, worlds might collide.

Owain and I strolled in the gardens after we had eaten, Tudur having retired to his bed earlier, worse the wear for sweet wine. His head would remind him in the morning—if it did not, somebody else would!

We walked, taking in the night's air deep with every breath while we talked about the readings. We knew the time was near when Owain would have to come out of retirement, self-imposed of course. So long ago, when we first started to honour the prophecy, neither of us had realised we would be well past our middle years before our true part in it would begin. This thought made me smile as closer to the truth is that we both hovered a little before our fiftieth year. Astoundingly, of course, I must remind myself the prophecy foretold of great battles yet to come! At our age, that did not put me at ease. Mind, you may recall me saying that every day I felt younger, not older, so whatever will be, will be. Owain spoke quietly so only our ears may be privy to his words.

"There is no doubt we are upon the cusp of great change, Crach. I feel it in my soul. The English Crown is already under threat due to the actions of that terribly devious Henry Bollingsbroke. I have had to suck up to that dreadful man ever since I was cajoled into being his Squire. Do you remember, Crach, at the Battle of Radcot Bridge over ten years ago?"

I nodded my head and added.

"He is an arrogant man and no good will ever come of it if he succeeds the King, although we know he will, it is so written."

Owain smashed his fists together, remembering how Bollingsbroke betrayed Sir Gregory Sais, a Welsh Knight, whose chivalry was well known. The Lords Appellant had disabled Richard II, who was now King in name only. I continued to speak softly.

"It is only a matter of time, My Lord before Bollingsbroke will take the throne, so it is written. We cannot change that because, like it or not, he will close his ears to you. He will not recall your past duties and achievements for the Crown, he will not honour your intellect and moreover, My Lord, he will deny you the Principality and your rightful place as Prince of Wales. He has two faces, and both are clear to those who look beyond his words."

I bowed in respect to Owain Glyndwr, soon to become 'Prince of Wales.' Who honoured me by saying,

"Thank you, dear friend, your council, as ever, is wise."

He bowed his head to me, smiling when suddenly he raised an arm and pointed at the moon, urging me to turn around.

"Crach! Is that who I think it is?" He quizzed.

I turned around and looked up to where Owain was pointing and saw the moon, glittering and shimmering in the heavens. I then spotted a silhouette flying high across its face. It was that of a dragon, and in this part of the world, there was only one.

The shadowy silhouette flew through the sky with great speed, twisting and turning, coming ever closer with every beat of its enormous wings. Suddenly, one minute outstretched, muscles taut, the next relaxed as these great wings folded into a slow descent with muscular legs twitching in readiness to meet the earth.

Tan-y-Mynedd the Fire-Dragon landed heavily on the ground, sending stones, rocks and mud scattering and splattering in all directions. His huge tail swished back and forth as his body stilled from flight. He bowed his head low, great golden eyes peering at the valley far beneath. He extended a thick muscular neck and turning his great horned head, stared down at me. I saw my reflection playing and dancing in his eyes, blinking back at me. He spoke in his usual booming manner.

"A good night for visiting, Dwarf?" Tan-y-Mynedd laughed, sending steam shooting from his nostrils. "It is good to see you, Crach, and My Lord!"

Tan-y-Mynedd bowed his magnificent head and snorted,

expelling air at force from flared nostrils, blowing our hair in all directions, as would the wind.

"My Prince, I am not here by chance. There is a great reason behind my visit. Time is short, as is the hour when I must take flight before the sun rises in the morning sky."

Tan-y-Mynedd gave another great snort and shook his head slowly from side to side, as if in resignation to that which awaited him.

"Tan-y-Mynedd, you are always welcome here!"

Owain took a few paces towards the great dragon and looked up into his eyes, becoming lost in his own reflection therein. I stepped forward confidently to stand at Owain's side.

"I am here for three reasons." Tan-y-Mynedd's voice was full of authority.

Yet, know well, my friends who share this story with me, magic was at hand that night as only we could see and hear him. At this late hour, it was unlikely any other than a creature of the night would be out and about. But even if Tan-y-Mynedd did happen to be seen by human eyes, he would simply spray green smoke, ushered forth in clouds of steam from those great nostrils. Resulting, of course, in smothering the onlooker in clouds of green vapour and whatever was thought to be seen would vanish, to be replaced by several hours of deep sleep and a guaranteed headache upon waking.

We waited patiently to hear his reasons as Tan-y-Mynedd scratched under his wing fiercely with a flicking leg, catching whatever irritated him. Settling momentarily from the itch, with the moon shining behind him like a halo, Tan-y-Mynedd looked down at us again, grunted and began to deliver his reasons for calling upon us.

"Hear my words for they speak of what is to come, not in years, but in months!" Tan-y-Mynedd shook his great head from side to side.

"The first reason for my visit is to say that fires will be lit and know that your neighbour, Baron Grey de Ruthyn, takes what is yours. The second reason is to advise you that any appeal will fall on deaf ears. Do not waste your time in wait. When you are called a traitor, hear no more. At this time you will take up your sword!"

Tan-y-Mynedd again shook his head, swishing his tail from side to side impatiently.

"Do you understand, my Prince?"

He stared down, almost swallowing Owain in his golden eyes with a penetrating look. Owain gazed up at our heavenly winged messenger, saying.

"I understand everything, Tan-y-Mynedd. Everything!"

We both stepped back as Tan-y-Mynedd raised his enormous wings, stretching them outwards as far as it was possible for his muscles and tendons to achieve. He spoke again.

"My final reason for coming here concerns you, Crach!"

Tan-y-Mynedd looked down seriously, his great horned eyebrows furrowed. I looked up somewhat amused and curious, thinking, 'concerns me?'

"You are summoned to the 'Great Council of Blue Stone,' Crach. There is much at hand, and your presence is required, and it is required now!"

'The Great Council of Blue Stone' is a sacred and most secret ancient order. Both my old Masters were members and had been so for many years until their respective deaths. Once a member, it was for life, death was the only exit. Tan-y-Mynedd, together with the few remaining dragons, was also a member, as are the Faerie Kingdom and the Elven folk. This was indeed a great honour. *'But how would I get there?'*

"By Dragon!" Tan-y-Mynedd informed me, answering my thoughts!

Owain stepped towards me, extending his hand in testament to our friendship.

"Until your return, Crach!" We clasped each other's wrists.

"Enjoy your flight, my friend. Rather you than me!" Owain laughed.

Suddenly, without any warning, Tan-y-Mynedd sneezed, sending clouds of dust peppering the air. I stepped boldly towards him and was just about to climb up his leg as I had done before, when he bent his head, opened his mouth and with his great teeth he gently nipped the back of my collar, hoisting me off the ground. With one powerful twitch of his neck, I landed firmly between those armoured scaled shoulders as he released his grip.

"Hold on tight, Crach, we have far to go before the sun arrives."

Tan-y-Mynedd's enormous wings flinched, muscles fluttered in readiness and with one great flap he sprung into flight, twirling, spinning and twisting in ever increasing circles, upwards towards the moon. I held on tightly, gripping onto his neck as if my life depended on it, which of course it did! Twisting my head around to look down at the rapidly disappearing ground, I could see Owain as a dot so far below, then gone. Fields, mountains, and valleys became smaller and more distant as we climbed higher and higher. Every beat of Tan-y-Mynedd's great wings taking us further, ever onwards to our destination, 'The Great Council of Blue Stone.'

HISTORICAL NOTES 1375 – 1398

This book is the first in a series of novels introducing *Crach Ffinnant, magician, wizard, prophet, and seer.* In reality, the story is total fantasy, but some of the characters did exist, and some of the events are historically accurate, but many are figments of my imagination. Obscure and lost in the mists of time. Crach Ffinnant is reborn from history as the narrator of 'The Prophecy.'

Crach Ffinnant—Very little is known about this fascinating man, but his name appears in various historical text. R R Davies, in his narrative 'Owain Glyndwr Prince of Wales' (2009), describes Crach Ffinnant as 'prophet and seer' to Owain Glyndwr. 'Crach' means 'scab, scabby and, possibly, dwarf.' 'Ffinnant' would have been the name of his place of birth. Davies suggests that Crach Ffinnant would have been *master of the rich heritage of legends and prophecies familiar to the Welsh people who rooted the miserable present into the glorious past and foresaw the day of the return of such glories.'* It is said that in the same way, politicians today have their 'spin doctors' to interpret the signs of the times, so Welsh leaders of the period had their 'seers,' and Owain Glyndwr had Crach Ffinnant. We know they were acquainted as far back as 1384 as Crach accompanied Owain Glyndwr and his brother, Tudur Glyndwr, during their military service under Sir Gregory Sais to Berwick on Tweed. Crach Ffinnant was at Owain Glyndwr's side on the 16 September 1400 when his

Lord was proclaimed 'Prince of Wales.'

Owain Glyndwr Prince of Wales—said to be the only true Prince of Wales, he was a direct descendant of the Royal Line of the Princes of Powys. He was born sometime between the years of 1335–1359, disappearing from history around 1415. After his father, Gruffyd Fychan, died, Owain, still under age, became a Royal Ward. In 1375 the young Glyndwr studied law at Lincoln's Inn, sent by his appointed guardian, Sir David Hanmer, which is not surprising as he himself was a lawyer, Kings Serjeant and legal advisor to Richard II. In 1383 Glyndwr married Sir

David Hanmer's daughter, Margaret, and together they had five sons and four or five daughters. He began his military experiences the next year, in 1384, along with his brother, Tudur, fighting in Scotland and Ireland under the banners of King Richard II. In 1397, possibly by seeing the gradual demise of Richard II, who was essentially by now King in name only, Glyndwr switched sides to Henry Bollingsbroke, who would later become King Henry IV.

Tudur Glyndwr—Brother to Owain Glyndwr.

Margaret Glyndwr—Wife to Owain Glyndwr and daughter of Sir David Hanmer.

Iolo Goch (1320-1398)—was a highly trained professional bard whose long career spanned a period of profound social change in Wales. He was a frequent visitor to Syncharth, the home of Owain Glyndwr, and records life as it was in his poetry, some of which still survives today. In his work 'Praise of Owain Glyndwr,' he alludes to magic and prophecy and also to the good and generous nature, abilities and intellect of Glyndwr. He may have had a brother but Master Healan (as he was known in his role as Apothecary in London but returning to his true name of Myrddin Goch ap Cwnwrig upon his return to his homeland of Wales) was not he that is my fantasy.

Lincoln's Inn—can still be found in London today and has been training Barristers at Law since 1310. Owain Glyndwr studied law there in 1375.

CRACH FFINNANT

Volume Two
RISE OF THE DRAGON
Chapter One

Hanging on for fear of my life's imminent demise, I used every drop of strength I could muster, blood pulsing through my muscles, straining with effort in the name of survival. My arms wrapped around Tan-y-Mynedd's thick muscular neck, thighs, and heels digging into a scaly armoured body provided me with some illusion of safety. Allowing myself to be cajoled into flying at such great speed aloft in the heavens, riding a dragon, in itself warranted an examination of my sanity. But I had been given no choice in the matter, none at all. Tan-y-Mynedd's great wings flapped, glided and flipped this way and that, as we flew on through the night. Our destination, the 'Great Council of Blue Stone.'

The full moon illuminating a dark night sky gave light to all below and the stars above twinkled. Tan-y-Mynedd the Fire-Dragon glided with ease, trapping draughts of air beneath huge wings, tail swishing left then right and back again. With the dip of an appropriate wing tip, gathering speed, he hurtled on. The great Dragon flew in and out of large fluffy clouds, limiting vision to the end of my nose, reminding me of the many times I had been temporarily blinded by a mountain mist. But as he flew on, the clouds dispersed and I could see for miles around, above and below. Peaks of mountains glistened, seemingly so small, far below. Valleys flashed into sight - there, then gone. Rivers wound their courses from source to sea, criss-crossing, twisting, splitting and turning, giving the appearance of an enormous spider's web guarding the earth so far below.

Tan-y-Mynedd the Fire-Dragon twisted a wing, dipped downwards and flipped his long, scaled tail. He glided down through the sky slowly from the heavens in ever-decreasing circles, the mountains, valleys, pastures, lakes, and rivers getting closer and closer with every twist of his tail. Suddenly, he turned back on himself, shooting off at an angle level with the ground below. Following a river through a shadowy gorge, flying just above the treeline of the forest, Tan-y-Mynedd the Fire- Dragon soared skilfully ever onwards. The ground below rose and then dipped away again into a deep valley, shrouded by mountains on all sides. The darkness of night began to fade, rose-pink and magenta flecks and flashes streaked across the ever-lightening sky. Dawn lingered in wait upon the horizon.

The great Dragon pulled back both wings, thrust out a proud armoured chest, extended four thick, muscular, scaled legs, flexed talons and swished his tail high. Expelling hot air from both nostrils in clouds of steam, he landed rather less than gracefully on a scree covered mountainside. Scree, rocks, dust, and debris flew in all directions. As the dust cloud settled, a morning sun was just beginning to rise, shrouded in streaks of multi-coloured cloud—a landscape in the sky, and painted by wizards.

Scrambling from this 'steed of the air,' legs shaking like jelly clothing brawn, my feet touching solid ground again, I heaved a sigh of relief. After hanging on to dear life on a dragon's back for heaven knows how long and also not knowing how far we had come, I had a need to take a deep, deep breath.

Standing perched on a rock while looking down the valley at the lake below, Tan-y-Mynedd the Fire-Dragon pointed with one great wing towards a cave set back in the rock-face and quietly spoke in the ancient language.

"The Great Council of Blue Stone."

A golden sun rose across the horizon. I stared in wonder at such magnificence, lost and yet immersed in the glory of this immense universe where all created therein is truly one. An early morning daydream would be an easy indulgence amidst this beauty. Standing high on this scree-covered ledge, I saw mountain ranges, deep, craggy valleys and great forests lurking beneath blankets of green. I was looking far into the distance when I was disturbed by a voice from behind.

"Crach, it is time," Tan-y-Mynedd spoke softly.

Turning at the sound of the Fire Dragon's voice, I did not immediately see Tan-y-Mynedd as he stood almost invisible, hidden in darkness inside the cave mouth with just the end of his great snout protruding ever so slightly out into the light. Sliding rather clumsily over the scree, I scrambled in silence up to the cave entrance. The great Dragon edged deeper away from the sunlight. Such brightness stung his eyes. Spending life for so many years in the great darkness of those deep subterranean caverns, emerging to fly only at night, had created difficulties for all dragons, not just Tan-y-Mynedd.

There was a moment, not far off in the mists of time, when dragons flew in dark or light, day or night. Wars and hunting had put an end to that. Either battle or bloody-minded cowardly actions in the name of sport had depleted their population considerably, almost to the point of extinction. Eventually, all the surviving dragons sought safety deep underground, emerging only in the darkness and safety of night.

The last female dragon was slain by the English over two hundred years ago as she attempted to protect her eggs. She had drawn the murderers as far away from the nest as she could before falling from the sky, punctured by hundreds of arrows. She lay on the ground, her broken body staining the dust crimson when her last breath came, but not before she managed to bite the head clean off an archer when he got too close. This tale was told to me long ago when I was a young apprentice by my old Master, Llwyd ap Crachan Llwyd.

None knew how many dragons survived, but it was known that all were male. The time of the dragon would end one day because of this great travesty, and for many, they were already nothing more than folklore. Of course, as I said before, dragons do possess the gift of making folk forget they had encountered them. If they do happen to be seen by unwanted eyes, green vapour sneezed from great nostrils always does the trick. But the reality, as plain as the wart on my face, means their beauty will one day be nothing more than a tale to be told around a warm blazing fire at the 'time between times.'

A rumour had been buzzing amongst wizards and seers across our great land for many years that somewhere a batch of dragon eggs lay hidden deep in the caverns of Ffestiniog. Tan-y-Mynedd and his brothers had long searched for them but to no avail, although admittedly there were still many hidden depths yet to explore. Whilst ever one dragon still lived, there was always a possibility, slim though it may be, that the eggs could be found and thus hatch. Hope always sprung eternal in the heart of a dragon.

Tan-y-Mynedd leaned against a craggy wall at the back of the cave and in a dim half-light, his deep voice echoed our arrival. I saw the wall in front of me begin to shudder and watched as shafts of pure light flickered through small cracks, appearing here and there across the rock. A small triangle etched into the rock wall started to glow brightly and suddenly a secret door, shimmering in the silver light, opened up in front of us. Tan-y-Mynedd stepped through, one huge leg after the other, wings folded, his tail dragging behind. I followed in the wake of his shadow. Once I had stepped across its threshold, the magical door closed behind us.

The great Dragon trod clumsily along a huge tunnel opening up in front. Clusters of quartz leapt from the rock walls, providing dim natural light. The tunnel ended as we stepped into an enormous cathedral chamber. Waterfalls sprung from cracks in the rock, showering to pools before forming a small lake. A constant sound of falling water filled the air. This was a world below our world, a magical and mystical place.

Voices bounced off the walls, ancient languages merged with each other to form musical sounds, resonating in haunting beauty. Silent shadows danced across the walls, aided by flickering flames ushering from huge candles burning here and there. The atmosphere reminded me of how the air feels just before a huge storm, full of power and energy.

A long table, carved from stretched ancient oak, stood further along the chamber. Several figures, hunched in conversation, sat opposite one another on huge benches strewn from beech and oak. The silhouette of two dwarves leaning against the wall behind another dwarf who was seated at the table took my stare.

Tan-y-Mynedd suddenly stopped and sat down with a thump on his great haunches. Fortunately for me, by side-stepping intuitively, I avoided being crushed but fell head-over-heels, tripping over a rock jutting from the cave floor. Tan-y-Mynedd turned his huge head and seeing me sprawled upon the ground, boomed with laughter. Suddenly I felt a strong hand grip my shoulder as its owner lifted me to my feet.

"Well, I never!" A familiar voice sounded.

Even though my ears rang from the Fire-Dragon's guffaw at my clumsiness, I recognised the voice instantly. Gathering as much composure as I possibly could after such an embarrassment, I looked up and there he stood, Fwynedd the Shepherd!

"Crach! How good to see you after so many years, old friend. Do you remember, I told you we would meet again?" Fwynedd the Shepherd, my guide so many years ago at the beginning of my adventures, patted me on the shoulder.

His words reminded me of our last evening together in the shelter of our cave on my last night in Wales before I became a mute performing dwarf in a travelling circus. Yes, I did remember him telling me we would meet again and here we were at the Council of Blue Stone with the prophecy still unfurling after so many years.

"Fwynedd!" I exclaimed with joy, as we grasped each other's wrists in warm welcome. "You certainly did say we would meet again and here we are. You are looking well, but much older of course!" I laughed.

"I have walked through portals in such timelessness for so long now, Crach that I do not remember the years and they seem to not remember me." He smiled with a familiar twinkle in his eye.

The years clearly did not remember him. His hair and legendary beard now as white as driven snow, curtaining a well-weathered bronzed face. His cheekbones, high and slender, his face as deep-lined and craggy as the walls of this great cave in which we now stood. With shoulders stooped, Fwynedd the Shepherd seemed less tall than the great height I remembered him to be, but not by much I will wager.

Fwynedd, waving his arm, silently beckoned me to look around at the folk gathered in this sacred place. I had seen dwarves earlier, of course, seated at the great table. Glancing around the enormous chamber, I saw at least another two dragons, and I thought maybe I could see a third. I had never seen nor known more than one dragon in my entire life, and that was Tan-y-Mynedd. I mused quietly, wondering how four dragons could be gathered together in the same vicinity, given the dragon's reputation for being a solitary creature, their propensity to fly into rages and the likelihood that in one puff of a flared nostril they can fall out with themselves without even thinking. This could be very interesting indeed with four of them under one cave roof! I could not help but titter under my breath at the very prospect of such a thing.

I then noticed Carron who was busying himself nattering away to other ravens, all gathered in deep conversation high on a precipice above my head. I did wonder how he had arrived ahead of me – 'raven magic'! A huge eagle perched majestically on a branch, a branch that was alive and twitching. The ancient Tree Folk were here too. Such beauty and wisdom shone from every golden feather adorning this 'King of Birds' with its huge all-seeing eyes.

Goblins chuntered to Elves, Faeries fluttered here and there, whispering to everybody, leaving wisps of light in their wake. Two wolves, huge and furry, one black, one white, with golden eyes shining wisdom, sauntered across to the table. They reminded me of the great wolves I travelled with in my time with the circus as a mute performing dwarf. Spectres fluttered in and out of view, phantoms called from the 'other world,' summoned to the Great Council of Blue Stone. As Tan-y- Mynedd said in Glyndwr's garden only a moon ago, this was an important gathering, but I was yet to see how important.

Fwynedd tapped my shoulder, saying.

"You have other old friends here too, Crach." Fwynedd stroked his chin. "You do know, of course, Llwyd ap Crachan Llwyd is attending."

I did not! Perhaps my old Master was one of the spectres from the 'other world' I had just seen. He always told me that both in life and in death he would never leave my side. He had been, as ever, true and honest in word and deed, often popping up in the most unlikely places and situations. It was certainly true, once a servant of the prophecy, always a servant, both throughout this life and the next. This is an adventure to behold with still so much more for the telling.

A dwarf standing by the pool lifted a great horn to his lips and trumpeted slowly. Three times it sounded, heralding a silence throughout the great chamber. All became calm, only the waterfalls echoed through the stillness. The great Eagle stood erect with wings outstretched, the living, shaking branch he perched upon, now still. This mere gesture alone would have stopped all in their tracks, such was this great bird's majesty and presence. The old Tree Man raised a branch, and the Eagle flapped his great wings in readiness of making an announcement. The dwarf raised the great horn to his lips and blew once more. All within the chamber fell silent. The Eagle spluttered and cleared his throat.

"Friends, fellow members of the Council of Blue Stone, I beseech your indulgence on this most auspicious of occasions. Soon, all those yet to come will have arrived, and our meeting will begin in earnest." The Eagle paused and flapped his massive wings. "Until then, please enjoy the food and eat heartily. The wine is sweet and strong, I ask you to remember this as you will need clear minds to deliberate on the matters at hand." Heads nodded around the room with mutterings of agreement, lost in the wake of the falling waters. "It is done!" The Eagle folded his wings, and the old Tree Man gently lowered his branch.

The humming of chatter amongst the gathered throng, mingled with the sounds of falling water, soon began again. Fruit and fresh trenchers of bread filled with vegetables and venison covered the oak table. Its length, unimaginable in my eye, seemed to go on for ever, as did this cavern. A dwarf who carried large flagons of wine, suddenly tripped, landing in a heap on the ground. As he cried out in surprise, I thought I recognised his voice. In fact, there was no mistaking it at all, but I moved closer to take a good look just to be certain. Stepping towards the dwarf, left me in no doubt as those all too familiar features came into view. I nearly screamed with delight, but remembering where I was, curtailed my enthusiasm.

"Is that you Crow?" I called out, not too loudly but with such excitement!

The crumpled dwarf sat on the hard ground, rubbing bruises with the unbroken flagons laying around him. Now, this was a familiar vision to me and most welcome in the extreme to see my old friend Crow who had taken such good care of me, when I first joined the Travelling Circus all those years ago in Shrewsbury. He was by far the most accident-prone dwarf one would ever meet, and the most loyal. A good friend indeed. Turning his head towards the sound of my voice, he leapt from the floor as his eyes met mine.

"Crach! Is that you?" His smile lit up a now much older face than the one I remembered. "Yes! It is you! Of course, it is you!" He exclaimed excitedly, answering his own question.

We embraced each other warmly and, as usual, I forgot my own strength, nearly squeezing all life from his small body. Crow was thinner than I remember, but then age does that to us. We either become fatter or thinner and why is it our ears always get bigger? I could see by the size of Crow's ears that he too, like me, suffered from this affliction.

"It is so good to see you, Crow. How are you, old friend?" I could not stop shaking his hand, nor he mine. "I knew we would meet again one day, but this was most unexpected." I paused for breath.

"I am well, Crach. The years have been good to me. I can see they have been kind to you also. And Crach, you are still talking!" We both laughed as Fwynedd strode towards me with his finger pursed against smiling closed lips, gesturing a need for composure. Standing at my side, he grinned, looking first at Crow before resting his gaze on me.

"Yet more old friends, I see, Crach?" Fwynedd spoke quietly, but he too seemed to have difficulty in containing his excitement.

"Yes, indeed," I replied. "This is my dear old friend, Crow." "And this Crow, is my old friend, Fwynedd."

The tall man shook hands with the dwarf.

'OWAIN GLYNDWR'

He was a prince in shining armour
Riding North and South
Jousting with the Kings of England
Words of justice from his mouth

Owain Glyndwr Owain Glyndwr
As he rode across the land
Our Prince in shining armour
Protector and bold man

Owain Glyndwr Owain Glyndwr
With a hawk upon his arm
A shield upon his shoulder
His visor closed and down
Riding for the Welsh people
Through village and through town

He was a knight in shining armour
He was chivalrous to the core
Protecting dear old Wales
From the sword of the English whore
Owain Glyndwr Owain Glyndwr
With a hawk upon his arm
A shield upon his shoulder
His visor closed and down

Riding for the Welsh people
Through village and through town

Lazarus Carpenter

THE AUTHOR

Lazarus Carpenter has lived in Wales for over twenty five years. Born in North Yorkshire, he is now an actor, musician, song writer and author, previously being a therapist, trainer, and researcher, specialising in mental health. He was educated in Middlesbrough, Sheffield, and Cambridge. With a fascination for Welsh History, he creates worlds within worlds; magical, haunting, spirituality permeating sound moral codes of life. He lives quietly with Debbie Eve and their dogs, Hennie and Noodle in a small cottage surrounded by the beauty of the Brecon Beacons in the Valleys of South Wales.

OTHER TITLES BY LAZARUS CARPENTER *THE*

BALLAD OF PENYGRAIG

COMING SOON

Crach Ffinnant
Volume 2
Rise of the Dragon